Death Lost Dominion

A novel by
Susan Adair Harris

Sojourn Publishing, LLC

Sedona, AZ

Printed in the United States of America
First Printing: May 2015
Published by Sojourn Publishing, LLC

ISBN: 978-1-62747-127-5
Ebook ISBN: 978-1-62747-128-2

To my beloved David
who has always believed.

"Death is our constant companion, and it is death that gives each person's life its true meaning."

Paulo Coelho,
The Pilgrimage

"So since I'm still here livin',
I guess I will live on.
I could've died for love–
But for livin' I was born."

Langston Hughes,
Selected Poems

Prologue

U ntil this moment, Marguerite could order breakfast in a favorite restaurant in any of several different countries, paying in local coin. She could live for weeks from a single suitcase and a packet of laundry soap. She could recite the names, birthdays, and name days of every person in her new husband's birth family. She knew how to be attractive, intelligent, and charming. But in this moment, she knew too much. She had seen and felt too much. Marguerite's mind—usually sure-footed and obedient—suddenly found the present intolerable and decided to run away–deep into the tangled undergrowth of her subconscious.

1

*H*e left her standing there watching him as he walked away. His walk was unsteady, supported by a cane. There was a rhythm about it—irregular like his heartbeat, fading like his life.

She held back the tears that burned inside her, gasping for expression. She wouldn't cry. She wouldn't speak. That time was past. She could feel herself rotting inside, the tears turning to acid in her soul. She had wronged him. She knew that. But there was no going back, no do-over. Just the thump, thump, thump. Somewhere a woman screamed.

The lamps were lit now—strange yellow glows in the gathering fog. London was a perfect place for losing people—the dark, narrow back street—the London that was. Clopping horse hooves stomped inside her head. Was she utterly mad or was she living in two times—unintentionally, accidentally, saying goodbye to the husband she adored—goodbye to the woman she might have been if she hadn't betrayed him.

She stepped into a pub. She needed a drink. Within, the time was indistinct, a place with no date.

The barkeep grinned at her. Perhaps he was no more real than her out-of-time self. The redness of his cheeks seemed to shimmer.

She asked for ale, brown ale, and he served it, frothing. She drew coins from her pocket and whatever they were, he took them. Her head hurt. Her heart hurt.

"All right, Luv?" he asked—the barkeep who was or was not there.

"Not so much," she answered truthfully.

"Y'er a Yank, then, aren't you?" he asked without a question.

"Yes, I suppose I am."

He handed her back the coins. "On the house, then, Miss, on the house. We serve the wounded here without cost. House policy."

She stared at the coins—quarters, pence—a jumble, as she was herself.

"Thank you."

A handbag hung from her shoulder, a stained handbag. It could've been a gargoyle for all the sense it made to her. She dropped the coins inside. "Why do you call me wounded?" she asked without looking at him.

"Why would I not?" he answered, this time a question that didn't answer.

She sipped at the ale. If she were mad, would she taste the foam?

He moved away from her, and she wanted to lean across the bar and grasp his sleeve. He was her anchor. He couldn't go. But he did and then the beer tasted bitter.

She left it there and looked for the door, half expecting it to have vanished. It hadn't, and she returned to the chill night air. Had it been night before? Where was the thump, thump, thump?

"He's dead, Luv." The barkeep was outside now, leaning against the window frame, puffing a cigarette. "He's nearly dead."

She didn't ask how he knew. Only a mad woman carries on a conversation with an illusion. But who was the illusion—him or her? Was this death?

Death sounded like home. Soothing. An end. People underestimated endings. A period was the most glorious punctuation. Dot. Done. And finis. No more.

She knew better. Endings were an illusion. Nothing ended. Not good. Not bad. Nothing.

She had done it to herself. No, she had done it to him.

"Matias is the one." Saved by the words that killed her. Killed by the words that saved her. And he was tortured. Not in London—old or new. Where? She strained. Argentina. Buenos Aires, Argentina, home of the soccer World Cup.

———◦◦◦———

She had met Matias in a meadow. What a silly place to meet a man, a head among the sunflowers, a man sitting beside a dog, a smile disconnected and glowing above the weeds. A Cheshire moment.

He greeted her in his deep baritone voice that rubbed against her.

She smiled. What was there to say? He was already a part of her heart, her soul. She didn't yet know his name. His hair was a halo of glistening black curls. His large, dark eyes glinted with sparks like the first moments of a new fire. He wasn't handsome, exactly, but he was magnetic. She could feel him deep beneath her consciousness, already making himself at home, drawing her ever closer.

They talked of the birds and flowers and butterflies. Their words were like dandelion fluff, drifting above their deep conversation that went without words. When he kissed her, the universe fell into harmony. Suddenly, they were sunlight together–a fresh star born of a quiet collision.

They made love before they found their last names, unselfconsciously because it was right and real and as inevitable as darkness. They lay in the flowers and she told him she was Marguerite, and he laughed and told her she was perfection, a dream he had invented once on a very good day.

And she kissed him as she had kissed no one before.

———◈———

She had never allowed her soul to touch anyone, to let anyone touch her, before him. She remembered his eyes as she spoke to the soldiers– that cool non-expression that said he had expected better but he could tolerate what she was because her imperfect self was the one he had chosen.

She thought she could hear his screams. A man screaming. A man SCREAMING. She could feel his screams on her spine, in her mouth, in her soul. People were cheering.

"God, I hate myself," she whispered to God, but no one answered. No one said, "It's all right, Marguerite." Only Matias would've said that–if he could speak. But he had no words now. No tongue.

Oh God, he had no tongue!

She was repulsed. He was a horror. Her horror. She had created him.

Without warning, he was there in her mind—misshapen, bloody, torn. No one she knew. If he were in a field, he'd be fertilizer. He was meat. He was a thing.

"I didn't mean to!" she wailed to the darkness. But she was lying. Of course she meant to. She wanted to be someone—anyone—else. She wanted to be the hero, the brave one, the good one. She wanted to disintegrate, because she refused to die. If she died, she might have to answer for what she had done.

But if she couldn't die, what was left? How could a person not die?

———◈———

Gradually she could feel the hard floor beneath her body, smell the sweat and feces and urine and the sickening odor of blood. Her mind was forcing her back from her delusions, back to the place where her body had waited, back to the agonizing reality she had been running from. Blood oozed down her leg over her torn stockings. Blood soaked the new blue dress she had worn for Matias. She was in a torture room in the ESMA, one place in Buenos Aires closed to the tens of thousands of rowdy tourists. It was a place where demons looked like men, where humans were ripped from their souls.

Marguerite pushed herself to her feet, feeling sharp pain. She was standing beside her Matias, the man who was all the best of her life, as he lay restrained on a bloody table. Outside, only ten blocks away, people were crushed into the stadium for the 1978 World Soccer Cup finals game between Argentina and the Netherlands. People cheered and shouted, never knowing how very close they were to Hell.

2

Marguerite had paid dearly for the plane tickets from New York to Buenos Aires—tickets she was lucky to get at any price. She had given two or three times what they were worth, but she needed to be with Matias for the games. Not that either of them wanted to attend—they shared no desire to be swept along with the crowds– but to Marguerite, missing the excitement would be like missing Christmas. The city would nearly explode with the thrill. If something wondrous happened and the Argentine team won this, the World Cup, as the coaches promised they would, the citizens would go mad with celebration. There would be parties in the street. Everyone would be in an ecstatic mood—a bright contrast with the mutterings that had been common since the removal of Isabel Peron. Yes, Argentina was due for a little happiness, as was she. She had her fill of mourning.

She had traveled all night from the tiny studio apartment she kept in New York. Her time away from Matias had stretched further than her patience could endure. Could a person go without a peaceful night's sleep for two months without going mad? She never slept well away from her new husband. He wanted to arrange his business to come with her to New York when her most recent travel book—about his homeland–was presented to the public. This time, however, she excused him so he could pursue his own dreams. He said 1978 was a golden doorway provided by God who had brought the world to Buenos Aires for a reason. She couldn't let him come away to the

7

States—especially since she knew this trip would last far longer than she usually needed to handle book signings. Her mother was dying.

Marguerite's mother Irene wasn't a warm person. She wasn't someone whose distress made family members yearn to rush to her side to comfort and honor her. She was the embodiment of necessity. Her wiry gray hair was no more than a scant covering for her white head; her featureless brown eyes, merely a place to hold her sight. She had stopped allowing herself to care about anyone years ago. She worked. She cooked. She cleaned her house. She didn't bother communicating with her daughter or her son Stan, Marguerite's older brother with the long, dirty hair. He died in a car accident. Stan was a kind of hippie. He played in a band. He was probably high at the time of the crash. He probably asked for it. He probably dodged the time he was supposed to die in Viet Nam. He was probably high then, too. Irene didn't cry—then or now. She never cried. What difference would it make?

When Irene fell terminally ill, she called her daughter.

"Marguerite, you're going to have to come. I'm dying. You need to sell my things." And she hung up. No point in spending extra money on a long international call. No point in getting all knotted up over something that was going to happen, regardless. Nobody was sorry. She wasn't sorry, herself. She had been waiting impatiently for the end for years, watching the soaps and game shows on her little black-and-white TV while she played endless hands of solitaire on her TV tray. Life was no picnic. Getting old made her hurt. Living was an assignment. Too much trouble. Too many worries. She was glad to go.

And so, Irene's care during her final days fell to Marguerite. Irene never liked Marguerite much. Marguerite was too smart, too appealing, too independent—thought she was somebody special. Her father had named her, and his stamp was all over her. He should've taken her with him when he walked away and left them all to fend for themselves. Marguerite wasn't practical. She had his high cheekbones, his impulsive personality, his thick, sandy hair and dreamer's blue eyes—reasons enough to hate her. When Marguerite ran off to South America and ended up marrying Matias Garcia, that suited Irene fine—high time Marguerite stopped flitting around the world looking for trouble.

Matias was polite and talked with big words like all those teacher types—not a sensible bone in his body. He was careless with money. He bought her and Marguerite both flowers–a scandalous waste because they just wither and you've got nothing to show, but Irene supposed he meant well enough. He was hard to understand with his accent and all, but he was okay. He didn't smell bad. Except that she didn't want to think that her grandchildren would be dark and they probably wouldn't know English. No, she wasn't sorry to be dying. She didn't want some kid who looked like a Mexican trying to hug on her and call her Grandma in that other language.

Irene had done her best to raise her children to behave—not that they listened much. She told them parenthood was an obligation. You had to do what had to be done. You couldn't think about yourself any more. You had to think about groceries and clothes and schoolbooks. You couldn't think about enjoying. That was for single people—men, mostly. Men always thought they were single even when they weren't. A wife and mother had to give up everything. Irene didn't care what her children thought about the job she'd done raising them. (They'd complained enough!) She'd done all right by them—nothing fancy but they sure hadn't starved. Now Marguerite owed her. Stan had got himself killed in that damned car he never paid for, and now

Marguerite had to tend to her until she was dead and then get rid of all the stuff left behind.

———◆◈◆———

Marguerite sat by her mother's bedside in her mother's barren New Jersey apartment almost constantly for two months, counting and recounting the bumps in the ceiling paint. The neighbors above fought. The neighbors below listened to religious music. Outside, horns honked and traffic roared and squealed. Someone in the hall yelled at someone else—day after day. Who had that much to yell about? Cussing. Blaming. Loud laughter. Was it all a noisy joke?

Marguerite listened to the radio. She filed her nails. She started reading *War and Peace*, which was her form of penance for any transgression she did. She never finished it. She hadn't done anything that heinous.

No time had ever passed so slowly. Her love and apathy wrestled one another daily. She had nothing to say to a mother who had never talked with her about anything, convinced her mother wouldn't respond if she had. When Marguerite's first menstrual period had terrified her, persuading her dramatic pubescent mind that she was dying like *Camille* in the tragic story, her mother had tossed her a booklet entitled "What to Tell Your Daughter." It had been packaged *"Free!"* with the sanitary napkins. "Don't mess up your bed," her mother ordered. When a boy stood Marguerite up for the prom, Irene said, "Good. You can help me clean the bathroom."

Now Marguerite wanted to mutter, "I'm sorry. I have to go." Then she would leave her dying mother and the dreary mustard-yellow apartment with the stick-on flowers forever. But she remembered her childhood and her mother holding a cool washcloth to her forehead for her fever and a wastebasket to the side of her bed for her vomit. It was the most time her mother ever spent with her, but Marguerite couldn't deny it. When she had really needed help with finding a place to retch, her mother was there. Irene wasn't much of a mother, but she was the only one with the job. And so Marguerite sat.

Irene would grunt and point because it hurt to talk, and Marguerite was supposed to understand what she meant. If she didn't, her mother would create a sound like a wail. It made the dog in the apartment next-door start to howl.

Matias called to offer help. "*Mi amor*, I should be there beside you. I am wicked to leave you alone for these weeks. My heart is torn. This is a profound moment for your family—now *mi familia*, as well. Tell your *madre* I pray for her. My family prays for her in the church where we were married. My mother lights candles daily–she is a good woman and God will hear her pleas. We pray *your madre* will find her peace. She had such emptiness in her eyes when we met. Sitting with her must be like sitting beside an open grave. I love you more than life, my darling. If you say to come, I will go to find a plane ticket immediately. I swear."

She sighed. "No, there's nothing you can do here. Do your good works, Matias. Make me proud."

"*Gracias, mi amor. Muchisimas gracias.* Your generosity humbles me."

He was glad Marguerite didn't agree. She could hear relief in his voice.

He hurried to finish talking before their time on the telephone was over. "Now that the world is coming to Buenos Aires, this might be the best chance to get health care for the poor. People are often better, nobler when they are being watched. There is so much to do to give

Argentina back its conscience. I am trying to teach my college students to think of those beyond the college walls. I am writing articles."

"Yes, I understand. I miss you, but I understand. *Adios, mi corazon.*" Marguerite was secretly thinking he was lucky she loved him so much.

———※———

Her mother died one day early in June. Irene looked at Marguerite, grunted, and then peered at an invisible someone at the foot of her bed. Her brows furrowed, as though she were trying to understand that which was incomprehensible. She released a puff of stale air which was her desiccated soul leaving to find succor elsewhere, and she was gone. Her body looked no more like her than an old rubber ball looks like a beating heart.

Marguerite cried a little. After all, this was the last member of her family she knew about, the last chance to make memories to call her past. She cried for what had never been between mother and daughter. She cried for her mother who had died inside so many years before and left her two children as emotional orphans. She cried for herself. And then she set about handling all the details—the burial, the distribution of her mother's things to charity, and vacating the apartment. No one cared that she had lost her mother. They wanted their money. Not only was Marguerite exhausted, she was drained.

She had hoped to sleep during the many hours on the plane. But most of the passengers were the last ones to make the trip in time for the World Cup finals. Their excitement was unbearable. They shouted, laughed, and waved flags. They chattered in different languages. They sang songs. A fight of sorts broke out, but the other passengers intervened. Leave the fighting for later when there was a team that had lost the Cup.

The man in the next seat tried to kiss her. He already stank of beer. She didn't understand what he said, but she imagined he thought a glorious soccer match made all behavior acceptable. She held her latest travel book between them, knowing the cover would be too soiled to sell or give to Matias for his students to use to practice their English. She could sleep when she got home. Yes, Argentina was home—wherever Matias was. She would sleep in his wonderful warm arms.

Marguerite knew about the military junta that ran the country, of course. They had taken over the government from Isabel Peron a couple years earlier—supposedly to protect the country from Communist terrorists. The leader of the junta General Jorge Videla, a man the people nicknamed "the pink panther" for his light build, wasn't especially fond of soccer, but he wanted to prove to the world that he and his soldiers had made Argentina a world power. They would win the World Cup if he had to buy it. Matias had told her so. Matias clearly did not respect the military leader, but one tolerated what one could not change. Marguerite couldn't imagine what the World Cup or even General Videla had to do with her or her life.

Her taxi arrived at the Buenos Aires apartment Matias had rented as two uniformed soldiers were ushering him out of the front door of the building. Marguerite climbed from the cab and then stood, not able to think of what to do next. "Matias!" she called.

The soldiers stopped to stare at her as Matias hesitated. The taxi driver, who had been chattering happily about the games ever since they left the airport, fell silent. He rushed to drop her suitcase on the steps to the building and take her money without bothering to check the amount. He didn't look at the soldiers, as though by not looking he could prevent them from seeing him. He hurried to return to his cab and sped away. They didn't interfere.

Matias was ready to greet her arrival, dressed in his best pants and the bright shirt she had bought for him because red made him so handsome. Yet, instead of rushing forward to lift her into his arms, he stood stiffly between the uniforms. His expression was grave, maybe frightened. Marguerite stared. She couldn't think. She hadn't slept in nearly three days. She could barely focus. Suddenly the world made no sense. Why was her husband with soldiers?

"What's happening?" she asked Matias. The soldiers prevented him from approaching her.

"Go into the apartment, *por favor*! I need to take care of some business," he told her. His voice was tense and strange. "Go, now!" he ordered. In his tone, she heard the warning, the awful realization.

Dear God, this was a disappearance! These men were here to make her husband disappear! She had heard of such things. Their neighbor Marta had told her of the mothers who met in the Plaza de Mayo on weekly vigils for family members who were simply gone. But weren't disappearances a problem for someone else? Matias had done nothing wrong. He was a teacher. There was no reason to take him away. Surely, there was an error.

"He didn't do anything bad," she muttered. "He's a good man." Speaking was a mistake. The soldiers glared at her. She was an ant before their boots. How dare she address them.

"*Tu esposa?*" one of the soldiers asked Matias.

"She's an American. She knows nothing of our affairs. Please!"

The soldiers said no more to either of them. They pushed them both into the back seat of a dirty green Ford Falcon and drove them to a nether world where decency had never been born.

3

Marguerite hugged Matias' arm as they sat in the back seat of the green car. He placed his hand over hers and she could feel his muscles, taut and cold. "You should've left when you saw them," he whispered almost without sound. "I tried to tell you to run away. I tried not to look at you, but I could never do that. I love you too much." He kissed her on the top of her head when the soldiers weren't watching. It was a sorrowful kiss, even through her hair. She could feel her heart dropping through her diaphragm, her stomach, and into her intestines.

"Please, God," she prayed silently. "Please let us end this day at home together, returned to our lives." Her soul heard no answer. God had abandoned Argentina.

She could see Matias' eyes. He might have been praying, too.

They pulled up to the tall building of the ESMA, only blocks from the *Estadio Monumental* where the battle for the World Cup was raging. Although no one spoke of it and most knew nothing about it, in the last few years the Navy School of Mechanics (known as *Escuela de Mecanica de la Armada*) had become a concentration camp, a place to send thousands of dissidents and anyone else the military chose to punish. Most never returned.

Marguerite and Matias were taken past a stench-filled hallway where sorrowful, bloody prisoners stood in the doorways of tiny fetid cells, forced to cheer for soccer goals the guards were watching on the small black-and-white television at the end of the hall. The soldiers took Marguerite and Matias to the basement, to one of the pale blue rooms where screams and moaning acted as gruesome counterpoints to the cheers. A military officer waited for them. He was of a moderate, lean build and had thick dark hair that curled around his ears. His shirt was stained with blood. His heavy mustache nearly hid the hideous grin that transformed a face that might have been attractive into a mask of depravity.

"This is Matias Garcia and his wife, *Señor* Silva," one officer told him in Spanish. "They are the ones investigated."

Silva nodded and waved the soldiers away. They waited.

"Good day, *Señora*," the officer said in formal English, looking Marguerite up and down, taking extra time to leer at the curve of her breasts beneath her dress. "I hear you are a writer. Do you also write the articles about the poor people of our city?"

Marguerite could feel Matias about to speak, so she hurried to speak first. She guessed they wouldn't be as tolerant with him. She had the officer's attention. Sometimes a woman's soft voice, blonde hair, and blue eyes could be persuasive. "No, Matias is the one. He's the one who cares for the people. There's been a mistake. I see you are a man of discernment. They have the wrong Garcia. This is a man of learning. Please, let us go!" She did her best to look appealing but dignified.

"Thank you, *Señora*. You have done well! You make my work easy. A dissident, as we thought," said Silva grinning at the other soldiers. "We have ways of dealing with such men." He gestured for the soldiers to strip then secure Matias on the next table. "He can watch as I take you—a compliment, I assure you—entertainment for your husband's final moments. You will know the power of Santiago Silva. Then you can watch as we kill him."

"No!" yelled Matias. A soldier struck him hard enough to make blood run down the side of his face.

Marguerite had done the unthinkable. She had said what they wanted to know. How could she have been so foolish? She had betrayed her love.

"No, he's no dissident! He's a patriot! Matias! I'm sorry! I'm so sorry!"

"It doesn't matter," he muttered groggily as they bound him. "It's all the same. I love you. Always."

She dropped the handbag she had clutched to her the way a child clutches a teddy bear as she struggled against them. They strapped her to the table and tore away her panties. Then Silva raped her, first with an electrified cattle prod over and over again, and then by himself. The soldiers cut away Matias's tongue so he couldn't protest as she screamed.

She was barely conscious when they threw her to the floor and began working on Matias. She screamed in his place. A soldier struck her, knocking her head against the floor. The sounds Matias made were those of an animal. They thrust the prod in his anus, then shocked his nipples, genitals, and gums. They beat him with a stick until his skin hung in shreds. The skin on his feet was peeled off with a razor. Then they stuck him with a hot nail—here and then there. Blood was everywhere.

Marguerite lost consciousness and began to drift through time and space.

———❈———

On the table, Matias himself crawled on his belly down a long tight tunnel of excruciating pain, feeling the aloneness he could never escape. His heart reached out with boney fingers, grasping for the woman he loved, and found nothing. Perhaps they had killed her. If she were lucky, she had died. He had lost his manhood and he had lost his soul. His blood flowed around him. He had struggled in vain to grip living. He would die soon.

He had tried to think of his reasons for being, but pain smashed each image before it could form. He could fight no more. Death beckoned, promising relief. Why did anyone cling tightly to a life that was no longer a friend?

There was no future left–nor did the past matter any longer. Now he was dying, bit by bit, mortally wounded in slow motion—a study in agony.

She was there when he passed, as he knew she would be. She had dragged herself to his side. Her tears slipped down her face like desperate rivulets falling from a dry, barren cliff. He couldn't't think of her pain. He couldn't think. He couldn't...

Marguerite stood without moving, watching the life force escape the face of her husband who had been all her hope, all that was beautiful in her future. She longed to go with him wherever he was bound. She yearned to take his place. She could feel her soul being tugged by his—abandoning the pointless heartbeats echoing inside her. Pain shrouded her thinking. Her tears evaporated. She was a shell, an insect sucked empty in a relentless web.

She stepped back as the soldiers unfastened his bonds to take his body away.

"Would you like to kiss him goodbye?" asked Silva with a smirk. "You have pleased me. You spoke truly about your husband, so I am going to let you go. It is my gift. I have already chosen a woman to accompany me to the parties, or I might have favored you. But she is younger, prettier, tighter. She came here a virgin."

Marguerite leaned over to kiss her dead husband, not wanting to, exactly. As she touched his lips, she could feel his body cooling. They weren't his lips. He was gone. He had left her behind at last, as he never would have done in life.

Silva laughed. "Don't forget your purse, American lady. We don't need your charity. And don't forget that I was generous with you—you who married a dissident. Now get out of here. I have other entertainments before I leave for the parties. Peru lost—no goals at all against our six. Can you imagine? We needed only four goals above them, and we had six. The blue-and-white is in the finals against the Netherlands. The triumph is at hand!"

As though in answer, upstairs a cheer went up.

He looked down at his stained shirt, made a face, and tore it away from his hairy chest. "What a man you have had, eh? If you say anything to anyone about this day, next time you'll know the thrust of *all* my men!"

The soldiers laughed, guessing the gist of his English.

She staggered from the room. Were her legs attached? Had she gained a thousand pounds of dead weight? Had the men torn her in two from the bottom up?

One of the soldiers threw a dress at her and told her to change. Hers was too bloody for the festive streets. They watched as she dressed and it occurred to her that this was the dress of one of their other victims. Later, her neighbor Marta would tell her the owner was probably a broken body in the tides of the ocean, a woman dropped naked and alive from a helicopter onto the concrete of the waves. The woman might wash onto the shore one day—if the creatures of the depths hadn't eaten her body.

A thought struck Marguerite's vacant mind as she stumbled through the exterior door. She loved Matias more than breath. What great timing. What irony. The words he probably wanted most to hear as he died and didn't were now the only words she could think. A vocabulary of three. "I." Yes, that was her favorite word—a bitter, lonely word, a letter standing like a monolith in the desert. The second and third words felt foreign in her mouth—an exotic taste she thought she would never know again. "Love you."

She vaguely recalled her mother throwing a handkerchief to her as she sobbed after her father had closed the door. "He's not coming back, Marguerite. Get over it."

4

Marguerite walked all the way to the apartment where the nightmare had begun—slowly, hurting with the movement. She couldn't bear the thought of entering another taxi. Besides, she would probably bloody the seat—not that anyone would want to notice. There was no point in looking for help or justice. No one in the city was in the mood for trouble—theirs or anyone else's. Now she knew what she had avoided knowing before. People here didn't dare know what she had learned. Anyone could disappear. One woman had told her she had seen the soldiers seize three pretty young girls just for pleasure—right in front of the rest of the riders on the bus. No one saw anything. *Surely the girls had done something.* They never returned. Thousands of people of all ages—even babies—never returned. Only the mothers complained, and no one listened.

Marguerite's suitcase was gone from the front step. Someone had seen her and Matias depart in the green car with the soldiers. Someone had guessed that neither would be coming back. Good guess. Nearly right. She opened the apartment door. Whoever had taken her suitcase had not yet dared to empty the apartment. It wasn't much as apartments in Buenos Aires went—not for a man who was so smart, so respected, so experienced. Matias spent his money elsewhere. The rooms were messy—unlike his being. Inside himself, Matias had been the neatest man Marguerite had ever known—all his emotions tucked into their cubbies, taken out only when the situation commanded it. Of course, the soldiers had ransacked the apartment. She should have expected that. Matias wasn't this careless. His papers were strewn across the room like dayflies in their final moments. Dayflies. A lifetime in a day. Matias's life had felt like a day.

She picked up the papers, tapping them into a tidy pile as though she would bind them or maybe deliver his lecture: "Here we have the final musings of Dr. Matias Garcia." And the students would shift in their seats, dreading the long talk to come. They never dreaded Matias. They loved him. They would sit up when he came in—especially the girls. He was handsome in his serious, funny way. They loved him.

She looked at the bed. She could feel the rough texture of his cheap sheets on her skin, the touch of his hands. She shivered. She wished she could burn this bed. No one else should ever sleep here. No one else should ever make love and moan in pleasure into this mattress. Maybe she could burn it. But the fire might kill everyone on the block, maybe in the city. She turned away.

His dresser drawers stood open, the contents sticking out helter-skelter as though they were trying to escape. If only they could. Escape. Escape. She wanted to escape. She pulled his boots from under the bed—his hiking boots—and they laughed at her, reminding her of the long hike on the mountain, of making love beside the stream, of the heavy clomping sound he made in the hallways of the university. She would let someone else have them—maybe one of the poor people he had died trying to help. What good were they now?

She stared at the bag of Matias's personal belongings she had gathered on the bed–such a pitiful collection for a vividly colored life. His ring—not the one she had given him as they married; someone had taken that...from his body. His identity cards. He looked so serious in his photo, so young, so unblemished. His keys. For what? The rental car he had gotten for her—that was one key. What were the others?

Who cared! She threw the bag against the wall and instantly regretted it as the abandoned items scattered across the floor, clattering, clattering, clattering. They were her kin now. All abandoned. Men leave. That was the lesson from her mother. Men leave.

She tried to remember how the scene had looked. Boots, guns, sneers and blood. SCREAMING. That was what she remembered. And her, standing there watching.

Maybe the soldiers had shoved and she fell. Maybe that was the huge scrape on her leg—scraped from falling.

She would forever hear herself saying, "Matias is the one." What a fool she was. Had she betrayed him on purpose so he could never leave her? Oh, please, God, say it wasn't on purpose.

At last, she collected a small pile of his belongings on a chair—the things she wanted to keep just a little longer—things she would take back with her as she retreated to New York and the things she wanted to give to his parents. His papers. Maybe there was a dissertation or an insight or a masterpiece in there. She could show them to Charles, the obnoxious photographer who helped her compile her travel books. He read Spanish well. He would recognize valuable academic papers as opposed to sheets of bombastic prose. She would pack the photograph of her and Matias on their wedding day— a million years ago when they were still young. Was it only months in the past?

She drew the lock on the door and went to the bathroom. First, she would take a long, long hot shower, soaping herself as many times as she could bear. She needed rest before she could think, but she didn't dare stay here, where the soldiers could easily find her.

She would dress in the clothes Matias had helped her choose from the city shops, traditional Argentinian clothes to wear to dine with his parents. Then she would go to the tiny apartment of the sweet elderly lady Marta for whom she and Matias often bought groceries. She would sleep on Marta's stuffed chair as long as sleep would come. And then she would cry, if she could, and keep crying until the pain finally grew worn and dull and she could breathe again—if such relief were possible. For the moment, horror had crushed her tears.

And then tomorrow, she would take the suitcase Matias usually used and stuff it with the things she wanted to keep. She would call Charles. He was going to tell her to forget, to get on. Stiff upper lip. Yes, he actually said things like that. He could forget people, wipe them from his memory. "Marguerite who?" he would say if someone asked. She had no doubt he could forget her if the need arose, although he claimed to be waiting for his chance to prove that she had married beneath herself.

He would help her close her affairs here—for a price. It was time to leave Argentina. It was home no longer.

——◆——

Marta answered the first knock, she whose aged body was so bent that it was easier for her to examine the floor than to meet the gaze of the person in front of her. But she always saw more than anyone knew.

"Come in, my friend," she said in her heavily accented school English. Marta had once been a teacher, too. Marguerite followed her to the little table that was Marta's kitchen. The tiny apartment had only one room and a toilet. Marta heated her water on a small wood fire housed in a miniature horno. The chimney pipe ran out the window. She had complained to Matias that mice ran in.

"The soldiers came," Marguerite told her. "They took Matias."

Marta nodded as she walked with her cane, thump thump thump. "I'll make tea—nice calm tea."

Marguerite felt the pain as she sat. "They took him, Marta. They tortured him. They mutilated him. Matias is dead."

"Yes, yes," murmured Marta, checking the heat beneath the pot. "It is a bad business. They take the good. They keep the bad."

"Matias!" Marguerite repeated. "Marta, they killed Matias!" Was Marta not hearing?

Marta clomped to her side, laying a soft, wrinkled hand on her shoulder, stroking her hair with arthritic fingers. She kissed Marguerite's hair, as Matias had done in his final kiss. "Your Matias was an excellent man. He has gone to a better place. We cannot change that." She clomped back to the water, pouring it carefully into her best blue cup with a precious bit of tea. "At least you know. So many are left with nothing, just a hole in life." She came back to the table, walking more slowly now to avoid spilling.

"May I stay here tonight? I'm afraid to stay in our apartment."

"Yes, of course yes. You can stay as long as you like. No one will come here. They have no time for the nearly dead. I will disappear on my own."

The old woman lowered herself slowly onto the other chair. Marguerite could see Marta's tears sliding down her face. She had loved Matias.

"You must go away from this place," Marta told her as she wiped her eyes with her shawl. "Go back to your own people. There will be no space on the airplanes now. All are crazy with the football. But when there are seats again, you must go. No one knows how long evil will choke our country. Too long for me." She crossed herself. "Too, too long for me."

"Why are they doing it, Marta? Why did they kill Matias?"

Marta sighed. "Evil hates goodness. Goodness has power. They know one day truth will destroy them. They forget that this is not the side of living they should fear."

"It was my fault. I told them he'd written the articles about the poor. I thought I was setting him free. I wanted them to send us home—to see the mistake. Oh, God, Marta, I killed him! I should've demanded they take me, instead." Marguerite reached into her stained handbag for her handkerchief. The sight of it made her sob.

"Drink your tea. You can use my bed. I sleep in the chair these days. The bed hurts my back." There was a long pause. "There is no cure for your loss. Your good Matias deserves your tears. But he knew what would be. He knew in time he would be taken. He brought me much food. He wanted to tell you to stay away, but he told me you would refuse. You and I know he was right. You are a woman of will. He was afraid for you. He is looking from Heaven now, glad to see you alive, hoping to watch you leave this place and find another life. You are young."

"I should take up his work."

Marta strained to stand, leaning heavily on her cane. When she was as vertical as she could manage, she paused. "No, the time for such work is not now. Matias did what he did for his students to give them vision they can use in the future. There is no help for the people while evil rules. Go where you can do something meaningful."

Marguerite drained her cup. "There's nothing meaningful about my life. I write books to make money. I'm selfish."

Marta came to pick up the empty cup. She placed a heavy hand on Marguerite's shoulder. Even standing, her eyes were level with Marguerite's. She pinned her guest in place with her watery gaze.

"Hear me well, Dear One. For Matias to die was both selfless and selfish. He knew he would die. He wanted to stand against the evil–this is selfless. He thought you might die with him. I can see you were harmed–this is selfish. He died with his blame. His name will be forgotten—maybe a line on a list one day. For you to stay here and die would be foolish. You would change nothing but your life. To die without reason is to flout God."

Marguerite was too weary to try to talk or think more. She accepted the gift of the bed and surrendered herself to her unconscious.

5

Argentina won the 1978 World Cup finals, and the country celebrated a brittle veneer of joy that would crack and fall away soon enough. In the crush of fans, teams, and media personnel, finding an affordable seat on an out-going flight to the United States took Marguerite weeks, even with Marta's help. She cowered in Marta's apartment, jumping at every unfamiliar sound, staring without seeing into the space around her. She washed herself over and over again. As soon as she could bear to sit long enough, she drove to the country to meet with Matias' family. Hers was news that had to be delivered in person.

They lived in a modest but cheerful farm on the pampas where she had often visited even before the wedding. It was a glad, prosperous place—green and fertile—a place where sunflowers and corn couldn't refuse to grow. Most of the family lived nearby. They had reserved a corner of land for Matias and his dream of creating a vineyard. His father Nicolas had forbidden Matias' brothers from mocking his dream. Nicolas Garcia had never given any indication that he favored his oldest son above anyone else, but admiration shone from his eyes when Matias was near.

Matias often spoke to Marguerite of his respect for his father, who had done so much with so little. Even those who disliked Nicolas respected his honest word. When his eldest had chosen to pursue an academic life instead of taking a place on the land near the family, Nicolas had not objected.

"I am proud of you, my son," he told Matias. "You must go where your heart directs you. But I tell you, do not allow a storm of words to cloud what you know to be right, as some have done. Use your learning well. Some look down from tall buildings at a man on a horse, as the man on the horse looks down at the man who walks in the dust. Use your learning to look inside a man without being fooled by his position or his appearance. Listen only to the wisdom of your soul."

Matias knew his father had worked diligently over many nights to teach himself to read and write not only his own language, but English, as well, to give him an advantage in the marketplace. He used his language carefully, as one uses precious porcelain dishes. He was a man of pride and honor, and so it was to him first, that Matias came when he had found a woman to marry. He had already brought her home to dinner—on that momentous day when they first met and made love among the sunflowers and to several dinners since. Matias had watched his father's approving gaze, so he knew Nicolas considered the lovely dark blonde Marguerite to be a rare find—like a special heart-shaped stone in the bottom of a stream or a butterfly that dared to rest on your palm. Matias waited until she had gone back to her country to complete the process of her book before he approached his father.

"Papá," he said as they walked along the rows of corn. "I want to make Marguerite my wife."

Nicolas thought for a few moments. He tried never to respond without thinking, and Matias did his best to emulate him.

"She is of another culture and has different ways," Nicolas said slowly. "She has been here only a short time. There is much about us she will not understand and much about her we will find confusing. More than an American, she is a girl of the city. She may be restless living here, tending the vineyard you imagine."

Matias couldn't help grinning. He wished all his college students were as thoughtful as his father was. They made judgments too easily. They were swayed by glittering arguments. "Yes, that's true. She tells me she's excited to learn what it is to be a part of the land, but of course, she doesn't yet know what she's talking about. At least we'll always have something to discuss. Sometimes we'll disagree."

His father crushed a beetle beneath his boot. "All couples can disagree if they speak to each other truthfully. The heat of the argument, once the problem is solved, can make a warm bed." Nicolas allowed himself a small smile, perhaps an echo of a good memory. "As your wife, she will want you to travel with her to her home to visit. The trip is costly, and Americans are a busy, arrogant people."

"Not all of them, Papá."

"No. I am being unjust. I have met few Americans. Your Marguerite is not arrogant—not like that woman you brought to dinner long ago, the one with the large chest and small brain. Her photographer is, but he is a Brit. Does she feel like home to you, my son, in spite of her foreign ways? Does she feel like more than a lover—also a friend?"

"Si, Papá." Matias leaned over to pluck a withered corn stalk. He tore it apart, examining the inside without realizing he did. "I can talk to her of my work, and she listens and asks questions—good questions that make me think. She says she admires me for my idealism and my work ethic, although she wants more of my time to belong to her and

33

less to the students. She's proud of my education. She educated herself. I can talk to her of my family, and she wants to know each of you. She says Nita is the sister she dreamed of having. Already, she loves you and Mama. She's hungry to have family. I can talk to her of my dreams, and she makes them her dreams. I feel like I've known her forever."

Nicolas drew a long breath and released it slowly, as though he were tasting it. "I would ask if you love her as I love Maria, but your love is in your eyes. You have looked at no other woman with the same light. Everyone in the family could see your intention when they saw the two of you together—perhaps before you knew it yourself. In the past, you were drawn to women who were not worthy."

He looked at his son, and Matias knew his father was thinking of the lust that had distracted his oldest son when he first lived in the city. Matias merely nodded. He couldn't deny the foolishness that had marked his youth. He understood his students all too well.

Nicolas continued. "Your mother is sad to think that she may have grandchildren who speak English. It is a difficult language, one she says was invented by madmen. I have to agree. She says her mouth does not like all the sounds, and her ears hear only a tumble of noises when people speak quickly. But your mother wants your happiness so much that she will try again to sort out the words. I promised to help her. She says a blonde grandchild would bring sunshine to the family photos. Matias, we will be glad to have Marguerite as our newest daughter."

———— ✥ ————

From the first day, Matias's family of two brothers and two sisters had warmed to Marguerite as they rarely did to strangers. They couldn't resist her fierce determination to please them. They loved the way she would meet their gaze without wavering. They told her she looked like an American movie star with her blonde hair and blue eyes, yet she didn't act like a celebrity. She was genuine and unafraid, even when she fell from a horse and had to be rubbed with liniment and sent to bed. Her temper was quick but short-lived and entertaining in its way as her face flushed and she pressed her mouth into an irritated line. The entire family would gather around to hear her speak in Spanish, chuckling at the cute accent she used to pronounce the words.

They laughed outright at her ignorance of farming, but went out of their way to take her to special spots where her unhappy photographer Charles could capture the best vistas of their beautiful country. They shared their stories and brought neighbors to do the same. And when Marguerite returned from America, her travel book about Argentina released, they combined their funds to be able to buy it, although it was in English—a language only Nicolas, Matias, and his closest sister Nita could read. They placed their purchase on the mantelpiece like a prize, beside the copy she had given them as a gift. It was used as a part of the centerpiece for the wedding table when she and Matias were married in the fall. The family members nearly smothered her with embraces. They danced with her and the children sang to her. Matias's sister Nita even took her aside at the reception party to tell her of the secret love she felt for a man she had met in the city. Everyone agreed; Matias could not have chosen better.

Today, they all sat with somber faces around the long table Nicolas had built. They had already seen the gravity of the news in Marguerite's haggard face. She looked ancient and ashen and bruised.

She had a swelling on her head, her hair had lost its sheen, her blue eyes were ringed with purple, and she limped. The youngest grandchildren were sent from the room with Juan's wife, who was given to melancholy in her pregnancy. No one spoke as they strained to hear and understand Marguerite's description of Matias's death. Nita translated for the ones who didn't understand English, because Marguerite knew no Spanish words for the horrors she had seen.

When the story had been told—Nicolas insisted that Marguerite include the details she remembered–the family members departed one by one to find a private place to weep and mourn or to rant and curse the military junta. Maria was sobbing so hard that she could no longer stand and had to be carried upstairs to her bedroom by her second son Juan. Nita went with them. Only Nicolas stayed to speak of Matias.

Nicolas was a spare man, not an ounce of excess flesh, the muscle of his life pulled taut and browned with use. He had borne many blows. His first child, the son who carried his name, had died of a fever when he was a boy. To Nicolas, life was a journey with many sad turns. He directed Marguerite to sit on the sofa by his fire. The June chill of winter was in the air. He poured her a full glass of his best wine.

"Thank you for bringing us the news," he said, standing with a straight back and speaking in carefully enunciated English. "I know it gave you fresh wounds to tell it. Our Matias honors us with his love for his country. He was a son to talk of with pride. I am not surprised they killed him. I knew they would and warned him, but he could not keep silence. It was his greatness and his doom." He took a long drink from his glass. Marguerite thought his hand trembled just the smallest bit.

"I will direct our other children to stay away from the city if they can. We must try to be invisible until the madmen lose power. We have seen much insanity in this country, and we are not free of it yet."

Marguerite gulped her wine, wondering if she dared drink until the sorrow was dulled. Was there enough wine in the country—in the world? Could she secret herself away forever in one of Maria's unused bedrooms—the crazed American woman screaming into her nightmares?

Nicolas continued. "You speak of your blame. This is wrong. A sparrow has no blame before a hawk. If the hawk does not kill you, you thank God and your strong wings. You will need very strong wings in the future days, my child. You have lost your husband."

He came to sit facing her on the sofa. She thought she could see tears in his eyes. "You are free to stay with us as a daughter of our family where you are loved, but this country is poisoned with fear and hatred. The soldiers can no longer tell which are the enemies and which are the strength. As the wife of my son, you may be in danger still. More of his writings may surface. We may not be able to protect you. You have suffered enough. Please return to the United States where Matias wanted you to stay. If he were here, he would tell you that knowing you are beyond harm would lessen his loss. One day when Videla is gone and our country has recovered its greatness, you may return. You are a Garcia–welcome on these lands and in this house as long as another Garcia lives. But, for the time being, please go to safety."

Marguerite sat for a moment, trying to recall what thinking logically felt like. Nicolas made a show of going to the kitchen for more wine, but she suspected he needed a moment to steel himself. He was not one to endure helplessness easily.

She stared at the fireplace. Her eyes hurt. Her face hurt. Her heart hurt. The pain in her crotch was as bad as ever. She had sat on this sofa with Matias after the wedding. She could almost see again what the scene had been.

———※———

Juan had teased his brother, singing off-key and tugging his wife from her seat to help him perform his exaggerated imitation of the tango Matias and Marguerite had danced at the wedding. Matias had laughed his sexy baritone laugh until the dimple in his cheek appeared. When Juan wandered off to find more beer, his arm around the waist of his moon-faced wife, Matias spoke to his new bride of children and the kind of house he and his brothers would build, the kind of vines he would grow to make their wine.

"With you in my life, my dreams are plans," he told Marguerite, kissing her hand. "Are you very sure you want to live here, near my family? We sometimes quarrel and have cruel words for one another. Sometimes the weather is bad and the crops are poor. Of course, if we fail at the vineyard, you and I can return to the city permanently. I can teach. I'll always work part-time in the city. I need to make a difference. I suppose it's my mission and my pride. But are you sure you want to live here and not in the States?"

She had leaned over to kiss him. She liked any excuse to kiss him. When their lips touched, the universe sent tiny potent particles of space zinging through her veins. "I'm happy to have a real home at last," she said, smiling.

But times had changed. The tie that had bound her here was destroyed.

———◆———

Nicolas returned. Matias had once looked out from the same knowing eyes his father focused on her. Even now, she could barely stand to look into them. If she were to go on, she needed to find a new place, different eyes.

She stood. "Thank you, *Padre de Matias*," she said. "I can't stay here where there are too many memories. Please tell all the family, I respect you. I love you. I return the land Matias and I had claimed. I hope someone else will be able to fill it with love and laughter."

Maria came down the steps, sobbing but walking on her own power. She was a short woman, a condensed package of affection. She wore a traditional long skirt that she held up to ensure good footing on the stairs. She shooed away Nita, who was trying to help her, and walked to Marguerite. Nicolas told her Marguerite's plans in Spanish. She shook her head sadly. "We love you," she said to Marguerite in halting English, "*muy mucho*." She hugged her tightly. "*Via con Dios, mi ángel.*" She slipped a necklace that suspended a cross over Marguerite's head. *"Desde mi madre."*

She and Marguerite wept together for a long while, before Marguerite finally pulled free. There were no more words to be said. It was time to leave.

Nita walked her to her car. Nita was the most like Matias of any of the family. She was tall, dignified, and intellectual. She attended the college and had great plans for a future in business beyond the farm. Today, her face seemed dim. Her eyes were red and swollen.

"*Mi hermana*," she began through tears. "My heart is broken to lose both a brother and a sister at once. When I think of the pain and humiliation you've suffered here, I hardly know what to say. I think I need to apologize."

"No apology," said Marguerite. "What happened had nothing to do with you."

Nita squeezed her. "Don't hate us for this. Some of us will keep working to right the wrongs."

"No!" Marguerite jerked away. "Please do as your father says. Please stay out of sight. You can't reason with madness. The men I saw had no conscience, no morality—no place someone could touch with emotion. They were far worse than beasts. They were demons. Please stay as far away from them as you can. Promise me."

Nita kissed her cheek. "I spoke to you of Franco, the man in the city. I will stay near him. What happens to us is in the hands of God."

Marguerite kissed her in return. "Please take care of yourself, Nita, and know the soldiers have no god but General Videla."

Since there were still few accommodations to be had in the city, Marguerite spent the night in her rental car just outside the airport. She wanted to be invisible. She didn't want anyone to see her. She couldn't bear attention. Charles, her photographer, was waiting for her in the lobby when she finally dragged her suitcase inside–Charles with the sunken cheeks and lavender, anemic skin that seemed to be contaminated by photographic chemicals. Combined with his oddly colored flesh, his faded red hair gave him the aspect of an exotic vegetable that had gone bad. Matias had barely tolerated him—for her sake. She had stopped taking Charles with her when she went to the Garcia farm—even when the goal was to gather material for her book. She borrowed his camera, instead—over his vehement protests.

Even though his skill with a camera was undeniable, Charles was a walking insult—certain he was just a little better than any native peoples, anywhere. He didn't pay attention to local customs or manners. He didn't care if he offended. He considered himself to be a grand gift—a human vial of precious superiority ready for the fortunate few who knew how to appreciate him. He liked the weather and machismo he could find in Argentina, so he stayed. From the time he met Matias, he decided Marguerite was too good for him–too good for Matias. Charles was as dense as his milk-infested tea. He was waiting to save her.

"Hello there!"

She hated his cheer. She had told him on the telephone that Matias was dead. She had told him how her husband died.

"I suppose he knew he was playing with fire," Charles had responded. "Knowing when to keep one's opinions to oneself is a talent that requires subtlety. Also, one needs to cultivate the right sort of friends—if one has access."

Charles couldn't imagine how irritating and insensitive he sounded. He couldn't guess how much she detested him—especially in this moment.

"You look terrible. A bit of make-up could do wonders. And sleep. You wouldn't believe the shadows you have. You're going to have to make sleep a priority if you're going to do any business. You look like two weeks in an opium den. How about some lunch?" he asked. "But I give you warning–I might persuade you to stay!"

Her mouth filled with venom. She wanted to swear at him, to use the most hateful, hurtful words possible. She wanted to run him through with sharp consonants and poison-laden vowels. But she just shook her head and took the packet of photographs he had brought for her final travel magazine article.

"Go home, Charles. I'll send you a check."

"What's this then? Self-pity? Blaming ourselves for not dying, are we?"

"Go away, Charles."

"None of that, Dear. None of that. You have to get on, you know. You have to get on. You and I could take a nice working vacation on the Continent. A few days on the Riviera and you'll be right as rain. This was never your kind of place."

She walked to him. His expression said he thought she was going to embrace him.

She slapped him–hard–as hard as she could. He nearly lost his balance.

"What's that, then? Losing it, are we?" He didn't sound cheery now. She had slapped a red mark of her reality onto his face.

"I'm losing you." She grasped the handle of her suitcase and started toward the ticket counter. "I'll take my own damn pictures." He had the good sense not to follow.

"I'll be waiting for you when you return to your right mind," he promised. "We could have something wonderful together as partners, you and me. 'Gather ye rosebuds' and all that."

"You can go to Hell," she said quietly.

6

B ack in the States, Marguerite took a cab from the airport directly to her friend Dorothy's apartment. The sturdy dark red brick building was a relic of an earlier time when apartments were larger, but it hadn't weathered the years gracefully. The brick was almost black with age and dirt, and the peeling white trim had turned as gray as the rotting wood beneath. Children played in the yard and up and down the block as their grandparents might have done, screeching and running and throwing whatever wasn't fastened down securely enough. The scent of diesel perfumed the air.

It was Sunday and Dorothy would be at home, washing clothes in her precious stacked machine and waiting for Marguerite to arrive. They had known one another since the early days when Marguerite had barely begun to make a living writing articles, advertisements, and thousands of cover letters. Dorothy was the ageless woman who compiled recipes for the Hanover Publications and Media Events newsletter when she wasn't performing secretarial duties. Her body was layered and pink and warm and always smelled of TV dinners and soap. Everyone in the Hanover office loved her, although most took advantage of her good nature. "Dorothy, would you mind..." "Dorothy, do me a favor..." She was the resident mother figure and patsy.

Dorothy opened the door to Marguerite's knock and stood for a moment, staring at the woman she knew so well. "Oh my goodness, Maggie! Look at you. Oh my goodness!" She moved her bulk aside for

Marguerite to enter. "Leave your suitcase here by the door for a moment, and come sit down. You look exhausted." She meant *defeated*, but she was afraid to say it.

She led Marguerite into the living room where a folding table stood in front of her threadbare flowered sofa. She hurried to remove the remarkably convenient tin plate that still held remnants of food in the corners of the partitions, taking it to her tiny kitchen. The room smelled of turkey and caustic laundry detergent powder. When she returned, she turned off the baseball game that had been on TV and dropped herself onto the sofa, creating a rush of dust that fell back to earth in slow motion through the sunlight.

Marguerite selected the chair angled into the corner. She sat gingerly. Her flight had been almost endlessly long and brutal.

Dorothy clamped her hands together in her lap, perhaps to prevent them from flailing. "I don't want to pry, but my goodness, Maggie, I can't help myself. You have to tell me what's happened! Please! You look dreadful—just so different. Your eyes are all sunken like you haven't slept in ages—like you got older. If I saw you on the street, I might not even recognize you. Were you mugged? Is there a war or something? All you said on the phone was Matias is dead and you need a place to stay. Something unthinkable has happened! I'm so glad you felt free to come here, but if you don't tell me what's going on, I'll get nervous dyspepsia and die trying to guess."

With effort, Marguerite smiled a little. The expression felt odd, as though another woman had done it using her face. She had wandered into a peculiar, distant world that didn't seem to have anything to do with her. She wouldn't be surprised if she were a phantom or a memory or a nameless character in a dream. "May I have a drink first?" the woman who was operating her mouth asked.

"Yes, yes, of course, yes." Dorothy pulled herself up. "What a hostess I am! Do you want water, coffee, or something harder?" She paused to look at her guest again. "I'd guess something harder. How about a little brandy? I have a bottle from last Christmas."

Dorothy's fussing felt safe and homey—like waking up in your own warm bed. "Brandy would be nice."

When she had her glass and Dorothy was settled again, Marguerite took a long, slow drink of the brandy, sighed, and recounted what had happened. Only her weariness made the telling possible. It was a report from another distant lifetime. The words felt clumsy and uncooperative. The images made her heart race wildly. A woman in her brain started to scream without sound. All the pain returned. She drank again—longer this time—and choked, but didn't allow herself to stop. Finishing was an assignment—proof she could survive. Maybe her chest would explode and excuse her from living. Were there tears streaming down her face or were they acid leaks from her soul?

Dorothy made little exclamations throughout, but managed not to interrupt. "Oh, Maggie!" she exclaimed at last. "Oh, Maggie!" She was crying. "How could they? How could they! Can't you report them to the State Department or something?"

"Dissidents are considered to be a local problem—nobody else's business. Individuals aren't worth upsetting international relations. The truth is I could've disappeared, and no one would look for me."

Dorothy shook her head. "It's not right, Maggie. It's just not right."

Marguerite pulled a soggy tissue from her pocket and blew her nose. She expected to see bits of her heart and lungs on the white. "You told me once you have an extra bed. Would it be okay if I used it for a while? I'm afraid to be alone. I have nightmares—even when I'm not asleep. Noises, sounds, shapes set them off. Anything. Anywhere.

45

It's getting worse instead of better. I can't face our apartment yet. I can't stand having people stare at me. I just can't."

"Oh, Maggie," Dorothy repeated as before. "It shouldn't be true. They're devils—Nazis! What happened to those people? How did they turn evil? Oh, my gosh, poor Matias! How could they do such a thing to such a nice man? He was a professor! It simply shouldn't be true. It's so sick. Like the Spaniards murdering Indians because they were there—the stories you told in your Central America article. Sick. Do you think it's something in the Spanish heritage?"

Marguerite finished the brandy. "I doubt it. No culture has a corner on evil."

"Oh god! I feel terrible!"

"Why?"

"I watched that soccer game on TV and cheered!"

"It doesn't matter." Suddenly Marguerite heard Matias's voice say the same words. *"It doesn't matter."* She saw his body being strapped to the table. *"It's all the same. I love you. Always."* The agony rushed back. She began to sob.

"Oh my goodness!" Dorothy stood up and came to put her arm around her friend. "I shouldn't have made you tell me—not yet. I've been inconsiderate. You poor thing! Oh, Maggie, I'm so sorry. I had no idea it was so bad—no idea."

"I'll need to stay a while," muttered Marguerite, trying unsuccessfully to calm her sobs. "I'm a mess."

"Well, of course you are! Don't you worry about it. I have an extra bedroom. I got this apartment when I had my mother with me, but she's been gone a couple of years. I was thinking of getting a smaller place, but I like it here, and now you can be my roommate. You can get rid of that darned studio. It wasn't very nice, anyway. Everything happens for a reason. That's what I always say. Everything happens for a reason." Dorothy stopped herself. "Well, maybe not *everything*." She stood staring. "I should take you to the emergency room. You don't know how injured you are."

Marguerite waved a hand. The brandy was churning in her stomach. She was going to vomit soon. She staggered toward the bathroom. "The ER is too expensive. There's no emergency—not anymore."

"We don't know that," Dorothy said, following. "After what you've been through? We don't know that. I'll call my doctor tomorrow. You need to see somebody. He's not too chatty, but he's good with female problems. And he's old—real safe. I'll go with you. For now, go ahead and use the face cloth in there to clean up. Then we'll get you to bed."

———

Marguerite had to wait a week to get an appointment, and—true to her word—Dorothy took the day off from work to go with her. She was worried about her friend who seemed to have lost all her characteristic optimism. They sat side-by-side on the tacky navy blue vinyl seats in the waiting room, Dorothy rattling on about the weather and the dated magazines and the TV programs she looked forward to on Saturday nights. The air reeked of antiseptic. Tired lounge music oozed from dusty brown speakers above their heads. A seriously pregnant woman sat nearby, reading a pamphlet for parents.

Marguerite asked Dorothy to wait for her in the anteroom when a nurse called her in. She suspected she didn't want to share what the doctor would say.

He was neat, white-haired, and slightly bored. His blue eyes were magnified by his thick lenses and bracketed by his black frames. At first, he didn't bother looking directly into her face. He just set about his business with automatic precision born of routine. He was boney and his fingers were cold. The speculum was colder. Marguerite had to grit her teeth not to pull away when he touched her. She wanted to cry out. She had to hold her breath.

"Just relax," directed the doctor. "Think of something calming. I'll only be a minute."

He made little involuntary sounds deep in his throat as he examined her. "Tell me how this happened," he said at last. He seemed to really see her for the first time as he rolled his seat around so he could peer into her face.

"I was raped," she said as flatly as she could manage. "Tied down and raped by a military officer in Argentina—first with an electrified cattle prod." She spoke quickly so she wouldn't hear what she was saying. She left out the details about Matias. "...And then they killed my husband."

"One of those political things," concluded the doctor, talking almost to himself.

"Yes."

"When was this?"

"June 25th. The day of the finals of the Soccer World Cup."

The doctor drew off his glasses. "I see things like this sometimes." She could almost hear him add, "And it makes me sick," but she was pretty sure he didn't say it aloud.

"You have some damage." He wiped his glasses. "And we'll need to do a pregnancy test."

She could feel her heart slime into a gooey mass. "Pregnancy?"

"It would be prudent. There are certain signs."

She sat bolt upright on the table, not caring that the modesty drape fell aside. "No! No signs! No! Not him! Not the demon! I can't be pregnant by him! Please, God! No!"

The tall, skinny nurse who had been standing in the background as an assistant stepped forward to restrain her, but the doctor waved her aside. His voice was softer now, kinder. He didn't try to touch his patient.

"Perhaps your husband? Perhaps you were already pregnant?"

Marguerite couldn't see the doctor clearly any longer. Her eyes were filling with tears. "Please, please, *please* tell me Matias could be the father. We hadn't been together for a couple of months. My mother was dying... We wanted to have children together so badly..." She held her hand over her mouth to mute her sobs.

The doctor replaced his glasses and stood up. He had probably used just such a motion many times to give himself time to pull his professionalism close around him. "We won't make assumptions until we can determine the results of the test. Then you can decide what comes next. As a victim of rape, you have choices. You can opt to terminate. The fact that you have choices is an important factor here. It makes the next step easier. I've seen it protect the mother's sanity."

Mother: the word that should have meant joy and love and a family with Matias. But today it was paired with *sanity*—a danger of losing sanity. Sanity was already lost.

Marguerite lunged to the sink to throw up.

———— ⚜ ————

When the test results came back, Marguerite wasn't surprised. She could feel the dreadful truth inside her. A baby. His baby. The baby of the devil. *Rosemary's Baby.* Dorothy sat beside her on the sofa, holding her, rocking her, as she wept.

Dorothy was Catholic, so Marguerite was surprised when she whispered, "You can kill it, if you want to, Maggie. You can have an abortion. You don't have to do this."

"I don't know," moaned Marguerite. "I don't know. I want to kill it. It doesn't belong inside me! It shouldn't be there! Actually, I want to kill Santiago Silva. I want to stab him right through the heart—over and over and over again. But I don't know. More killing? Blood to honor my Matias? I can't think. I can't think about it right now."

As the days passed, the crimson smog in Marguerite's mind refused to clear. Dorothy became alarmed. Marguerite was crying out in the night more often. Dorothy insisted she attend a support group sponsored by Dorothy's church—a support group for rape victims.

7

A sign written in crayon and taped on the wall directed the support group members down a flight of stairs to the nondescript basement of the church. It was a sign that could easily be removed each night.

> Assault Victims Meeting Downstairs
> Tuesdays and Thursdays 7-10 pm
> Only Meeting Participants Allowed
> No children or men
> No loitering

Even the church didn't want to use the word "rape." It wasn't an auspicious beginning.

Marguerite tried not to meet the eyes of the other women tromping down the steps, hoping that made her less noticeable. She wanted to be invisible. Inside, she was cursing Dorothy for sending her here. A ring of gray metal folding chairs awaited like a pagan sacrificial circle in the large room at the base of the stairs. Marguerite slipped onto on empty chair, vaguely aware of a young girl settling into the chair to her right and a buxom platinum blonde slouching in the chair to her left.

The harsh fluorescent lights in the ceiling made the walls hard and the shadows stark. The air carried the aroma of cooked tomatoes and fried hamburger. The mere fact that she was in a basement made Marguerite sweat so that she could smell herself and feel the moisture running down her back. She imagined herself escaping up the stairs. She could escape and walk back to Matias's apartment. Her heart began to beat against her chest. She had to escape! Another part of her brain made her squeeze her eyes shut and take a deep breath. She could see blue walls behind her eyelids and...no! Her eyes flashed open. She was in New York—not Argentina–in a church, Dorothy's church. She would have to keep reminding herself. She pulled off her windbreaker and draped it on her seat.

A couple of the women elsewhere in the circle were chatting about nothing in particular.

"No, I don't watch TV in the evenings, Con. I like to sew. I sewed this shirt."

"Really? I'm impressed. I can't sew a button. My mother always told me I should learn, but I never did. Maybe you can sew me some baby clothes."

At last an older woman with tightly permed gray hair stood up. She was wearing big brown glasses and a fuzzy gray sweater dress. Her oddly pink lips smiled as she adjusted the clipboard of papers she held in her hand.

"We should get started now. I see a couple new faces. I'm Harriet Blackwell, community counselor and facilitator of the group, and this is a safe place." She smiled again but no one responded. "We're here to share our experiences and our strength. We're here to support one another. You're not alone. I was raped by a janitor in a building where I was working late long ago, so I understand what you feel. We have a few rules here. Everyone can talk, but don't interrupt. We don't judge. We accept our differences. We respect feelings. No one is allowed to put anyone else down. And no one is allowed to carry the confidences we share here outside this room. Is everyone agreed?"

A few women said yes, while the others nodded.

"Very well, then. Christie, do you want to begin?"

Marguerite followed the gazes to a young Black woman sitting glumly apart. Her arms were tightly wound over her chest, mimicking the tight rows of her hair. She was young—perhaps twenty. Her eyes were locked on her shoes, men's sneakers. No one was sitting beside her.

"No, thanks."

Harriet Blackwell sighed, a tiny exhalation of disappointment. "Very well. Maybe later. Connie? How about you? Tell us your first name and how you came to be here, if you will, please."

Connie was a young woman, probably in her thirties, who sat nearly hidden behind long straight curtains of brown hair. Under Harriet's attention, she abruptly tucked one side of her hair behind an ear. The features of her weary face had been outlined and emphasized with dramatic make-up that had smeared slightly, creating shadows beneath her eyes. Her pregnant belly stretched the wording on her rock group t-shirt as it bulged above the waistline of her pants. "I'm Connie, and I already told everybody that I was at a party. I guess I drank too much or maybe my drink was drugged. I'm not sure. When I woke up, this creep was climbing off me and I hurt like hell. I don't know if he was the only one. The doctor says probably not."

"Sonofabitch!" exclaimed the platinum blonde at Marguerite's left.

"Did you go to the authorities, as you said you would last time?" asked Harriet Blackwell preventing the blonde from continuing.

"I called. They said I waited too long and they wouldn't know nothin' if I had multiple partners. They'd have to test the baby to see if they can tell who to tap for child support."

"Sonofabitch!" exclaimed the blonde again, so loudly this time that she made Marguerite jump.

Connie shrugged. "The doctor put me on somethin' like antibiotics and told me to make sure I got somebody I can trust with me when I go to parties." She glanced at Harriet. "You know, *later* after the baby comes. And who am I supposed to trust, I wanna know?"

The skinny young woman beside her patted her leg. Marguerite recognized her nasal voice. She was the one who had talked about sewing. "I'll go with you, Con. You call me next time."

Connie made a disparaging grunt. "Like you can take care of me. You who left your bedroom window open. That was how you got done, wasn't it? You left the damn window wide open. You might as well have sent an invitation. You got no sense. If you go with me drinkin', I'll end up having to haul your sorry butt home."

The skinny woman looked like she might cry. "It was hot. The screen was closed. It was hot, Con!" She picked at the embroidered yellow ducks on her blue sweatshirt.

Harriet Blackwell reached out to pat the skinny girl's hand. "That was kind of you to offer to help Connie, Rhonda. We need to support one another. I don't think you responded kindly, Connie. I think you made Rhonda feel bad."

Connie sighed. "Sorry, Rhonda. I didn't mean nothin'."

The skinny girl brightened. "That's okay, Con. That's okay."

A woman sitting across the circle sat up straighter. Her hair rose in tidy lumps like a soft brown helmet stuffed with dumplings. She was wearing a rose cardigan over a tightly buttoned white blouse and a pleated navy skirt. The thick lenses in her glasses disguised her age, but she was clearly much older than the others. "Harriet, I thought you were going to say something about avoiding bad language. You said you'd say something."

Harriet nodded. "Yes, please, Everyone. Try to avoid bad language."

Connie made a noise that no one could interpret and the platinum blonde shrugged.

"Thank you, Harriet." The lady with the lumpy hair drew a long breath that she exhaled in an audible sigh. She leaned toward Connie. "No hard feelings. I would go with you to parties, Connie. No one would fool *me*."

"No, thanks," replied Connie, rolling her eyes.

Rhonda giggled.

The lady with the lumpy hair pursed her lips and looked to Harriet who was instantly absorbed in writing on her clipboard. At last, the lady turned to Marguerite. "My name is Abigail—not Abby, *Abigail*– and I was assaulted as I walked home from the market. It was disgusting. I went to the police, but they couldn't locate the criminal. Men are often victims of their baser nature. I'm working on forgiving the rapist. I pray for him."

"You wouldn't think anybody would've bothered you–you know, since you're old," offered Connie, as Rhonda giggled again. "You don't have to worry about gettin' pregnant."

Harriet Blackwell frowned. "As you well know, Connie," she said brusquely, "age doesn't matter when we're talking about assaults. Only the very, very young and the very, very mature don't have to worry about pregnancy."

The little girl sitting at Marguerite's right whimpered softly. She leaned forward so her short blonde hair fell across the pale creamy skin of her face. Her scuffed leather shoes stuck out in the air at the ends of her thin white legs. The tops of her white socks were ruffled and her pink dress was patterned with puppies. She didn't look old enough to be thinking about sex. She looked like she should be dressing dolls and building tents with dining room chairs and blankets. Long tears stretched down her flushed cheeks.

"Let's take a break—five minutes," suggested Harriet Blackwell. "There are snacks in the kitchen to your right. Help yourself, but please, Connie, don't stuff your purse. When we return, perhaps our new member will introduce herself." She smiled at Marguerite, who didn't return the smile because she was thinking this would be a good time to exit.

"Come on," the platinum blonde urged Marguerite. "Harriet wants to talk to Janet. And if we don't hurry, Connie will have eaten all the Twinkies. Harriet doesn't buy that many."

Marguerite reluctantly followed the woman who had been beside her, noticing as she did that the woman's white pants were so tight that Marguerite could see the little red hearts printed on her panties.

"I'm Mona," the woman told her as she snatched a chocolate cupcake from the table and started picking at its plastic wrapping. "You want one?"

Marguerite shook her head. Watching Mona stuff half the cupcake in her mouth at once killed her appetite. White frosting filling hung on Mona's chin. Marguerite handed her a napkin.

"Oh yeah, thanks." Mona gestured with the crumb-laden wrapper left in her hand. "I love these things. I could eat a million of them, so I don't buy any. I'd be a fat cow in a heartbeat. When you got a big chest, you can get a big butt real easy." Mona dragged the napkin across her face. "You want a Coke?"

"Sure."

Mona grabbed two cans from a tub of ice and handed one to Marguerite. They pulled the rings from their cans in unison, hearing them pop and fizz. Mona leaned close to whisper in Marguerite's ear. "The father of Janet's baby is her own dad. Can you believe it?"

"Oh dear god."

Mona pulled Marguerite away from the other women who were arguing over the last Twinkie. She was still whispering. "And her mom is going to make her have the baby."

Marguerite dropped her can of soda into a waste bin. "She seems too young."

"She's a little older than she looks." Mona downed the last of her Coke and, with a glorious belch, dropped the can into the trash. "Are you pregnant?"

Marguerite stared at her for a moment. "Yes." The room fell silent. The others were listening.

"You wanna talk about it?"

"No."

"You think you're gonna abort it?"

"Yes, I think I am."

Harriet stepped into the kitchen. She picked a can from the ice, watching it drip water from the tub onto the linoleum floor. "Okay, Everybody. Let's get back to group."

Marguerite followed Mona back to their chairs. As soon as everyone was more or less settled, Harriet came to hand the soda to Janet. "Who wants to start?" she asked, looking at Marguerite.

Ignoring Harriet, Mona launched into a monologue. She leaned forward, hugging herself so tightly that her massive cleavage bulged dangerously from the purple bra she was wearing beneath her knit shirt. "My aunt told me I *asked* to be raped when I wore a tight top. I was so pissed. So I have big boobs. Am I supposed to hide them? Some women pay to get plastic boobs, and I'm supposed to hide mine? I don't think so! Besides, it's not like I was running around nude. They were covered! I had underwear! No one *asks* to be raped. Not even whores. That sonofabitch caught me alone. That's all. He trapped me." She turned to look at Marguerite. "I'm not ashamed to say I aborted that creep's baby. Zip. Zap. No more baby. Take that, Superman."

Abigail hurried to rise, making the legs of her chair screech across the floor. She bustled around the interior of the circle, hurriedly passing out sheets of paper. When Marguerite looked at hers, she saw a color photo of a bloody fetus. It was a thing. She couldn't make herself stop staring at it.

"A murder is a murder," instructed Abigail pompously, focusing on Marguerite. "Thou shalt not kill…"

Harriet Blackwell interrupted. "Now Abigail," she said as she walked after her, taking the photographs back. "You know we don't preach here. We can talk about pregnancies, and even whether to keep the baby and what the options are for adoptions and such, but no photographs or preaching. We aren't here to tell one another what to do."

"I think that's wicked," sniffed Abigail. "There are commandments regardless of how the precious life was begun."

Paying no attention to Abigail, Mona poked Marguerite. "So, do you think you *asked for it*? Do you?"

Marguerite folded her hands into a white knot in front of her and stared at the floor. Sights and sounds that didn't exist were crashing from one side of her consciousness to the other. The tension in her body drew the attention of the others. She was the new presence everyone had been wondering about. The room was quiet.

"No," she said almost without voice. "I didn't ask for it."

The skinny Rhonda moved to the edge of her chair. Her voice was high and grating. "But did you put yourself in a compromising situation?"

"*No.*" Louder this time.

The little girl Janet leaned close. "Was it a family member?"

"No!" Marguerite shifted in her chair, angry without reason. "And it wasn't a party and I didn't leave the window to my bedroom unlocked." She stood up, not realizing she had. Words gushed from her mouth in a torrent. "It was political domination, military punishment for my husband's ideals. I didn't do anything but try to stick up for my husband." She started to cry. "I didn't do anything but try to stick up for my husband and they cut him up like cheap steak and now I'm carrying that monster's baby! I hate myself and I hate this child!"

Chairs screeched on the floor as the women came to hug around her. She knew they meant well, they meant to support, but Marguerite felt smothered and restrained. They made her want to strike out in self defense, to hurt them as she was hurting. There was no one present who could imagine what she had known. She jerked herself free and stood facing them as though she were defying hostile beasts.

Mona's voice slithered in to strike. "So, are you gonna kill that bastard's seed?"

The silence was suffocating. Everyone was watching. Waiting.

Marguerite shoved Mona away. "You don't know. You didn't see." Her voice choked with tears. She let her eyes travel around the circle of bodies that were recoiling from her. She pinned Abigail with a vicious glare. "How could you show me that picture? How *could* you! Don't you know? It looked like my husband! It looked like my poor murdered husband!"

Marguerite grabbed her jacket and purse and rushed from the room. She had her decision; she was going to bear Silva's child. She felt herself plummeting down a cliff.

Dorothy was waiting when she arrived home. Neither spoke until after Marguerite had changed to her nightclothes. She snapped off the only lamp in the living room as she sat near her friend on the sofa. The yellow light from the street muted the colors in the room.

"I'm going to have the baby," she said at last in a voice heavy with resignation.

"Are you sure about this?" asked Dorothy in the darkness.

"No, but I can't do anything else right now. I just can't. I *can't*, Dorothy!"

Dorothy patted her hand. "Okay. That's okay. It'll be fine."

Marguerite leaned back into the sofa. "I need to go back to work. I'm going to need an income. I have to keep up my insurance premiums. There'll be bills. I have to keep working, but I can't face the office. I'll need to work from home. Can you set up a lunch with Lester for me?"

"Of course. I'll talk to him tomorrow."

Marguerite held her abdomen. She felt sick all over.

"I don't know anything about mothering," Dorothy began. "Except I had one. So I don't know how much help I'm going to be." She paused, perhaps waiting for a response. There was none, so she continued. "I have this idea that we don't have to tell anybody about the rape, if you don't want to. I mean, your husband was murdered. That explains your moods. Talking about it all doesn't seem to do you any good. Nobody has to know this baby isn't his. It's nobody's business. And if we raise this child the best we can—I intend to do all I can to help, you know. You aren't alone–If we make him a credit to Matias, then that's a good kind of revenge, don't you think? We take that sicko out of the picture entirely. Kind of like an adoption."

Marguerite stood up and started pacing back and forth in the pool of light, creating odd shadows that moved around the room. "I don't know. I don't know if I can lie like that."

"This is your child, Maggie. Your child—no lie. Think on that."

Marguerite headed for the bathroom. She wasn't ready to think at all.

———❧———

Lester Pullman was a tall, stout man with thick white hair and a bushy salt-and-pepper mustache. His blue suit still bulged around his middle as it always had. He might have been wearing the same pale yellow shirt he had worn the last time they met. Seeing him sitting in the noisy working class restaurant where they had lunched together many times before, watching him check his watch and doodle nervously on the paper napkin, gave Marguerite a sensation of being outside time. Had she really gone to Argentina and had her life explode? Once he spotted her approach, Lester stood up, stuffing his pen into a pocket of his suit coat. He was an automatic gentleman out of habit instead of respect. But his smile was genuine. She knew he liked her. Without meaning to, he treated her like a little sister.

He almost hugged her, thought better of it, and shook her hand vigorously. "Maggie, Maggie, Maggie. It's good you're home. You look beat. Have a seat."

She sat and ordered a salad when the waitress hurried over.

Lester grinned at her. "That book of yours was a major hit. We rushed it out just in time—before the Soccer World Cup in Buenos Aires. I read there were something like 71,000 spectators for the finals—mostly not Americans, of course. You probably heard about it. But we still cleaned up. The best reference on the market. They loved the local flavor you put into it. Blew the competition out of the water. They'll have to go some to come up with a better guide. You should be proud of yourself. Gonna make us look good this year. We sent a check to Charles. Damn good pics. Liked the follow-up stuff, too. It's in the newsletter."

She couldn't think of a response.

Her silence seemed to remind him of something. He made a face without knowing he had and adopted a more serious tone. "Dorothy said you lost your husband. I'm real sorry, Kid. How did it happen?"

She considered lying for a moment. "He was murdered."

"Murdered!" he spouted so loudly that the people at the next table stopped to listen. Lester scowled and dropped his voice. "What the hell?"

She avoided his gaze. "It was political."

The flat period at the end of her sentence didn't invite more questions. Lester nodded slowly as though he understood. "Those countries down there get into a lot of that stuff." He thought for a moment. "You know, you could write a book about that…"

She cut him off. "No. No book about that."

"Sure. Sure, Kid. Sorry. Books about political stuff don't go big, anyway." He stuffed a french fry into his mouth to cover the awkward silence.

"Lester, I need a favor."

He swallowed. "Name it."

"I'm having a hard time. I don't want to come into the office any more than I have to. Lester, I'm pregnant."

"Well, congratulations!" He grinned and then realized she wasn't smiling back. "Oh. And your husband's dead. Damn, I'm sorry, Kid. That's hard."

She stared at the salad the waitress had just delivered. All at once, it looked sickening. "I don't think I could stand to have a baby shower. I don't think I could stand it. I don't want any fanfare—no cards or gifts or parties. I don't care if no one knows. I don't want to be around people. Please, Lester."

He was studying her. He had never seen her look like this before. She seemed so much older and sadder than the young woman he knew. Her bravado and the toughness he had admired were both drained away. "You want something you can write from home, am I right?"

"Please?"

"Sure." He ate a couple more french fries, thinking as he chewed. "Maybe a how-to...how to...how to get ready to travel overseas. Yeah. That would be good. You've been all over and people are traveling more. What do you do to prepare to travel for the first time— maybe from the point of view of a single woman?" He caught himself. "Or whoever. How about that?"

"I could write that. Dorothy could bring you pages."

"Sure. We'll put Zak in charge of pulling the thing together. You work well with Zak. You're living with Dorothy, huh? Is that what she was telling me?"

"Yes. She took me in. I'm selling the studio apartment."

"Good idea. Dorothy's a peach." He checked his watch. "Damn. I gotta run." He stood up. "I'm sure we've got enough stock pics on file—plus the extra footage Charles shot–to back you up. Or Jerome can do some artwork. We'll see what we need. Work on your own schedule. You always work fast." He motioned to the waitress to take his credit card. "This is on me." He made a face at Marguerite's salad. "We need a box."

He came around the table to kiss Marguerite on the head—as Matias had done. At the touch, she started to cry.

"Listen, Maggie," Lester told her quietly in her ear. "You need something, you call me on my direct line. No joke. Just call. Even at home. Louise loves you—so do the kids. Or come on over. We've got a guest room. You have friends, you know—not just co-workers, friends. We won't mention our arrangement to Alice Hanover. She's by the book, but she won't argue with profits."

"Thanks, Lester."

"You're gold, Kid. Everything will be okay."

She watched him walk out before she stood to leave. Dorothy would enjoy the boxed salad.

8

In spite of Dorothy's best efforts and Marguerite's best intentions, the pregnancy wasn't an easy one. The damage that had been done by the rape complicated the process. The doctor insisted on periodic checks that grew expensive. Marguerite had to spend time in bed. She hated it. As she lay there, visions plagued her. Even the good memories of Matias scraped the sides of her mind raw–what might have been. The other visions were as horrible as her nightmares. She imagined a baby that looked like Silva—had the same evil laugh and lecherous grin. When she slept, she slashed the baby into bits in her dreams. Matias accused her, hated her. Left her there in that blue room. Walked away. Abandoned her. She awoke sobbing. Dorothy brought her warm milk laced with whiskey.

She finished writing her book and took up drawing, but her pictures tended to be dark and foreboding. She couldn't imagine joy. She worked crossword puzzles that she never finished. She tried to learn to knit, gave up, and turned to cross-stitch sewing that was nothing but counting from one hole in the fabric to another–anything to keep her mind too busy to think. Dorothy tried to distract her with programs on television, but the characters were too happy, the music too loud, the stories too distant from reality. The roar of spectators cheering a football game made her tremble and weep uncontrollably. Dorothy couldn't miss the games, but she turned the sound off.

Marguerite's hypersensitivity grew worse with time. A sound. A flash of light. A texture that reminded her of the straps. A person on the street. Her flashbacks intensified. The doctor thought maybe her tumbling hormones were at fault. He didn't dare prescribe more potent tranquilizers. In an instant—even in the middle of the day, even in the middle of the grocery store—she would be back in that room, feeling the agony, feeling the loss. If Dorothy dropped silverware, Marguerite jumped and wept. She began believing she was the monster. She ceased believing in reality.

Even when she didn't make a sound, the screeching frozen horror in her expression alarmed people. Marguerite guessed they thought she was mad. She did her best to hold it all inside–to go rigid and blank. That scared people who knew her more than the grim expressions. The doctor sent her to a therapist named Judy. But even Judy's imperturbable calm couldn't make it all go away. Marguerite quit going.

She thought about abortion again—the illegal kind now that the window of opportunity was past, but the thought of what a fully developed aborted baby would look like, what she would have to remember for the rest of her life, intensified her guilt so much that she pushed the thoughts aside. Another killing, and this time it would be her unequivocal blame because she had waited too long. She would be the murderer. She could end up in jail. She could end up in Hell where Matias would never find her.

She thought about suicide—killing both the baby and herself. She could leap off a bridge or take pills or poison. She could step in front of a bus. And Silva would win. He could laugh. He had triumphed over all possibilities for happiness. The only prospect worse than living was granting him victory.

The doctor sent a social worker to talk to her about adoption. The idea was appealing. Have the baby and let the nurses take it away.

Never see it. Never even know the gender. She took the papers and stared at them for weeks. Would the adoptive family discover how the baby had come to be? Would they look at him or her with frightened eyes, watching for insanity? If the baby reflected South American heritage, the mixture of Spanish and native tribes, would people shun him? Would the adoptive family understand that this baby hadn't done anything wrong and deserved a chance—a chance to be innocent?

The life inside her kicked her as often as possible, reminding her that the person to come had a mind of his own. This baby was a victim as Marguerite was–certainly no less.

New York was still cold but braced for spring when Marguerite's water finally broke. Dorothy drove her to the hospital swathed in towels. The doctor had to take the baby with surgery. Marguerite was glad. The baby wouldn't exit the way Silva had come in.

"It's a girl," Dorothy reported to her as soon as Marguerite was coherent. "I told them I'm your older sister and they let me see her."

"I don't think I can look at it."

"*Her*," corrected Dorothy. "You don't want to look at *her* not *it*. We're talking about your little girl."

Marguerite squeezed her eyes closed, wishing Dorothy would go away.

Dorothy was not deterred. "They're cleaning her up now. The doctor wants to do some tests, considering this hasn't exactly been a normal pregnancy. So far, they haven't found anything wrong. A nurse will bring her in when they're done."

Marguerite sighed heavily. "I'm serious, Dorothy. I don't know if I can go through with this. I don't know if I can love her. I hate myself. I don't want to hate my child. I don't even want to be unfeeling like my mother was. What if she looks like him? Can I still put her up for adoption?"

Dorothy sighed and shook her head in mock disbelief. "You'll be fine. Wait until you see her! She's a sweetie pie. You'd better start thinking of names."

Time slipped a click and a nurse entered.

"Mrs. Garcia, meet your beautiful daughter." She placed the tiny bundle beside Marguerite. "She's a fighter, this one. Her eyes are open already. She wants to eat and she wants it now. I'll let you see if you can nurse her. Do you need any help?"

"No." Marguerite didn't want the nurse to see how much she wanted to push the baby away. "I'll manage." She pulled back a corner of the swaddling blanket.

The baby looked back at her with new eyes—haunting and pure–watching the blurry world as best she could. She tried to focus on Marguerite. Her vulnerability was overwhelming. She rested on the precarious ridge of living, looking for a champion. Her body felt warm and soft. Her tiny heartbeat throbbed bravely. She was as angelic as Silva was not. Matias would have loved her.

"What will you call her?" Dorothy asked, cooing unashamedly over Marguerite's shoulder. "Have you thought of anything yet?"

Marguerite didn't want to admit it, but she had been toying with names for a while—just in case. Now, as she looked down on this, her daughter, for the first time, she knew what her choice would be. "*Lympia*."

Dorothy stopped cooing for a moment. "Did you say *Olympia*?"

"No, *Lympia*, from the Spanish word meaning 'to clean.' It will be her job to clean away the evil, to make a fresh start."

Dorothy snorted. "Big job for such a tiny baby. You could've called her something like *Lucy* or *Sally* or even *Patty*—you know, from *Peanuts*. When she goes to school, the teachers won't know what to do with a name they've never heard. She'll have to spell it for everybody." She picked up the baby and held her close. "Hello, Lympia Garcia. Welcome. I guess it's not such an odd name–*Lympia*. Kind of Greek or something. Look at those fists! She'll be as stubborn as you are—I can tell. You know, I think she might be up to the challenge."

"After I feed her," said Marguerite, reaching for the baby. "My daughter can take on the world after I feed her."

When she and the baby were released from the hospital, Marguerite called Nicolas Garcia. She wasn't sure how he would respond, but the doctor and the psychologist Judy had advised Marguerite to tell the truth. After all, she and the baby were family, regardless—weren't they? "*Hola, Padre,*" she began. He interrupted.

"I have terrible news," he told her, his voice cracking. "Juanita is one of the disappeared. They took her boyfriend Franco, and she made so much trouble that they took her. Juan is making inquiries, but no one is hopeful."

"How is Maria?"

"Not good. Please stay away, *Hija*. This is a land of death."

"*Si, si, Padre*. I will do as you ask."

Dorothy was waiting when she hung up. "Were they excited? I'm sure they'll love your baby as their own."

Marguerite sat on the sofa. Nearby, Lympia was stirring in her new crib. Marguerite stood to pick her up.

"I didn't tell them." She took a moment to feel the baby's heartbeat against her, so much calmer than her own that was pounding against her chest. "Their oldest daughter just disappeared. They think she's dead. I have a bad feeling they're right." She let the tears in her eyes slip down her face and onto the baby's sleeper. "I guessed it would happen. Nita was so like Matias."

"Oh dear God." Dorothy placed a wide, warm hand on Marguerite's shoulder. "I'm sorry, Maggie. I'm really, really sorry. Is there anything we can do from here?"

Marguerite pulled the baby close. "No. I don't think so. But hearing that I just bore the child of one of the men the family hates most won't help."

"Maybe not right now," Dorothy conceded. "But they'd love her if they met her."

Marguerite could feel a last hot tear creeping down her cheek. "Not necessarily," she said, carrying the baby to the bassinet to be changed. "Not necessarily."

———◈———

They called her Pia as she grew. Her eyes became huge and dark beneath long lashes. She was bright, curious, and willful. Her hair tumbled in thick dark curls that might have been reminiscent of Matias, if that were possible. She copied everyone—including the rhythm of the commentators' speech on television. She hooted over cartoons without understanding what was going on and built precarious towers with her plastic blocks.

When Pia was barely three, the military junta in Argentina invaded the Falkland Islands, intending to seize the land from the United Kingdom. The newscasters said Argentina was trying to exercise its might and prove to its people they were right to maintain military rule. But the generals had misjudged their opposition—including the help sent from the United States—help that was the reason the story warranted space on the American evening news.

By the time Pia was four, a civilian government was replacing the Argentine junta. Marguerite heard the report on television—toward the end of the national broadcast. She called Nicolas. She imagined the celebration the family would be planning. Maria would prepare her specialties. Nicolas would hang lights and bring his best wine up from the cellar. Perhaps Juan would dance the tango with his wife. Their baby–who had been no more than a slight bulge the last time Marguerite saw them–would be older than Pia, or maybe there would be another baby, as well, by now. Marguerite imagined the couple dancing the tango with Juan holding a small child clinging to his back. She was smiling as she waited for the operator to connect her.

The son Juan answered. "*Mi padre es en el hospital con mi madre*," he told her, speaking as he would to someone of limited intelligence. "*Muy enfermo.*" He hung up abruptly. Was he merely upset or was he angry? Did he blame her or Matias for Nita's death or for whatever was wrong now? Was Maria dying? Juan obviously didn't feel that Marguerite needed to know.

Marguerite paused to send a silent prayer for the family that had almost been hers.

"Who are you calling, Mommy?" asked Pia.

Marguerite drew the little girl onto her lap. Pia's beautiful eyes were so like Matias. In this moment, she wanted her daughter to know the beautiful heritage that had come before her. She wanted her to know about the self-sacrifice, the courage. What did it matter if the genes weren't exactly hers? The legacy was. "Can you remember that I told you your daddy died far, far away from here?" she asked.

Pia nodded.

"Your daddy was a wonderful, loving man. He was a teacher. He tried to help lots of people. One day you'll help people like he did. And one day—a long, long time in the future, you'll meet him in Heaven."

Pia made a face. "He should have waited for me. He died too quick." She blew a kiss to Heaven. "There you go, Daddy. There you go."

"Yes," agreed her mother with a sigh. "Too quick." As Pia scampered away, Marguerite told herself she was doing the right thing.

———

Pia liked to charm visitors by singing and dancing to odd off-tune compositions of her own design. Or she might hurry to paint huge bright pictures on her art board with her sadly splayed brush. Marguerite told herself Lympia definitely took after Matias, and she almost forgot she was lying.

But as Pia entered school, she seemed to be less like him. She had a temper she would unleash when she was tired, stamping her foot and drawing her lips into a crinkled pout that looked like a heart that lacked ironing. Dorothy said she was too like Marguerite, but Marguerite knew better. One day, after a temper tantrum that lasted all afternoon so that Pia was sent to bed directly from dinner, Marguerite sat at the kitchen table, her head in her hands.

"What if she's going to be like Silva?" she asked as Dorothy approached.

"And what if she's just like any other little girl who gets too much attention and thinks she's the center of the universe?" replied Dorothy.

"She's your little girl, Maggie. She's yours not just because of biology. She's yours because you're raising her. I read once that Hitler wanted to be a painter. Maybe if he had a different upbringing, better parents, and more chances to do what he loved, we wouldn't have had a Holocaust."

Marguerite stood up, piling the dirty dishes into a precarious tower. "Nice. You're comparing my baby with Hitler."

Dorothy followed her to the sink. "Oh stop. I'm just saying that the way you raise a child makes a difference. The guy who started the Wendy's fast food restaurants was adopted. You think he would've created a chain of restaurants if he'd grown up with drug addicts?"

Marguerite was rinsing dishes in the sink. "Maybe *his* biological parents weren't sadists."

Dorothy made a disapproving noise in her throat. "You're being stubborn. That's like her, too. Maggie, we're crowded in this apartment. As Pia grows, she needs more space—her own room. We're too adult here. We need to find a place where she can run and play outside on grass with other children. Pia needs exercise and sunshine. And when I say 'we,' I'm hoping you don't mind if I come along. I've gotten used to being part of the family."

Marguerite agreed, but inside she was worried.

———⊰❈⊱———

The suburbs solved some problems and created others. Marguerite and Dorothy bought a tidy clapboard house in New Jersey with three bedrooms and two baths. It sat squarely on a large threadbare lawn beneath a protective weeping willow tree—the very stereotype of suburban life. Marguerite had to repaint the rooms to conceal years of dirt and fingerprints. She couldn't spend any time in her bedroom until she had hurriedly covered the blue walls. Dorothy bought a lawn mower, saying it was her fault they needed one, and Marguerite used it, cursing when she had to yank the engine into life—especially on hot days. The cheap metal window frames of the house glistened with indoor icicles in the winter and were almost too hot to touch in the summer. Mice escaped into the house at night from a secret tunnel beneath the kitchen sink, and the big willow in the front yard grew greedy for moisture, so they had to pay to dig up and repair the corrupted water lines. They couldn't avoid buying a secondhand car to go to the grocery or the hardware store or to shuttle Pia back and forth to her activities. They spent far more money than they had expected to spend. They told each other the move was worthwhile because now they had community. The neighbors pretty much ignored them.

Pia loved having a yard and a swing set, but the commute to work took Dorothy and Marguerite away for longer hours, leaving Pia in the hands of babysitters. Pia was quicker than they were, becoming contrary and manipulative, and before long, Marguerite was doing more freelance work from home. She wanted to be present when Pia returned from school bursting with her daily traumas and triumphs. She wanted to monitor Pia's friends.

"Are you and Aunt Dorothy lesbians?" Pia demanded to know without preface one day when she and her mother were folding clothes. She had just celebrated her tenth birthday.

"What?" Marguerite stopped folding and looked up at Dorothy who was standing in the doorway. Dorothy shrugged. "Where did you hear about lesbians?" her mother asked Pia.

"Louise Wright. She has an aunt who's a lesbian. She says you're a lesbian because you live with Aunt Dorothy and you don't date men." She looked at her mother, deciding she might need more explanation. She leaned close to help her mother understand. "Lesbians don't like men."

Marguerite sighed. "I don't date because I was married to the best man who ever lived. When you've been married to someone who was nearly perfect, you don't bother looking for someone else."

"And then you got to be a lesbian?" Pia's magnetic eyes focused on her.

"Lesbians can like men. They just like women better for some things. It's the way they're made. I am not a lesbian. I loved your father as dearly as I love you. Aunt Dorothy is my friend. She's adopted family. That's why you call her 'Aunt'."

"You said you love her. I heard you." Pia looked triumphant.

"People are supposed to love each other," Marguerite explained, throwing a look of exasperation to Dorothy who stood in the doorway, enjoying her discomfort. "All people are supposed to love all people. But there are lots of different kinds of love. Dorothy and I don't feel the kind of love that makes people get married."

The explanation had become too detailed for Pia's attention span. She patted the pile of pillowcases she had finished folding and stood up. "I think you should find a new man so I can have a dad. Michael Thompson says dads are cool." She paused to pull on the shoes that waited for her beneath the coffee table. "I'll tell Louise you're not a lesbian, but she isn't going to believe me. She thinks she knows everything. She doesn't. I get better grades. Can I go outside now?"

"Sure."

She flounced past Dorothy and out the front door, letting it slam behind her as an undefined statement.

Dorothy was laughing. "Just wait until you have the sex talk! I hope I'm nearby."

"Sex!" Marguerite felt her stomach roll. "It's not time for that yet, is it?"

"I hear it's never too early these days. Look at Pia. She's ten going on twenty-five. It won't be long before puberty."

"Oh god." Marguerite gathered the piles of clean clothes into her arms. The old dread had returned. She tried to force the memories to disappear. They never had. She still rarely slept peacefully all through a night. "I can't stand the thought of a boy on top of her. I want to hurt someone."

With effort, Dorothy leaned over to pick up the socks her friend had dropped. "You can't be anti-love forever. One day she'll need to care about somebody. Remember how it was for you and Matias—the love, not the rape. That wasn't even sex. That was assault." She draped the socks onto the top of the pile Marguerite was holding. "Somehow, I think the sex talk you eventually give Pia is going to scare the crap out of her so badly that she never wants a boy to touch her."

"I hope so. I'll do my best."

Marguerite laughed at Dorothy's grimace. "I'm just kidding," she said, unsure if she was. She carried the clothes to the bedroom and piled them on the bed. Dorothy was close behind her. They busied themselves sorting items into drawers.

When she had finished her pile, Dorothy straightened, her hands on her lower back. "Are you ever going to tell her the real story about Matias and Silva?"

Marguerite sat at the side of the bed, feeling a sensation of sinking more deeply than even the worn mattress could explain. Her knees felt weak. "I don't have a choice, apparently. The therapist told me if a child discovers her life has been a lie on her own, that's worse than knowing about the rape. But not yet. Let her have her childhood without that burden."

Dorothy nodded thoughtfully and then smiled. "Well, seems like you and I are a topic of gossip. Maybe it's time for you to give that guy in the library who keeps flirting with you a chance. Moms are role models, you know. It's time for you to date."

"I'm too old," said Marguerite aloud, but inside she was screaming again.

9

The search for a suitable date began. Richard White matched his name. He could've been one of those kinds of tasteless bread that are packaged in brightly colored white plastic to disguise the fact that they look like toy food. The old advertisement chirped, "Builds strong bodies twelve ways!" He was like that. He was religious about working out, so he had a nice physique, but he felt like additives—artificial nutrition. The good part about him was he was totally nonthreatening. He hadn't had an original thought for years.

He was delighted when Marguerite agreed to go to dinner and a movie with him.

"I saw your note on the bulletin board about the children's books you had to sell," he told her with barely concealed glee. "I know something about graphology, and you have the same intelligence and creativity as I do!" He was amazed. She wasn't.

In her mind, Marguerite was saying, "Oh god. I'll kill myself." But she forced a smile. "How interesting."

He tried to slip his arm around her, in a patronizing, dominant sort of way, and she jumped. She nearly hit him, which even he couldn't fail to notice.

"I'm sorry," she told him insincerely. "I don't like to be touched."

He frowned a little, apparently decided she needed warming up, and returned to what he believed was his entertaining banter.

He took her to a romantic comedy *When Harry Met Sally*. When he laughed, he snorted—which would have been tolerable if he had laughed at the funny spots. He laughed several beats too late, when the rest of the audience had settled down to prepare for the next humorous line. After his spray of laughter spittle gleamed in the light from the projected film, Marguerite declined his offer to share his popcorn.

As they left the parking lot in his brand new red Porsche—his proud evidence that he was truly successful as a manager—he drove forward over the parking stop so that the concrete scraped the bottom of his car with a terrible SCEE-RATCH. She pretended not to notice. "I did not see that," he told her, as though the presence of a parking stop was peculiar.

"Would you like to come up to my place for a little drink?" he asked as he finally pulled into traffic.

"I don't think so, thanks. I'm pretty tired."

"I have space on Thursday nights," he told her. "I like you and I think you're a very attractive woman. I do see other women. I'll be up front about that. But I'd like to see you, too. Who knows if something could come of it? I'll make you dinner on Thursday nights. I'm a good cook. I can make Béarnaise sauce. And a little sex would do you good. You'd sleep better. You can't mourn your husband forever. I'm divorced and I was dating again in weeks."

Marguerite was thinking that he couldn't have been dating much; he was too socially inept. She hadn't heard the sleep line since high school.

"No, thanks. I need to be home with Pia."

"You're making a big mistake!" he warned as he completed a clumsy, heart-quickening U-turn in traffic.

"I'll take my chances," she murmured, and he heard her.

Dorothy laughed heartily as Marguerite recounted her experience later. "And if you ever tell me I have to date some oddball from the library again, our friendship will end," Marguerite finished with a flourish.

But it wasn't the end. "You need companionship," Dorothy insisted. "Pia needs a father figure." Dorothy found a pleasant, friendly man in the produce section of the grocery store. He was wearing a golf cap and an open-necked shirt. He looked like a mature male model without the sultry glare.

"Do you often shop for your wife?" she asked him as casually as she could.

"I'm not married," he replied, wondering if this aging, overweight woman was coming on to him.

"I'll bet you're a good cook," Dorothy continued, hoping he would answer yes.

"I like to cook," he admitted.

"Oh good!" Dorothy permitted herself a satisfied sigh. "I don't mean to bother you, but I have a friend who needs advice about how to select good cantaloupes. Would you be willing to give her a few tips? She'd be too embarrassed to ask anyone herself and she's driving me crazy with her complaints about the bad ones she's purchased."

Relieved that he wasn't about to be stalked by someone who reminded him of his mother, he followed her to meet Marguerite by the olive oil. In her jeans, green t-shirt, and blonde ponytail, Marguerite was a welcome contrast to Dorothy.

"Maggie, this guy can help you with your selection problems," Dorothy said by way of introduction.

"You have problems choosing cantaloupes?" he asked Marguerite, noting that Dorothy had discreetly withdrawn.

Marguerite made a face. "Yes, actually I do, but you've been dragged here under false pretenses."

"Oh?"

She took a deep breath and plunged into her confession. "My daughter's girlfriend thinks I'm a lesbian because I share a house with a woman—Dorothy, the woman who just accosted you. Dorothy wants me to spend time with men so my daughter can stop worrying. Apparently, you happened to be both attractive and handy, so you were nominated without your permission. I apologize on behalf of both Dorothy and me. You've stumbled into a middle school soap opera."

He laughed. "I'm flattered—at least about the attractive part. And I understand middle school soap opera perfectly. I work at the high school."

His laugh was easy and natural. She liked him.

"I'm so glad we aren't at the high school level yet," she told him, wondering if she might be flirting just a little. "I need more training before we hit the majors."

He pulled out his wallet and extracted a business card. "I'm Allen Pritchard. Let me know if I can assist. I'm a high school counselor, so I can help explain the mysteries."

She offered her hand. "Marguerite Garcia. Dorothy calls me Maggie."

His shake was firm but gentle. "I'm pleased to meet you, Maggie."

She dug in her purse for her business card and presented it to him.

"A freelance writer," he read aloud. "I'm impressed."

"Don't be too impressed until you read my work." She tried to peer into his mind through his eyes. What was he thinking? Without intending to, she kept talking. "You know, I don't mean to do business in a grocery store, but I really would appreciate a chance to talk to someone who's better qualified than I am about dealing with adolescent hormones–if you have time one day. Could I call the number on your card to make an appointment?"

"Not really." He was tucking her card into his wallet. "We don't do outside work from the school, and we don't have much time for lunch. I could refer you to a good psychologist, or you and I could arrange a business dinner some time."

She smiled her professional smile. "I'm not overly fond of psychologists so far—a long story I promise I won't share. A dinner would be nice—Dutch, of course."

"I'll have to give you a call after I check my schedule. I have a few obligations working."

"Until then," she offered her handshake again, conscious that he was touching her for the second time and she wasn't yet panicked.

His manner was smooth and professional but friendly. "Think about any specific questions you want to ask, and let me know so I can be sure my answers are well founded in current research. In the meantime, I'd better go make sure no one has replaced the items in my cart."

"Yes, do. And thank you."

Dorothy reappeared the moment he left the aisle. "So?" she asked. "Did you like him? Did he ask you out?"

Marguerite chose her olive oil and placed it in her cart. "He's a high school counselor, and I asked to talk to him about Pia. We're going to plan a business dinner."

"A counselor!" Dorothy almost clapped. "Couldn't be better! And what a great line about Pia. I've underestimated you. I'll call the school to be certain he is what he says he is, and you're on your way!"

"It's a business dinner, Dorothy," Marguerite reminded her as they passed the pickles. "I wasn't using a line."

The dinner was business at the outset. They talked about Pia and puberty in general. They talked about high school expectations and preparing Pia for college. And then they talked about living in New Jersey and how difficult it was to find honest, stimulating conversation. Allen Pritchard was easy to talk to about nearly anything. By the time the dinner ended, they had another date—not specifically about business this time.

The next evening, Marguerite took Dorothy into the kitchen for a personal discussion, out of hearing for Pia who was in her room.

"I feel like I'm leading him on," Marguerite told her friend, as Dorothy carried the cookie jar over from the counter. "There's no way I'm ready for a romantic relationship. I'd freak out."

"Oh, for Pete's sake," muttered Dorothy, eating her third sugar cookie of the evening. "You didn't promise sex or anything did you?"

"No, but that's how men are. Two dinners, and a little pay-back is understood."

"What nonsense." Dorothy accidentally sprayed crumbs across the kitchen table when she spoke. She hurried to brush them together with the side of her hand. "I'll bet you money this guy isn't going to pressure you. He has kind eyes. The school told me he does charity work."

Marguerite started munching a cookie herself, realized she didn't want it, and pushed it away. "Never-the-less, I'm going to be up front with him from the outset—up front and blunt, Dorothy. Nothing cute."

"Fine. Mess up the first nice time you've had since…since Pia. See if I care." And she took the remains of Marguerite's cookie and shoved it into her mouth.

Only two weeks later, Marguerite was sitting across from Allen in an Italian restaurant.

"I was raped long ago, and I don't 'give out' or whatever they're calling it these days," she blurted over the salad. "I just thought you should know."

He was quiet for a moment. "I'm sorry. I'm deeply sorry that happened to you." He dressed his salad and then paused. His eyes were a pale, winter sky blue. "I didn't ask you to dinner for sex, Maggie— just fettuccini and good company. I'd be content to be friends, if that's okay with you."

She smiled a quiet, sincere smile. "That would be fine."

He was careful not to touch her—especially if she didn't see it coming. He didn't even reach for her hand. As a counselor, he knew his business.

He slipped into Marguerite's life smoothly, almost imperceptibly, perhaps accidentally. He was tall and bald, sensitive and wise, and fascinated by everything. He felt like a warm comforter or maybe excellent mashed potatoes. Even Pia seemed to settle down in his presence. Dorothy adored him and said more than once that she would've competed with Marguerite for his attention if she were a couple decades younger and a hundred pounds lighter.

He took all three of them to see *Dances with Wolves*. The next day Pia asked him to walk with her, so they went to the park.

"You're a counselor… at the high school…right?" she began.

"Yes."

The guy in the movie did what he thought was right, even when people thought he was wrong and did terrible things to him and his animals. I think my dad was like that. He got killed for doing what he thought was right."

"I don't know much about him."

She took Allen's hand and pulled him over to a park bench where they both sat. "Do you think a girl—say, a girl like me—could stand up like that without being weird? You know–do what's right even if people get mad?"

"Do you have something in mind?"

"Not yet. I mean, I do little things at school—I stuck up for a kid who has problems reading. I complained to the principal that the teacher was picking on him in class. I wanted to be brave like my dad."

"What you did sounds brave."

"Yeah. I don't think the principal believed me. He said I wouldn't understand."

"At least you said something."

"Yeah, I guess so. Now my teacher avoids me, and the other kids call me a suck-up."

"If it helps, I don't think you're a suck-up."

She turned to smile at him. "Thanks. I'm just worried about going into high school with that kind of reputation."

Allen nodded knowingly. "Standing up means you have to take the consequences. People don't like you just because you're right. Sometimes the brave part is letting them *dis*like you because they don't want to feel wrong. You have to know what you said or did was worth the grief."

"Like a martyr."

"In a smaller way, yes."

She stood up. "Thanks, Mr. Pritchard. You're an excellent counselor."

"You can call me Allen away from school."

She grinned. "Allen, then. I knew you'd tell me the truth."

———◆⊰⊱◆———

Allen took the three to museums, apparently never tiring of listening to Pia's excited running narrative about whatever they were viewing. He and Marguerite enjoyed long walks, sometimes circling the park several times as they talked. They chatted about Pia and her impending adulthood. They discussed Dorothy's high cholesterol and the kinds of changes they wanted to convince her to make in her diet. They talked about books, the weather, and the foreign films they went to see. They never talked about sex.

"Are you sure we aren't boring you?" Marguerite asked him after spending a long day together as a threesome peering at Egyptian artifacts. "We take so much of your free time."

"I like the company."

Marguerite had the impression he had spent long years without companionship.

He invited the three to his house for Thanksgiving, where he did such a delicious job of preparing the feast that Dorothy made him promise to invite them to dinner again. They watched the movie *It's a Wonderful Life* instead of football—to Pia's delight and Dorothy's dismay, and Dorothy told Marguerite secretly that Allen was almost a perfect man. "If only he had been around thirty years ago."

Marguerite didn't reply. She couldn't compare him with Matias. Matias had been passion and joy. Allen was safety and home.

10

T he four of them—Marguerite, Pia, Dorothy, and Allen–were a patched-together family for Christmas, singing carols with the stereo and baking funny gingerbread men that Pia altered until their legs bowed in or bent ridiculously outward. Allen gave Marguerite a soft, deep blue sweater that emphasized her eyes, and she gave him an elegant green silk tie. Pia made paper mache ornaments for everyone.

"Why don't you marry him?" Pia asked her mother after Allen had left and they were preparing for bed. "Why don't you just marry him? He's here all the time, anyway. And he helps me with my homework."

Marguerite kissed her forehead. "You don't marry someone for helping with homework," she said. "We're happy as we are. Most people never have this much happiness." But she was wondering how deep the affection she felt for Allen went. And what kind of affection did he feel for her? If she told him the whole story about Silva and Matias and Pia's parentage, what would that do to their relationship? What kind of relationship did they want?

She decided to find out before the New Year.

The day was cold and painfully bright. Sharp crystals glittered from the new snow, diamonds that might slice you if you fell on them. The chill captured Marguerite's breath and froze it into little gray, misshapen clouds that slipped away with the wind. Passers-by drew their arms close to their bodies and tucked their faces into their collars.

It was an odd time for a casual walk through the park—especially one that had as its purpose the revelation of great secrets. Even Allen, who was usually impervious to cold, admitted defeat.

"I don't know about you, but I'm freezing. I haven't felt my fingers for the past fifteen minutes."

Somehow, they ended up at his modest brick house, sipping hot chocolate in front of his electric fireplace. Marguerite was acutely aware of being in his space, alone with him this time, smelling the lingering fragrances of his shower, seeing his neatly made bed through the doorway. She sat on his tan leather sofa. He sat across from her on a dark blue upholstered chair, looking a little like a therapist about to hear something difficult. He looked as serious as she felt. She didn't want to know what he was thinking—yet.

"I need to tell you about my husband and Pia's father," she told him, setting her cup down on an end table, and he nodded. She went through the story, omitting nothing this time, and he never interrupted. When she finished, he looked a little like he might cry, but he didn't. He sat silent.

She started to worry. What could he be thinking?

His voice was unsteady when he finally spoke. "I'd say I'm sorry, but what you endured is too big for sorry. What you endured is devastating—a disaster–an example of the worst, the very worst of people. How you can walk around, being as lovely as you are, after an experience like that is a mystery, a miracle."

Marguerite shifted her position on the sofa, fighting an urge to pull herself into a fetal position. "Allen, I need your opinion—professional and personal, now that you know us. I've been meaning to ask since we first met, but I was afraid of what you'd say. Should I tell Pia her father was a rapist or let her keep believing he was my husband?"

He finished his chocolate, deliberately taking his time, and replaced the mug on a coaster on the side table. "Yes. Yes, you should. You probably should've started that direction before now, but the present will do. She idolizes your husband and wants to be like him. You need to tell her she can certainly do that even if they don't share blood."

Marguerite kicked off her shoes and pulled her feet up under her. "But she's so young and impressionable. I can't pretend her father was anything but a monster. She was conceived in pain, hatred, and violence. What kind of pride is there in knowing that? What is she supposed to tell her friends?"

He leaned forward, resting his arms on his knees. "I'm not saying the truth will be easy for her, but we all have to live with who we are. She doesn't have to be defined by the past, and she doesn't have to tell her friends if she doesn't want to. The longer you wait, the bigger the shock is going to be, and if she finds out on her own that you've deliberately lied to her, your relationship will be damaged."

"I haven't told her because I don't want her to feel like less."

"Tell her you haven't told her because you didn't want to upset her. Make your lie an act of love. It was well intentioned. She's very intelligent. Once she adjusts to the facts, she'll understand why you waited. If you, the victim, can love her as you do, can separate her the person from the conception, she should be able to love herself."

Marguerite felt suddenly shy. "Does this change your opinion of me?"

He smiled. "I admire you for surviving. I admire you even more than I did before, and I've always thought you are an extraordinary woman."

She pulled a patterned throw pillow in front of her where she could hug it to her chest. She couldn't look at him. "I don't know that I could ever have sex with a man again, Allen. You need to know that and why. I don't mean to lead you on."

He came to sit near her on the sofa, at an angle, so he could see her face. She could feel her heart pounding, her nerves jumping with too much electricity. Surely he wasn't going to kiss her, was he? Could she tolerate his touch? Would she cry out?

"Maggie," he said quietly, using the nickname he had adopted from Dorothy as he always did. "Maggie, I love you as much as I have loved anyone else in my life—more. I love Dorothy and I love Lympia—she who cleans. I get that now. I love feeling as if I have a family. My own family disowned me when I was a boy. I would do anything for the three of you. But I'm a kind of lie myself."

He leaned forward a little, not touching her with anything but the invisible bubble of his self. "Maggie, I'm gay."

He waited for a reaction, a gasp perhaps. But she didn't make a sound.

"Please forgive me for not telling you sooner, but if the school district found out, I'd never work again. They consider my 'condition' to be an aberration, a sickness. They think gay people contaminate the students—as though I'm contagious. My parents felt the same way. They did their best to beat gayness out of me. I ran away and put myself through college bussing tables. I don't tell anyone. I just bury that part of myself and try not to think about it."

She rose and wandered around the room, touching different objects as though the physical sensation would help her think. "Gay. How ironic. I didn't guess. Isn't that funny? I always thought I was good at guessing."

"We know what we choose to know. Maggie, I'm deeply sorry if I've hurt you," he said. "You deserve more." His voice was husky.

She gave a half-laugh. "I was worrying that you were anxious for a sexual relationship."

"You're safe there, but I treasure our friendship."

She turned to face him. "So do I." She studied his face for a moment. "Oh, Allen. I think I understand for the first time what it feels like to be permanently disconnected from the mainstream through no fault of your own. Here you are, what Dorothy calls the perfect man, hiding a huge part of yourself because people think God made a mistake with you."

"Thank you," he said softly. "You're more generous than most."

She laughed bitterly. "We're a perfect match, you and I–two people who can't love as they were designed to because of the cruelty of others." She picked up a porcelain statue from a table, a miniature copy of Michelangelo's Pieta. "I'm the perfect cover for you, Allen. I make you look heterosexual."

His brows furrowed. "Maggie, I didn't spend all this time with you to use you!" She looked at him, and he shrugged. "Okay, maybe I thought of it in the beginning, but now you're my dearest friend."

She replaced the statue and came to sit by him again. "I'm not offended. I think I told you Dorothy hunted you down in the grocery store because she wanted me to look like a 'normal' woman for Pia. Dorothy pretended the lesbian rumors didn't bother her, but they certainly did." Marguerite reached out to place her hand on his. "You and I *are* normal for our circumstances. We do love one another—as friends. This isn't a lie, Allen. It's the Universe fitting the irregular pieces into the puzzle."

He smiled. "I never thought of myself as a puzzle piece, although I have felt irregular at times."

She stood up. "Let's get married!"

He drew back, his mouth gaping.

She continued. "Yes, let's get married—as friends—a permanent cover for both of us. No more stupid, annoying questions. No more sideways glances. We can have twin beds—separate bedrooms, if we find a bigger house. Lots of married people do. Lots of married people don't have sex."

He looked distressed. "But what if I meet someone? What if I fall in love with a man or have an affair? I'm not a saint, Maggie. I'm just gay."

She shrugged. "Lots of married men have affairs—some of them homosexual, I'm sure. If you have an affair, you'll be discreet as you obviously have been up until now. And if you fall in love and want to live with your partner, well, then we'll get a divorce. I'd miss you terribly, but I care about you enough to let you go. Couples have to lose one another someday, no matter what."

"I'll be in the way if you find a man to love or if one finds you."

She made a funny noise in her throat. "Not at all likely. But again, we could cope." She came to stand near him. "Allen, living with you, I wouldn't feel like I was betraying Matias—again—and Pia would have a father, a good father. I think you make a wonderful father, Allen."

"What would Matias say?"

She shrugged. "He'd probably hate the idea. He wasn't immune to machismo, but if he's looking down from Heaven and wants Pia and me to be as happy as possible, he'd agree."

Allen sighed. "I never dreamed I'd have a chance to be a father." Tears were slipping down his cheeks, celebrating a chance to be free. He took a long breath and exhaled it slowly.

"Let me think about the marriage thing. I'll take care of the legal preparations. And then, well, I can't think of a better way to start a new year than by embracing a family." He stood up and took her hands in his. "I can't believe you'd do this with me!"

He released her and set about self-consciously collecting their dirty mugs and napkins, thinking aloud as she had never heard him do before. "We'll invite Dorothy to stay with us, unless our kind of arrangement bothers her. She may not want to share space with a gay man. We'd have to tell her, wouldn't we? And she'd have to keep our secret. I don't know what we would tell Pia. Would she get the wrong idea if we don't sleep together? I'll have to think about that. I'm too close to the problem to think well right now. We'll definitely need a larger house. How about February as a possibility?"

She grinned. "February sounds perfect. Let's open some wine and toast our little adaptation."

He wiped a hand across his face, erasing his tears. "Yes, ma'am. Wine it is—the bottle I've been saving for a special occasion."

———◈———

Marguerite was doodling designs for a handmade wedding invitation on a pad of Pia's art paper when Allen called. January was nearly past, and he had not yet set an exact date for their wedding. She didn't want to tell anyone but Dorothy and Pia until she had a date—just in case. Perhaps the idea didn't sound as good to him once he'd had a chance to think it over. Perhaps the real prospect of acting like a couple all the time was more difficult for him to tolerate—felt like more of a lie–than he had expected. Maybe she was making assumptions that weren't going to work out.

She hadn't seen him for several days. He had been fighting a persistent flu, not unlike most of the country. She could already guess that he was going to beg off having dinner with the family. So much for the pot roast. Was he milking the illness to avoid facing her?

"How the heck are you?" she asked playfully over the phone. "Can I bring you something? More chicken soup, maybe? How about crossword puzzles?"

"No, thank you." His voice sounded strained. Something was wrong.

"Do you have a fever again?"

"Yes."

"Maybe you need to talk to a doctor about what might help."

She could almost hear him swallow. "I already did. Maggie, I have AIDS."

She sat down on the sofa, dropping like so much dead weight. "Oh dear God." She couldn't breathe for a moment. All the air in the room had been sucked into the telephone.

"I'm sorry, Maggie. I'm so very sorry. We would've made a good-looking couple."

"Are you sure? Are you sure it's AIDS?"

"Yes, they're sure. There'll be more tests, of course. But they already know."

She wanted to ask when he might have been infected, but she didn't. He heard the question, anyway. Allen was like that.

"It was long before I met you. He was young and beautiful and I thought I loved him. I was wrong. He didn't care about me at all. He was just collecting trophies—at least one too many, as it happened. My virus has been waiting since then to take over. Now it's moving fast."

She couldn't think. "We can still be married."

"No. No, there's no point. I can't be a family member any longer. I'm quitting my job, but as the disease progresses, people won't be kind. It's not a disease that's easy to hide, and people love a scandal. You'd just stigmatize yourself and Lympia. Life is going to be tough enough for you now."

"You *are* family," she insisted. "Sick or well, married or not, you're still family. You're my best friend besides Dorothy. We're going to help you fight. They find new treatments all the time. Not everyone dies."

"Stay away, Maggie. Keep Dorothy and Pia away. If I accidentally infected any of you, I'd go to my death despising myself—and maybe despising you for letting me do it."

"You aren't going to infect anyone. They know how to prevent contamination. We just have to avoid bodily fluids, I think. I think that's what I've read. I can find out. The hospital will tell us, I'm sure. We'll be careful, but we'll be there. Do you need anything now?"

He was quiet for a moment. Marguerite thought she heard him crying. "I love you all, Maggie. You're the best part of my life. Tell Dorothy I think an angel sent her to find me in the produce aisle. The three of you made my life worth living."

Marguerite wanted to say more. She wanted to tell him that he had helped so many high school students, affected so many lives, saved so many young people from suicide, that his life had been more than worthwhile. He had enriched their family and resuscitated her life. He'd been a gift. But she couldn't. She was weeping. She would have to save those words for another day.

11

Marguerite waited until they had finished dinner before she asked Dorothy and Pia to stay at the table to talk. She had thought she'd have Allen tell them himself—he was so good at dealing with terrible situations, but he was too ill. Besides, she couldn't be positive they wouldn't say something hurtful to him without realizing. Bad surprises sometimes brought out the stupid in people.

"Allen and I aren't getting married," she said first. "He's too sick."

"Can't you wait until he's well?" asked Pia.

"They don't think he'll get well. Allen has AIDS." The words squatted on the table, fat and ugly and inescapable.

"What do you mean AIDS?" asked Dorothy. "How could he get AIDS?"

Pia supplied the answer. "He's gay. That's it, isn't it, Mom?"

"Yes. He's gay. That's not the only way people get AIDS, but it's the way he did it. We didn't tell you because we didn't think you needed to know that. He's my dear friend. I love him as I love you. He was going to be the best darned dad you ever saw. He's a wonderful man. He loves both of you. But he's gay. And now he's sick and probably going to die."

"Being gay means a man in love with another man, right?" asked Pia.

"Yes, it does—in general. There's more to it, I'm sure."

"Brian Turner at school said gay people can get therapy and stop being gay."

Marguerite drew a long, painful breath. "Can you stop being a girl? No. Allen couldn't stop being gay unless he had been only pretending to be gay all his life. And he wasn't. It's biology."

Dorothy stared at her dirty plate. Her upbringing was battling her affection. "I should've known he was too good to be true." She glared at Marguerite. "How could you be married to a gay man? What kind of nonsense is this?"

"No nonsense. We love each other as friends. We weren't going to sleep together. Not all love is about sex."

Dorothy snorted.

"In a different world, he'd be judged by his character, not his sexual preference. But this isn't a different world. I guarantee it." Marguerite wadded her napkin in her hand. "We were going to take care of one another."

Pia was scraping her fork across her empty plate, a sound she knew agitated her mother. "Why didn't you tell us before? Why didn't you think we needed to know? Didn't you trust us?"

"If you had known, you'd have to keep his secret at school. You'll have to keep it now—at least for a while. He's quitting his job. If the administrators or parents had known he was gay, he would've been fired even if he weren't sick, and he wouldn't have any insurance. They'd probably investigate whether he was molesting boys."

Dorothy gaped. "Was he molesting boys?"

"No, of course not!" Marguerite was annoyed. "Being gay doesn't make you a pedophile. Most pedophiles are heterosexual. But people make assumptions—dumbass assumptions that fit their teeny tiny view of life."

Dorothy was hurt. "I just asked."

Marguerite sighed. "I didn't mean you're a dumbass."

Pia's face was turning red. "You should've told us. You should've trusted us. I don't care what Brian Turner says. I love Allen. I don't care if he's gay or has AIDS. I want to help take care of him as much as I can. Please don't tell me I can't. He's the only dad I know." She started to cry.

Marguerite came around the table to embrace her daughter. "We'll take care of him, Pia. I told him so. He said to stay away so we wouldn't take any chances, but we'll take care of him the very best we can."

Dorothy nodded slowly. "I'll help, too, but I'm glad he wasn't molesting boys. I'm surely glad about that."

Allen died slowly, month by month, the sores spreading to his most tender areas. He was sent to a special ward in the hospital. He lost much of his short-term memory so that Pia had to tell him the same story about her day at school over and over again. When she looked at his emaciated misery, Marguerite couldn't help thinking of Matias. At least his gruesome suffering hadn't stretched into weeks. From what she had read, for some of the estimated 30,000 of the disappeared, it had.

It was Dorothy's turn to sit by Allen's bed. He was asleep. She sat at a distance from the bed, watching the TV high on the wall. Marguerite decided to tell Pia about the ESMA and how Matias had died. She had an idea that the story might provide a point of comparison for the ugly death that was claiming Allen. She led Pia to a remote corner of the hospital lobby, facing the courtyard garden.

"The soldiers tortured him," she told her. "They shocked his private parts with a cattle prod and skinned his feet. They stabbed him with a hot nail. I watched as he died."

Tears streamed down Pia's face, but she didn't give in to them. "I come from strong people," she said at last. "I won't let you down—or him, either. I'm proud of him, Mom, really proud. No wonder you didn't want another husband. You should've told me all this before."

Marguerite hugged her. She had left out the part about what had happened to her that day while the crowds gathered to watch soccer. Allen wouldn't approve, but the time still felt wrong. Pia was only beginning to build an identity for herself. The deaths of two good fathers were enough for one teenager to handle. She didn't need to have a third, an evil father some of whose genes she carried, to confuse her—not yet.

"What a terrible place Argentina is," Pia muttered, shaking her mother from her thoughts. "I read about the Maya who sacrificed their own people. Were they in Argentina? Those people are cruel and demented."

"The Maya believe in reincarnation. Death meant something different to them. As for Argentina, governments everywhere make mistakes. There are terrible people everywhere. They're the minority, but they crave power, and when they get it, everyone pays. The military junta is out of power now. There's a civilian government that talks of human rights for its citizens–many good people such as the members of Matias's family. I used to think of going back to finish the work Matias began with his friends, but I don't have his talent for good works."

"Family? I have family in Argentina?" Pia sat up, instantly alert. "You never told me that before."

Marguerite felt her insides twisting, twisting, twisting. This couldn't be the right time to explain—not while dear Allen lay dying. This couldn't be the right time. She didn't have the strength.

"We'd better go back upstairs."

Allen didn't die without pain, nor did he die without family to mourn him. Marguerite, Dorothy, and Pia were all there. Marguerite held his hand. He mouthed, "I love you," as he left. Dorothy said anyone who died like that would certainly have a place in Heaven.

"He deserved a place for who he was," said Marguerite in a soft voice.

Pia agreed.

His birth family arrived soon after they received word he was dead. They were willing to handle his burial arrangements. They were ready to accept the goods he left behind. But he had willed all he had to Marguerite and Pia. The family left in a huff.

"Dike," someone muttered to Marguerite as they exited.

———⊲⊷⊳———

The strain of caring for Allen wore badly on Dorothy. His death brought back the pain of her mother's death, and Dorothy had no more reserves after her own medical issues over the years plus the shock of Allen's sexual orientation. She stopped going out. She stopped joining in the dinner table conversations. And then, one day, Pia found her staring at the TV with her jaw sagging. She couldn't talk. They called an ambulance that rushed her to the hospital. She had suffered a stroke. Her left side had stopped working. Her brain was badly compromised.

The two younger women had no way to care for her day by day. Marguerite had to take an extra job to pay the huge bills the sale of Allen's goods hadn't covered, and Pia was in school. They had no choice but to trust Dorothy to a convalescent care facility. Dorothy's weary brain couldn't process the change. She thought she had been abandoned. She died in the night.

"I feel terrible," Pia confided in her mother as they sat weeping in the funeral home, waiting for the cremains. "I feel guilty–like we could've done something more and we didn't."

"Me, too." Marguerite handed her daughter a tissue from the box she was cradling. "But I know guilt well. It doesn't help. Nothing changes except that you tie yourself in knots. Let it go."

"Have we done something wrong?" Pia asked, after blowing her nose. "First Allen and now Dorothy—so close together. It's like we're being punished."

"Sweetheart, death is a fact, no matter what you do. All we can do is to send them off with love. As for the punishment part, I have no doubt we've done some things wrong—at least I have," her mother told her. "But letting professionals take care of Dorothy wasn't one of them. She needed special care. So did Allen. I look at people who do evil…"

"…Like the man who murdered my father."

Marguerite hesitated for the smallest part of a second. "Yes…like him. And I don't think everyone is punished on this side of living."

"On the other side?"

"Maybe."

"I hope so."

She brushed Pia's hair back from her face, that lovely face. "I'm just so glad I have you, Lympia. You make the world around you clean and good. I thank God for you." She kissed the top of Pia's head. She knew her daughter would be an adult soon enough.

12

T he morning sun threw dazzling golden light against the reflective windows of the classroom building as Pia marched away from the university. She ignored the glances of appreciation she received from the young male students who passed her on the steps. Today, they offended her. She had dressed carefully in her professional blue dress and high heels–not for them, but for success—success that hadn't happened. The committee had rejected her line of reasoning. They had refused to approve her dissertation and, consequently, her PhD—told her she needed to rework her conclusions. Her mentor had warned her they were going to deny her. He said she had gone too far, stepped beyond the research, beyond their academic comfort zone, into idealistic ether, but she had hoped really hard he was wrong. Why were they all so painfully conservative! Her face was flushed and her step was fast and hard. The committee members were idiots–with no conscience. They couldn't recognize important substance when they saw it. How could the world ever change if those in charge didn't want change? Everything had to be their way. Control freaks! Why had she bothered with them!

She tucked her work under her arm and then, on a whim, dumped the dissertation into a nearby wire waste bin. She didn't need to be a PhD. What a joke it was, anyway. Doctor. They weren't doctors. They were just professional students—mostly followers, scoffing at any idea they hadn't suggested first.

Nick was waiting for her. His height made him look regal, even in his casual slacks and striped pullover top. He was already a PhD, but his dissertation had been something scientific, something to make the world better and wiser. Or maybe it had been the same old nonsense. She didn't care to know, but she knew he'd tell her, anyway, if she asked. And she would try to understand in-group terminology that sounded like a foreign language. Eventually, he would come up with an utterly new idea about something. He was like that. She liked Nick. He smelled delicious. She liked his changeable hazel eyes and brown hair that insisted on being independent. She liked the way he looked so much less interesting than he was.

"How did it go?" he asked, pretending to be unable to read her face.

"I'm done. I quit. It's over."

"So you did it your way," he concluded, not knowing if he wanted her to hear him. He strolled over to the waste bin to retrieve the tidy dissertation he had spotted—one of the things that was not like the others, one of the things that wasn't the same. It looked ridiculous there, like a top hat on a homeless person. He added it to the pile of books he was already carrying. "You might need this one day, you know."

He was so practical. And calm. Sometimes annoying.

"For what? I'm not going back to them, Nick. I don't give a shit."

When she used profanity, he knew she was seething. Usually, her language bordered on the prudish. He wanted to laugh, but he knew she wouldn't understand. "Maybe you'll use it to move forward on your own. The dictatorships aren't going to go away without strategy."

"They aren't going to go away at all—partly because of apathy. Duh!"

If he had known her mother better, he would've recognized Marguerite's glare, but he had met Marguerite only once. "Focus on what you're going to do next."

"I'm going to get drunk."

He should've been on his way to the library, but a chance to watch her drink was too delicious to ignore. Pia was an easy drunk. After her third glass of wine (yes, it had to be a nice red wine. She cared about what was good for the body), her nose would turn rosy red and she would grow more expressive, more emotional, her words a little fuzzier—especially the big ones. If he were lucky, she would end up kissing him, realize it felt extraordinarily good, and kiss him more. She never drank so much that she couldn't make love. She didn't like drinking enough to do that. She was the perfect girlfriend.

"Then I'm coming with you."

Her eyes narrowed. She suspected his motives. "I'm going to get really drunk this time, Nick. I mean it. Really, vomiting drunk."

"Okay. Then you might need an escort."

"Never mind." She read his thoughts through his eyes. She could do that. She had a way of knowing more than she should be able to know about anyone she liked. She would stand close, look at you with her large dark eyes, and suddenly your soul would tell her whatever she wanted to know.

She gave a huge sigh. "JUST NEVER MIND. You'll take me to brunch, instead, and you'll pay. I was too nervous to eat this morning. Do they serve wine in the morning? I don't like champagne. We'll have wine with brunch—something outrageously expensive."

He laughed. "Sure."

"And you can throw that damned dissertation away. I have plenty more copies. I spent my rent money on them. Mom's going to be very unhappy. She donated to the cause."

"I'll keep this copy as a memento then."

They walked in silence for a while.

"They truly are gutless wonders, you know—those self-important committee members," she said at last. "Mom used to tell me that university people were progressive liberals. Like hell. Things must have changed–not for the better, either."

"They have careers and reputations to protect," he added, knowing as he said it that he shouldn't have. She would hear him defending them.

"And THAT'S a good reason to be unreasonable." She glared at him, saw a reflection of her glare in his eyes, and laughed. "I'm fuming, aren't I?"

He nodded. "Just a little. Rightfully so. You put a lot of work into that dissertation. Most departments in most universities would've gone all gooey over it. You're fighting politics here. And jealousy, maybe. You could always take it elsewhere."

"Yeah, right." As though universities traded graduate students. As though they'd pick up her dissertation and say, "Hey, you've got something here. We're going to give you a PhD because you're so good. You don't even have to re-do all the coursework or the research—well, maybe you'll redo *some* of the coursework. Maybe *most*. Okay, *all*. We have our standards." She could hear that conversation in her head. She wouldn't give another committee the opportunity to reject her. She hated rejection—especially when she had earned better.

Nick could see her thinking. He was shaking his head slowly. She could be really stubborn.

She grinned at him. "How about we buy a bottle of wine after brunch, take it to your place, and then we could take a nap—you know, a *nap*?" She tickled his ear.

"You're going to use me?"

"The best I can. I have tension. Stress kills, you know."

He laughed. "You're on. And then we'll figure out how to put your ideas into coveralls and make them do something helpful."

"Honestly?"

He kissed her lightly, thinking of the afternoon to come. "On my honor."

They lay together in the warm summer light. Nick thought she was most beautiful with her mass of dark hair spread across his white pillow—a magical juxtaposition of white and black dancing with the afternoon sun, flirting with the shadows. Asleep, she could appear so vulnerable, so undisguised, and so magically elfin—a perfect contrast to the tough exterior she presented to the world. He had known from their first date that he wouldn't walk away from this one. She had a grip on his heart that he couldn't explain.

———❈———

His parents didn't care for Pia much. Harold and Cynthia Graves had higher aspirations for their son. They were terrified this erratic siren would lead Nick away from the scientific career they had plotted for him since his teens. They met Pia on the day she received her Master's Degree—in the humanities, nothing substantial. Nick was receiving his doctorate in climate science. What an odd name—Lympia, just the sort of silly artificial appellation some people liked. She looked especially

Spanish beside her blonde mother who wrote plebian travel guides—travel for the uninformed. Mrs. Marguerite Garcia had never attended college—at all. In spite of her high cheekbones and mostly natural blonde hair that might once have been striking, she looked slightly unkempt and distracted all the time. Her clothes shouted their kinship with millions of copies on racks in malls everywhere. She put her head together with Pia's and the two women giggled like girls. To Cynthia Graves, the scene was quite unseemly.

"Delighted to meet you," Pia told Harold and Cynthia as she offered each a handshake. At least she knew enough not to attempt to hug them. Perhaps Nick had prepared her. Her dark eyes had a way of looking into you. Her body made an unremarkable dress into something that turned heads. Even Harold grinned like a schoolboy. She was definitely dangerous.

"I made lunch reservations for the six of us—on Dad, naturally," announced Nick triumphantly. "I knew you'd want a chance to talk to one another."

He was wrong, of course. Cynthia had planned a strictly family celebration. Nick would know that. He enjoyed seizing control.

"How very kind," said Marguerite. She had to know Nick had invented the invitation on his own without permission. If she did, she feigned innocence. "I've heard such lovely things about you both from Nick–how you've supported him every step of his way. You must be very proud."

Nick stepped between Marguerite and Pia. "And we're all proud of Pia, too. She's already been accepted into the doctoral program. What a fine day this has turned out to be!" He presented his arms to both women and they started as a trio toward the parking lot.

Harold and Cynthia followed. There had been other girls in Nick's life, of course, but not as many as they had anticipated. He seemed to have his own way of sorting the possibilities. A waitress would lean over the table, offering him more than additional water, and he would look away. He was picky. This Pia was attractive, but they wouldn't have guessed he'd pull her out of the crowd. He wasn't usually drawn to ethnic types. They had never seen him so smitten. If they forbade him, they'd never see him again. He had his grandfather's rebellious streak.

They wanted Nick to make his mark—the mark the family had earned by pushing him forward all these years. Nick had extraordinary potential. All his teachers had told them as much since he was a boy. He was much brighter than his younger brother Peter was and less flighty than his younger sister Kathleen. He held the key to his parents' dream of moving out of the realm of successful business into a realm of scientific acclaim. (Wouldn't it be wonderful to attend a Nobel Prize ceremony?) Besides, they weren't prejudiced, but they didn't want to look forward to brown grandbabies—even a pale latté sort of brown.

Nick had never been the precise answer to his parents' prayers. He humored them and then did what he wanted. And now he wanted to spend as much time as he possibly could with the young woman in his bed.

Pia stirred, opened her eyes, and unleashed the full force of her smile on him. "Oh, you're good; you know that, Mr. Graves? You've totally freed me from my grand funk."

He kissed her soundly. "I could do it again, if you have the time."

"Of course," she held him back with a single finger. "On one condition."

"Which is?"

"You have to come with me when I tell my mother I didn't get my PhD." She sat up, holding the sheet against her. "Nick, I told the committee members to fuck off. Truly. I did."

He laughed. Only Pia would destroy a PhD at the last possible minute. "That might not have been your most prudent move."

"Are you disappointed?"

He pulled her close again. "In you? If you told them off, they asked for it, and you're the only person I know who has the guts to do it. I love it. I love you. You'll make a career without that damned sheepskin—which isn't sheepskin, by the way. What do they say, 'piled higher and deeper'? You stepped out of the trap."

She didn't bother responding. She kissed him, instead.

<hr />

When Saturday arrived, Nick sat glumly staring at the centerline in the highway as he drove Pia to meet her mother. Marguerite seemed nice enough and he thought she liked him, but what terrible transformation would occur when she heard the news about the lost PhD after all her sacrifices? He knew *his* parents would explode, if the situation were reversed. They would shout and threaten and start canceling favors regardless of who else was in the room—even now when he hadn't lived at home for years. His mother had no solid concept of how old he was.

Would Pia's mother blame him—his subversive influence? Hadn't Pia been doing well before she met him? He hated conflict—especially if he couldn't manage it. What could he possibly say in his own defense? She already knew how much time her daughter had spent with him this past year, helping him deal with his latest research, sleeping in his bed. Pia loved to brag about his accomplishments. Was it at least partially his fault Pia hadn't taken her mentor's warnings more seriously? Had he unconsciously encouraged her to fail? Would her mother think he was one of those chauvinists who was threatened by a successful woman? Was he?

He could only hope Pia's inspired plan about Argentina would soften the blow.

Marguerite had moved back to the city, to a nondescript apartment in a nondescript blonde brick building. There was no off-street parking, of course, and Nick cursed as he circled the area, looking for an empty spot. Pia was quiet, rehearsing the story she would tell.

Marguerite met them at the door of the apartment house. "The buzzers are broken," she explained. "A short or something. A man is supposed to be here tomorrow." She hugged Pia enthusiastically and hugged Nick politely, in turn. He had the impression Marguerite didn't want to touch him. Great.

When the three of them had settled comfortably in the living room, wine glasses in hand, Marguerite sat without speaking as Pia explained why she had insulted her dissertation committee.

"I didn't actually intend to tell them to fuck off," Pia was saying. "It just slipped out. They were so smug—as though they're better than I am, and they're not, Mom. They didn't understand the big picture at all. I had it spelled out for them with nearly a zillion references and research statistics and everything, and they didn't get it."

Marguerite laughed. "I wish I could've seen their faces." This wasn't the first time her daughter had chosen a grand gesture over prudence. Marguerite rather admired her. She couldn't imagine how

Pia would cope with Nick's stuffy parents, but she had stopped underestimating her daughter long ago. Pia could do anything.

Nick was smiling now. The perilous moment was past.

He was staring at Pia's animated face, focusing on her lips. His adoration was almost palpable. Marguerite hoped he was going to have the stamina to stay the course. It would be a bumpy ride, as Bette Davis would say.

"So, Mom, are you ready for the biggest, most exciting part?"

Marguerite took a sip of her wine. "Okay. Now I am. What's the most exciting part?"

"We're going to Argentina! Nick and me...er... I. He's taking time off from his research assistant job. We're going to investigate the transfer from military junta to civilian government and compare it to similar movements elsewhere in the world—from the point of view of the citizens who were most affected but not consulted. We're going to go to the place where they murdered my father—the Navy school. It's a museum or something now. And—are you ready for this? We're going to go to find my father's side of the family! I'll take pictures and interview everyone. It'll be a reunion! You can give me the contact information. Maybe they'll let us stay with them! I'm studying Spanish so I can do the interviews myself—or at least I'll know if the interpreter is being honest. I'm going to put everything I find into a book that's going to sell a million copies. Better than a stiff dissertation, huh?"

Marguerite had stopped breathing. Her face was slowly turning crimson. She took a huge gulp of rocky air. "No! You'll do no such thing."

"What?" Pia was taken aback. She looked to Nick, as though he could explain the abrupt change in the atmosphere in the room. He looked as surprised as she felt.

"Why? Why are you saying no? What's going on?"

"Argentina is not an entirely safe place, even now."

"Mom, they've changed. The country isn't the same. The government is civilian; I looked it up. And the inside stories I'll tell will make a great book!"

"No!" Marguerite stood and walked to the table where the remainder of the bottle of wine waited. She poured her glass full and downed half in a single long drink. The time she had been dreading for so many years had slammed into her without her seeing the approach. She felt dizzy, but she stayed standing. "You don't have any family you would want to find in Argentina, Lympia Marie." She paused to breathe.

Pia stared at her. "But, Mom, you said..."

"Matias Garcia wasn't your father."

The silence in the room thundered and crashed.

Pia's voice was small and intense—energy compressed into a black hole. "What are you saying, Mom?"

Marguerite took her wine to her chair and sat. She drank another long draught and then drew a ragged breath. "I haven't told you everything about what happened the night Matias was killed."

Nick reached out to take Pia's hand, tightly, as though to keep her from flying into space.

"Matias and I wanted to have children—more than anything. But we never had a chance. My mother was dying and I had to come to the States. When I got back home, soldiers picked us up before I could kiss Matias hello. They left my suitcase on the steps." Her voice broke.

She stopped to suck in more air. "Before Matias was tortured," she began again, her voice quaking as were her hands and then her whole interior. She used two hands to place her wine glass on the side table. "Before Matias was tortured, mutilated, and killed, I was raped, first by an electrified cattle prod, then by the man who murdered Matias, an officer in the junta. His name was Santiago Silva. He is your father."

This time the pause simmered and boiled like a molten pit of caustic lava that was about to engulf and incinerate them all.

"*I'm the child of a crazy sadist?*" Pia jerked her hand away from Nick.

"He impregnated me."

"You're telling me my father *raped* you? I'm the child of a rapist?"

"Yes, I was raped. And I had to decide whether to abort you or raise you and protect you from a world that creates such men. There was enough killing. I chose to keep you. You're *my* baby."

Another silence and then Nick spoke. His voice hung crookedly in the room—out of place and clumsy. "I'm glad you didn't abort her. She's magnificent. She's your daughter. That's all that's important."

Pia stood. "No! That's *not* all that's important. What does that make me? Have you thought about that, Mom? Have you thought about what you kept? Can you imagine your parents, Nick? Oh yes, we're fine with you being with a girl who comes from a South American Mengele. We would love for the two of you to have children, so we can see what they become. The family that murders together, stays together? Don't they, Mom? God, Nick, you've been making love to the child of a psychopath!"

"Pia, I don't..."

She cut him off. "Mother, you didn't think I needed to know that the man you kept praising as a near saint *wasn't* my father? I didn't need to know I was happy in a *lie*? Why didn't you just tell me my father was Gandhi? Or Nelson Mandela? Or maybe the Dalai Lama? All these years, I've been praying to a man who didn't have anything to do with me. I drew pictures of him in school. I wrote essays about him. My personal hero! My role model! What an exquisite joke! I should've drawn my father with a cattle prod! And you didn't think you needed to tell me? Oh god, Mom."

She strode to the door where her wrap hung on a hook. "Come on, Nick. Let's go. Next she'll be telling me she isn't my mother."

"Oh, I'm your mother, all right," muttered Marguerite, but Pia wasn't listening. She was already outside.

"I'm sorry, Maggie," Nick told her as he followed Pia. "This is going to take her some time. It might take me some time, too." He gave a kind of hopeless shrug and went out the front door.

13

At first the car was silent as they drove, Nick at the wheel, Pia sitting, staring intently at nothing at all.

"So what do we do now?" he asked as soon as he dared. "Do you still want me to give up my job offer for this year to go to Argentina?"

"No. Take the damned job."

"What about you? What are you going to do?"

"I'm going to stay as far from my mother as I can—until I find a way to forgive her, for one thing. It's not bad enough that my father has to be a rapist, but he's a torturer, too—perversion and sadism in one neat package."

She fell silent. He could sense her thinking, hard. He concentrated on the traffic.

"Nick, do you still love me—and don't bullshit me on this."

He pressed the brake for a red light. "Of course. How could I stop?"

"I think we know the answer to that one, don't we?" she asked sarcastically. "You won't really know if you *can* love me until you've had time for this reality to sink in. I'm not who I thought I was—who you thought I was."

"You're exactly the same person you were yesterday."

"And what does that mean when yesterday I didn't know about the genes inside me?"

He sighed. "Your birth father is history, Pia. Everybody has ancestors who weren't poster children. We have a slave owner and an

Army deserter in my ancestors—and probably worse characters that my mother doesn't discuss."

"Everybody isn't the child of a Nazi prince. Your parents aren't going to be generous with me."

"We don't have to tell them."

She laughed bitterly without warning, and it startled him. "If I don't think about it, will my evil dad just go away?"

"He's been away for all these years. I'm sure he doesn't know you exist."

She was quiet again, and Nick turned on the radio. Cher was wailing a song about being discriminated against for being a gypsy. He changed the station.

"Let me off at a bar."

He did as Pia directed, walking behind her into the smoky room. He pressed against her back to steer her to a booth where they slid onto the maroon vinyl seats.

"Double scotch, neat," Pia told the waitress. "And keep them coming. My boyfriend will pay."

"Ginger ale for me," ordered Nick.

"You don't have to stay here and babysit me," Pia growled when the waitress had left them. "I'm apparently one tough cookie and able to fend for myself."

"That remains to be seen. Besides, I'm the one with the bank account."

"So now I'm your cheap mistress?"

Nick turned his head to stare at the other patrons. "I'm not the enemy, Pia."

"But maybe I am."

The drinks came and Pia downed her first in several long gulps, shivering with the impact, and started on the second.

She was quiet for a few minutes, feeling the world slowly blurring. "I hate this, Nick. I hate knowing I have the potential to be a monster."

He sipped at his ginger ale. "You hate ugly surprises, but you need to read up on genetics. You aren't a clone, you know. This isn't a horror movie. You aren't going to turn into your father."

"And what about the generations to come? You can't say what's going to happen then, can you? You don't know what kind of maniacs our children might be. We can't have children, Nick."

"I didn't know we were working on that yet."

Her third double drink arrived. Pia commenced gulping. The waitress looked at Nick.

"Maybe some water with it next time," he told her.

"No water! I don't like being mal-leged."

"You mean *managed*. I know. I'm not managing. I'm just a bystander here."

Pia looked up at the waitress, realizing her focus wasn't keeping up with movement any longer. "I have the *ponential*..that's *potental*...to be bad. My dad was really, really bad."

The waitress picked up the empty glasses. "If she weren't with you, I'd cut her off completely," she said quietly to Nick.

"Let her get really drunk," he replied, ignoring the faces Pia was making. "It won't take long. She doesn't have much tolerance. She's had some unsettling news. She needs to be truly blasted this once. I'll take responsibility."

Pia was unbuttoning the top buttons of her shirt. She started singing, "I'm bad, I'm bad, I'm bad," over and over, unable to think of any more lyrics.

The waitress shook her head. "I'm sorry, but you're going to have to go down to the next block and buy a bottle from the liquor store. I can't serve her any more."

Nick paid the tab and went to help Pia to her feet.

"I'm bad," she told him, nearly falling.

He held her waist. "You're bad, alright." He half-carried her to the car. "You aren't going to barf all over my upholstery, are you?"

"Not yet." She grinned at him. "But I can't promise *anathing*. I like you, Nick. I do. I like you."

He fastened her seat belt around her and went around to the driver's side. "I like you, too."

He maneuvered the car back onto the road, trying to avoid as many bumps as possible.

Pia was starting to cry. "You're nice. You're too nice for me, Nick. Just too nice." And she vomited.

———✦———

When she awoke, she was naked in his bed–alone. "Nick?" she called, discovering that her head was roaring and she didn't want to move. The bed seemed to be slowly rotating.

"Nick?"

He appeared in the doorway to the living room. He was wearing only his briefs.

"Yeah?"

"I feel terrible."

He made a face. "You don't look so good, either."

She pulled the sheets around her. "Did you take my clothes?"

"What do you think? Of course I took your clothes. I rinsed the barf off them, but they look like you do. I tied them into a plastic bag.

You'll need to wear some of my things to go home. I set out some boxers, my smallest jeans, a belt, and a shirt there on the chair."

"They won't fit."

"Hence the belt. You'll need to eat something. Now that you're awake, I'll take my shower and make lunch." His hazel eyes looked murky brown today. They were ringed with dark circles.

"I'm not hungry."

He went to the closet, pulling out fresh clothes for himself. "I didn't ask if you were hungry. I said you need to eat."

She slid to the side of the bed, taking her time to lift herself to a sitting position. "You're crabby. Did I vomit in your car?"

"Yes."

"Oh. I was afraid I remembered that."

He paused to look at her, his arms stacked with clothes. "Don't move around too much yet, or you could be sick again. I don't need anyplace else to wash. You'll have to take it easy today."

"And I was going to insist on running a marathon." The thought hurt.

"Yeah. You can have the shower after me—while I cook."

She sat on the bed, watching him enter the bathroom. She had no intention of getting up. When she moved, she smelled vomit on her hair. If she were a better person, she'd insist on washing his sheets. She decided she wasn't that good—not today.

She could hear the whoosh of the shower water. It seemed unusually loud. She stared at the painting that hung on his wall. It was one by an artist from the university—not bad, really. The shapes seemed to vibrate. Gradually, around the throbbing pain, her brain reproduced what had happened the night before—the conversation with her mother, the way good Matias had been replaced by a fiend.

She could see a corner of Nick wrapped in a towel, shaving in front of his mirror.

"Nick?"

"Yeah."

"Do you hate me today?"

"No, but you're pushing it."

"Your bed stinks."

"I figured. I have more sheets."

"Did you sleep with me?"

"No. I slept on the couch."

"I wasn't very attractive last night."

"Not really, no."

"Why did you let me get so drunk?"

He appeared in the doorway, dressed in a pair of jeans. "You needed to hit bottom and start over."

"So what's next?"

He tugged his t-shirt over his head. "You take a shower—be sure to wash your hair–and I make lunch—with lots of carbs to soak up all that alcohol."

"I mean with us. What's next for us?"

He came to hand her a bath towel. "We get practical. You don't have the money for your apartment any more, so you move in here. I take the university job. You find something to do so you can contribute. And we both live happily ever after. We can get married if you want."

"Now that's a romantic proposal."

"I didn't have time to work on it."

"I'm not a charity case."

He scowled. "When I marry, it won't be out of charity. You should know that."

"What about my father?"

"What about him?" Nick went into the bathroom to retrieve his dirty underwear from the floor. His voice said he was irritated. "Pia, I don't give a shit about your dad. Like I said yesterday—if you remember—you aren't him. And I don't intend to give my parents a copy of your family tree. It's none of their business. I didn't ask them if I could love you when we met, and I'm not about to ask their opinion now." He threw his dirty underwear into his hamper with the angry vigor of a basketball player making a hopeless basket after the buzzer. "So, *please* take a shower now—I didn't clean you up all that well last night—you weren't cooperating—and I'll make lunch. Then I'm going to go see what I have to do to make my car habitable again."

He headed for the kitchen, and she called after.

"What if I don't *want* to move in here?"

He didn't answer and she knew she had better postpone any further discussion for another time.

14

P ia stood in front of the desk in her almost-former apartment manager's makeshift office, waiting to complete the paperwork that would finalize her move out of her studio. In spite of the utter lack of romance in his suggestion that she join him in his apartment, she had to admit Nick was right about the practicality of it. Without a stipend from the university, she couldn't afford to live alone, and she didn't want to consider moving in with her mother.

The manager's apartment reeked of cabbage. Mrs. Chandler, the frizzy-haired wife of the manager, sat before her, squinting through her bifocals as she wrote in her ledger.

"Of course, you'll forfeit your security deposit. We'll need to replace your carpeting."

Pia gave a little moan of dismay. "We cleaned really well. That carpet was there when I came in. I didn't hurt it a bit."

"It needs replacing."

"So I get the honor of financing your upgrade?"

Mrs. Chandler glared at her. "You signed the contract. You forfeit your security deposit."

"Nick said I would. He said it was a waste of time to clean everything, because you'd take my money, anyway."

Mrs. Chandler ignored her and continued highlighting blanks on the paper with bright yellow streaks. "Nick Graves. He's the one who pays to keep you here, isn't he?"

"He writes a check when I'm short. I pay him back. I'm not *kept*."

"And your forwarding address?"

Pia sighed. "You have it. It's Nick's address."

Mrs. Chandler pursed her lips and glared over her glasses. "It is written in *First Corinthians*, 'Flee from sexual immorality...The sexually immoral sins against his own flesh.' If I had known what kind of young woman you are, I never would have rented to you. I met your mother. Was she ever married to your father?"

Pia seized the sheet of paper and signed where Mrs. Chandler had highlighted. "My mother *was* married when I was conceived, if you must know. What does it say in the Bible about judging people?"

"In *John*, it says, '...Judge with righteous judgment.'"

Pia folded the paper into her purse. "Well, you have the righteous part down," she said as she exited. "Or should I say *hypocritically pious*?" And she let the door slam behind her. She could only guess what the self-appointed critic would say if she knew about her real father or even the gay man who had almost claimed the job.

Pia was still fuming when she and Nick sat down to dinner in his apartment. They had to squeeze their placemats and serving dishes onto one end of the table, since the other end was stacked with cardboard boxes of her things. "That little dictator made me so mad!" she told him, passing the asparagus. "She thinks she's superior to everybody."

"You're overly sensitive right now."

"My losing my security deposit when the apartment was immaculate doesn't bother you?"

"Oh that." He spooned extra asparagus onto his plate. "Yeah, that pisses me off, but I told you it was coming. They all do that."

"She gives a bad reputation to the word *religious*."

He nodded, but Pia knew he was thinking about something else. They ate in silence for a while.

"*Dictators in America*," she announced at last. "I'm going to write a book about the many dictators we have in America who manipulate public opinion and action—politicians, industrialists, media moguls, religious institutions, the power elite of education, and anybody else I think of. I'll compare them to the world dictators that we look down our noses at, acting as if such a thing could never happen here. I can use my dissertation as a starting point."

"You're going to call out religious denominations and educators?"

"I certainly am."

"Oh good. I thought you might do something controversial."

"Isn't the truth always controversial?"

"That depends on whose truth you're talking about."

"I'll show your parents that I have far higher moral standards than the man who gave me life."

Nick shook his head. Inside, he was thinking that his parents could deal with a shady ancestor far more easily than a provocative book, but he kept his peace. "You know, Pia, your mother couldn't help what happened."

Pia stuck her fork into her potatoes so that it stood like a sentinel, towering over her meatloaf.

"She didn't have to lie to me."

———◦≪≫◦———

The year passed quickly. While Nick was engrossed in both teaching and performing scientific investigation with his university team, Pia took a part-time job editing articles for a magazine. She spent every extra minute rushing from one resource library to another, doing research. Nick had to buy a bicycle because she monopolized his car. Her resultant book was passionate and lively, a cross between a scholarly discussion and a tell-all—heavily weighted toward the sensational. She suspected she was trying to vanquish her own demons by ferreting out demons elsewhere, but for the moment, she didn't care. She sent her manuscript out into the universe with her blessing and an indistinct feeling of foreboding.

The big publishers treated her content as though it were an incurable African virus. They couldn't get far enough away. Their minions stamped "NOT FOR US" in red across the cover sheet or maybe the table of contents, taking care not to touch another page. After some months, Nick thought he could relax, believing Pia's remarks would remain abandoned and isolated on the white ice floes of her manuscript pages forever. And then the situation changed.

A small, ambitious publishing house seized on her sensationalism as a show starter, hyping the book's promotion. They gave it a commanding red-orange cover—a dictator who looked suspiciously like Hitler standing in a church pulpit with students in caps and gowns being crucified behind him. They bought advertising spots on television near the most shocking interview programs. With the help of her publisher's hungry marketers, the talk show circuit pounced on her material. People were tired of arguing about weapons of mass destruction. A public lashing of the country's most sanctified institutions was diverting. Pia was touted as either a pariah or a harbinger of the new age. A publishing agent called her.

"Let me take you to lunch, Dear," the agent cooed in her nasal voice. "I think you and I can do business."

When Pia met the agent, she was sorry she wasn't a fiction writer. Barbara Bright would have made an ideal character—someone to provide comic relief. Even her name sounded artificial. Her eyelashes stuck out as huge, fringed awnings over her bloodshot eyes that were an unlikely royal blue, having been reborn behind tinted contact lenses. The neckline of her shiny blouse gapped over her concave chest, and she wore orthopedic shoes.

"I don't usually do this with my regular clients—buy lunch, that is," Barbara told Pia over their salads. "But you've created quite a stir. You're a hot topic on YouTube and MySpace. I keep up with the latest trends, you see. I think we can generate even more interest. I've heard of a new forum called Facebook. I hope you're prepared to be wealthy!"

Pia smiled, thinking that if this woman knew the secret to being wealthy, she'd look better.

"I take over the legwork, Dear. If we get you enough publicity, we'll be able to go back to the publishers, and they'll court us. Your mailbox will be stuffed with checks. How about it?"

The novelty of sending out manuscripts and cover letters had lost its charm. Pia wanted dependable income, but she was tired of chasing it. "Sure," she told Barbara Bright. "Where do I sign?"

Barbara turned out to be as industrious as she had promised. Before she had time to consider the wisdom of agreeing, Pia had been accepted to be interviewed by Don Watson, a popular talk show host on a local TV station. Barbara was delighted. Pia felt sick. Don Watson didn't deal with any subject in depth. He liked to mock his guests to make himself look clever.

Pia submitted to make-up and even some guy who fussed with the way she had buttoned her blue silk blouse.

"Do a little sexy," the fleshy assistant dressed in white told her as he unbuttoned her top buttons. "It sells books. If you got it, flaunt it, Sister."

In the studio, Don Watson appeared bored and disconnected as he swiveled right and then left in his leather chair, waiting for the floor manager to cue him. He defied his advancing age with a spray tan and sleek brown hair that puffed over his carefully camouflaged toupee. He wore an expensive designer suit and a Rolex watch. He didn't bother to look at Pia, although she was seated only a couple feet from him. An assistant somebody girl was touching up his hair, spraying down a cowlick that wanted media attention and dusting his nose with powder to take down the shine. Don Watson himself was reading the notes he had been given, supposedly the questions he was to ask Pia, his next guest. He frowned, as though he didn't understand or like what he was reading or maybe the print was too small. The floor manager gave the cue, and Don Watson lit up. He ignored the teleprompter.

"And we're back, this time with our guest Olympia Garcia and her book, *Dictators in America*. I understand you're a student, Ms. Garcia?"

Pia tried to look pleasant as she sat in the chair opposite him but lower—not by accident. "Not any longer, Don. I'm a writer."

"Your book has been described as inflammatory. Do you plan to take down the dictators you see running America all by yourself? You come off as a self-proclaimed, self-anointed crusader. What inspired you to think you were qualified to lead the masses to a greater truth? What have you led up until now? Olympia, aren't you a little young and inexperienced to go around criticizing some of the most revered institutions in our country?"

She could feel her blood start to throb. "My name is *Lympia*, not *Olympia* and no, I don't intend to rout the dictators by myself. The American people like some of them. They've been led to believe they need them. I just wanted to shine a light on the hypocrisy of people in authority who tell us whatever half-truths they think will help them maintain their power, misrepresenting or ignoring the facts."

"So this is yet another WMD book—Not-Oh-lympia?" Don Watson smirked for the camera, rolling his eyes. The camera operators laughed.

Pia shifted in her chair. "No, I wasn't writing about Weapons of Mass Destruction at all, although the failure of our government to openly admit the limitations of the intelligence they had before entering a war would be an example, I suppose. Other writers who have more patience with politics than I do are investigating that. In Argentina when the people were convinced they were in danger from Communist terrorists, they allowed a military junta to come into power. That junta eventually murdered tens of thousands of innocent citizens. Fear can grease the slide for bad decisions, although it makes the masses easy to control. I'm concerned with the leaders outside the government who contribute to fear and hatred with misinformation."

"What makes you think the United States of America is about to fall into the hands of a military junta? Do you know something the president doesn't know?" He chuckled.

"I didn't say we were, but losing control of a country isn't as difficult as we would hope."

"And just who is *we*? Who convinced you to go crusading about dictators?"

"I was thinking of my father..." She caught herself too late. "A man who was like a father to me. I wanted to write a book to make a difference, as he would've done. I wanted to empower the common people, the democracy."

"Just like a father, huh? Where have we heard that before? Don't let us pry into your private... affairs!" He grinned at the camera and the floor manager laughed.

Pia could feel herself redden. She was wondering how much more of his abuse would fit into her slim time slot. "My book isn't about losing a country as much as it is about degrading the independence and critical thinking of the American people by giving them incomplete or faulty information. When we talk about educational institutions that dictate the perspectives open to a student who is paying dearly..."

He interrupted her. "Critical thinking, yes. One portion of your book that's getting a lot of attention is the part in which you accuse church leaders and even churches themselves of taking away the ability of their parishioners to think critically. You advocate abortion. Are you anti-religion, Ms. Garcia?"

"No, certainly not, and I didn't advocate abortion."

He picked up his sheet of notes. "Are you, as some have claimed, an atheist trying to undermine the faith of the American people? You question the consistency and even the authorship of the Bible, suggesting that church leaders might be misinterpreting the intent of those being quoted. You say people should place their own whims of spirituality above churches." He turned to face the camera lens directly. "Take note, all you pastors, rabbis, and priests out there. You've been doing it all wrong. Ms. Garcia, what gives you the right to question practices and hierarchies that have sustained the faithful for centuries?"

As soon as he was off camera, he picked a bit of lint off his lapel and tightened his tie.

"Information," Pia answered him, in spite of the reality that he had stopped listening. "Information gives me the right to ask questions regardless of my private belief system. I take the time to research established historic and scientific facts. I didn't say anything about spiritual whims or what people should or shouldn't do in their places of worship. My remarks weren't limited to Christian leaders, but addressed leaders within every faith who practice questionable ethics. I didn't even talk about what followers should believe. Most of what you've just said about my book is not remotely true. I discuss only authority figures and their choices—hence the title. Have you *read* my book, Don?"

Pia could hear muted laughter from the camera operators.

"Of course." Don smiled for the camera that was focused on him again. "I can't say I agree with your conclusions, Olympia. I think our religious leaders are doing just fine without your naïve input, but thank you for joining us on the show." He turned back toward the camera that was on his face. "After the break, we'll be talking with Alfred Littleman who reads the minds of animals. Don't go away. This will be interesting. You'll want to hear what he has to say about your little Fluffy."

The floor manager signaled cut, and Don scowled at Pia. "You little bitch. *'Have you read my book?'*" he mimicked her in a falsetto voice. "Who do you think you are? Don't hold your breath until you come back to this show, Babe. It ain't happening."

The female assistant tugged Pia away from her seat so she could be replaced by a short man with huge hair and no neck.

Pia returned to the Green Room to retrieve her personal belongings. A pimple-faced young man with a headset draped around his neck handed her several papers.

"You stirred a hornet's nest with the religious stuff," he told her. "These are the calls that came in already. Half of them are death threats."

"Oh, that's nice." She took the papers and dumped them in the trash. "You have a really friendly show here."

The young man shrugged. "Don gets ratings." He followed her partway down the hallway. "I read your book. Did you mean to champion abortion?"

Pia was tugging on her jacket. She felt hostile and naked. "No, I didn't. I championed personal responsibility. But maybe some babies *should* be aborted—including me when I was a fetus, and no, I'm not going to tell you what I mean. Thanks for reading the book."

The young man turned into a side room and Pia continued down the hall and out the front door. She was looking for a cab in front of the building when the young man called to her. "Wait! Ms. Garcia, there's a telephone call for you. It's your mother."

Pia paused for a moment. She hadn't talked to her mother since the confrontation—not so much as a statement but because she hadn't taken the time. For a moment, she considered asking the kid to tell her mother he hadn't caught her. He was looking at her expectantly. She sighed and followed him through the revolving doors to the room where a telephone waited for her.

"Hello? This is Pia."

There was silence for a beat. "It's good to hear your voice."

Pia felt a pang—was it guilt? Relief? "Hi, Mom."

"You looked good on TV."

"Thanks, Mom."

"I'm down the street from you at that little Irish bar. Would you please come down to see me? I brought you something, and we need to talk."

The voice reminded Pia of just how long it had been. She had even spent Christmas with Nick's family in Hawaii—really just Nick while his parents frequented a country club. She could imagine her mother sitting alone in that drab apartment. For a moment, she wanted to cry. How could she have been so mean? "Sure. Sure, I can do that." She'd have to let Nick know she wouldn't meet him for lunch. "I have to make a couple calls and I'll be right there."

"Okay, I'll be waiting."

Pia stared at the phone after she hung up. How do you face someone you've wronged? How do you say you're sorry for ignoring someone for over a year?

She called Nick, glad for his soothing voice. "I'm going to skip our lunch. I'm meeting my mother."

"Your idea?" He sounded hopeful.

"No. Hers. She's down here already. She must have seen my name in the TV schedule or something. I think she was watching the show from that Irish bar."

"I'm glad. You've waited too long, Pia. It's not fair."

She felt a flare of temper. "So you've said—about a million times."

"Sorry."

She drew a long breath. She could recognize the real target of her anger. "It's okay. I know you mean well. I just hate it when you're right."

"Nervous?"

"That's an understatement. I'm sweating like a pig." She paused. "Do pigs actually sweat?"

"I have no idea."

"Me, either. I'll call when I'm on my way home."

"Okay. How did the show go? I was in class."

She grimaced, knowing he couldn't see her. "The Spanish Inquisition and the Salem witch trials. I'm only slightly less popular than herpes. Don Watson is a major jerk."

"I'm sorry, Pia. Some people look for certain words to hate without bothering to read the context—especially these talk show jocks. I suspected he wouldn't be fun. We'll hope most people missed the show."

"That would require luck which I, apparently, do not have. A couple viewers actually called in death threats. Don Watson attracts a sick crowd."

There was a pause as Nick thought about what to say. "Be careful and stay around crowds. Don't walk alone. See you later. Love you."

"Love you, too." She hung up. Suddenly she had to go to the bathroom.

15

P ia found her mother sitting sipping brown ale in a rear booth of the bar. Marguerite had aged perceptibly. Her sandy hair hung in limp strands tainted with white. Her face looked drawn and pale. She was wearing a navy blue suit that had to be at least a dozen years old.

She stood slowly as Pia entered the booth, and Pia delivered a perfunctory hug before they both settled down, opposite one another.

"How are you doing?" Marguerite asked.

"Fine."

"And Nick?"

"Fine, too."

"You looked good on TV—I watched here in the bar–but you look better in person. That blue blouse flatters your skin and your dark hair. The barkeep said you're eye candy. That was probably the real reason they interviewed you for Watson's show—sex appeal. Watson is looking old." She sighed.

"I thought your book was well done—very insightful. No wonder idiots like Watson don't want to talk about it. First of all, he probably can't process what you're talking about. He doesn't seem to spend much time thinking. Second, he just wants to stroke the knee-jerks who watch his show. They like believing they're smarter than everyone else because they don't contaminate their opinions with facts. Your book makes people examine aspects of our country they don't want to see."

"Thanks. How are you, Mom? You look tired."

The older woman fussed with something in her purse. "I had a hysterectomy. I'm still mending."

"A hysterectomy!" Pia could sense her guilt expanding exponentially. "I'm sorry, Mom. I didn't know. I should've been there. What was wrong?"

Marguerite waved a dismissive hand. "I'm getting old. I brought you something." She pulled out a folded sheet and handed it across the table.

"What is it?"

"Your birth certificate. I'm sorry I took so long to get it to you. I hope you didn't have to order a duplicate already."

A waitress arrived. "May I get you something?" she asked Pia.

"Coffee. Black."

"Be back in a minute." And the waitress left.

Pia opened the certificate.

"You'll need it to get a passport," her mother said. "Replacing a lost birth certificate is a real pain. You'll see I said your father was unknown. The doctor told me to do that. I didn't want to lie, and I didn't want to give Santiago Silva any claim on you. There are many dishonest birth certificates in Argentina. The military used to steal babies and give them to other parents; did you know that?"

"I don't know. I might have read something. I've been preoccupied with American dictators these last months."

"They changed their names and altered their birth certificates. Anyone born around those years has reason to wonder if they're who they think they are."

"What must that be like?" muttered Pia bitterly, but Marguerite pretended not to notice.

"I know saying I don't know who your father is makes me look bad as your mother—like a slut, but how many people read your birth certificate, anyway?"

Pia stared at the document, not really reading it. "Nick and I aren't planning to go to Argentina any longer. We shelved that idea long ago. I thought you knew. I didn't see a point, and I didn't have the money. Besides, we're busy. He has a university job and I have my book."

"That's probably wise. I don't know how welcome either you or I would be there these days."

The waitress brought Pia's coffee and placed it in front of her. "Anything else?"

Marguerite answered. "Not just now. I might want another ale later."

"Just signal to me," replied the waitress, doing what she could to appear cheerful. "Enjoy!"

Pia stared at the table. "I've done a lot of thinking, Mom, and I understand why you didn't tell me the truth. What you did, you did to shelter me."

"Yes. Yes, I did. Believe me, I wished more than anything that I could've written Matias's name as your father. I almost lied, anyway, but the doctor said it wasn't fair to the Garcia family. It wasn't honest. He wouldn't do it."

Pia made a sound in her throat. "You wouldn't want the Garcias to think I belonged with them."

Marguerite shifted in her seat. "They'd love you. They're good people. I'm sure they'd adopt you—would've adopted you. Coincidentally, Matias's father was named Nicolas—like your Nick. But Nicolas died last year. A horse rolled on him."

"How sad." Pia thought she could hear a chill in her own voice—almost sarcastic. What was wrong with her?

"Just the way of things." Her mother pretended not to hear the bitterness. "Matias's mother is living with his younger sister and her family. She's starting to sound senile. She had a heart attack a year or so ago. One of her daughters was among the disappeared—taken off the street as she walked from a class, except no one ever saw her again. They think Nita might be in one of the mass graves they're starting to find. Losing a son and a daughter the way she did, knowing how they died–it was all too much stress for Maria. I probably shouldn't have told the family so many details. I was probably hoping for pity."

"Did you name me for her—the Marie part?"

"Yes."

"That's nice." Pia opened her jacket. She was beginning to feel hot. "Mom, I need to apologize. I should've called you a long time before now. I've been childish and selfish. I don't recognize myself. I've been a brat."

"Yes. So are we all from time to time. To tell you the truth, I thought it was selfish of me not to die."

Pia stared at her mother, seeing something she hadn't noticed before. She was picturing a young woman, pregnant by a man who had brutalized her. "Did you think about suicide—back then?"

"Daily."

"Do you still?"

"I believe I'd have to face my choice on the Other Side, so no. I want all this to end one day. I'd like to think I might see Matias again. How about you? Do you think of suicide?"

Pia made a half smile. "I'm too busy making trouble. I wanted you to have killed me before I was born."

Marguerite didn't reply. Instead, she finished her mug of ale.

Pia studied her mother's face—the lines she remembered, the new wrinkles spreading across her skin like cracked glaze. "It's lucky for me that you brought the birth certificate. I was just investigating what I would need to do to get a copy for my passport application. Nick and I are going on vacation in Costa Rica soon. It's a present from his parents for Nick's birthday. We're going to lie on the beach and pretend the world has gone away. Would you like to come along? I know he'd love to see you. He's been asking about you—over and over. Don't tell him I said so, but he's a better person than I am. We can help you update your passport if you'd like to join us."

Marguerite smiled–an awkward, unfamiliar expression. "Thank you, but no. I need to rest. A mother doesn't belong in the middle of a romantic vacation, and I shudder to think what I would look like in a bathing suit these days. But thank you for inviting me. It means a lot." Her eyes looked so sad that Pia could feel the pain behind them travel inside herself. She rose from her seat as Marguerite rose. She went to embrace her mother. They stood for long moments holding one another. The waitress came and went.

Marguerite's voice was soft and low. "I love you, Pia. You're the meaning of my life. I hope one day you'll be glad I stayed alive and kept you."

Pia kissed her mother's cheek. "I'm glad you're my mother," she whispered, not trusting her voice. "I'm infinitely grateful to be loved by you. I'm not worthy of you." Quiet, slow tears dropped onto her mother's shoulder.

The waitress brought the bill and placed the black folder on the table.

"I've got this," said Pia, sniffing. She pulled a credit card out of her purse.

Marguerite kissed her daughter's forehead. "Call me when you get back. And bring me chocolate. I like the dark kind right from the beans."

Pia laughed. "Yes, yes, I will."

———◆———

The sun was a soothing blanket, hot and heavy on their backs, massaging its heat into their muscles as Pia and Nick lay on their towels on the beach. The trip to Costa Rica had been trying, but it seemed to have happened to two other people as they lay side by side, nearly nude, thinking of plantain daiquiris and sunscreen and making love in their little casita.

"You're white," said Nick as he turned on his side. "For someone with Hispanic heritage, you are so very white."

Pia scowled at him. "Have you looked in the mirror? You're a miserable gringo and your legs look like old chicken parts—with freezer burn. In a few hours, I'll be tan and you'll be a boiled lobster."

He laughed, knowing she was probably right. His sunburns were always quick and bad. "I guess we'll have to go back inside," he said, doing his best to give her a suggestive grin.

"I must have my father's skin," she said ruefully, moving to sit, her knees cradled in her arms. "Mom burns terribly."

He drew his fingers along her shoulder and then kissed it. "It feels like your skin to me. But maybe I'd better check it—all over. You can't be too careful."

She laughed, but she quickly fell serious again. "What will your parents think when my skin turns dark?"

He sighed a disgusted, frustrated sigh. "They'll think Matias–or whoever–was a South American man who probably had blood from the ancient Indians. And who cares what they think, anyway? I like the color of your skin—tanned or not tanned, light or dark. I'd like a chance to show you how much, if you can stop being tragic for five minutes."

She was smiling as he tugged her to her feet.

They made love all afternoon in the soft heat of their bed, laughing, exploring, dozing, and doing it all again. They went into the ocean again just before dark, when they could still spot jellyfish. Then they showered together in the stall by their casita, rubbing one another more than was absolutely necessary. Their eyes kept meeting over dinner, penetrating deep into the soul of the other as they sipped their drinks and swayed with the beat of the music.

"Marry me, Pia," Nick whispered to her as they danced together as one.

She kissed his ear. "Later. I'm having a good time being your mistress right now."

The week slid by in a mellow, delicious dream. Pia pretended there was no other world, no other reality, and the sun and the ocean cooperated. People around them smiled. Nearly all the guests were on vacation, and the workers who served them were content to encourage the illusion of paradise suspended in time. Happy patrons tipped better.

Once the locals found Nick and Pia to be sincerely interested and respectful–visitors who did their best to use their high school Spanish, they opened up with glimpses into their lives. A cab driver told stories of his boyhood and the brilliantly hued birds that squawked the dawn into being. Their concierge talked to them of the quirks of the monkeys and set up a guided tour so Pia and Nick could meet wildlife face-to-face along the trails of one of the preserves. A cleaning woman invited them to her home to join the family for a traditional celebration dinner of fish roasted in banana leaves. By the time the week ended, Pia and Nick had disconnected from their New York selves. Their bodies felt like different limbs of a single being—warm and drunk with loving. They weren't prepared for what came next.

16

The flight home was anticlimactic since Pia booked their trip on an airline that had figured out customers were going to fly whether they were comfortable or not. Profit had ascended into Heaven. Pleasing passengers was no longer a top priority. More people, more profit. Nick was soon in a bad mood. His airline seat was too small in every direction. For him, flying was a form of masochism because he had no space for his long legs. "We should have driven across Mexico," he said at last. "We'd have to drive really fast to avoid the banditos, but we'd have a chance to arrive as functional human beings. This plane is a form of birth control. No one on this flight will be fertile for months."

Pia laughed politely as did the passenger beside her. Nick had concocted his joke on the flight in, and he was proud of it. He might use it again if he had an opportunity. She opened the mail she had stuffed into her purse before they left their apartment for their vacation. It looked out of place beside the tiny tube of sunscreen and the postcards she hadn't sent. After a week in the tropics, the envelopes were warm, vaguely moist, and wrinkly—properly humiliated. She paused over one particularly virulent letter:

> *Bitch,*
> *You are the spaun of the devil. You want to turn*
> *people away from God. I will find you and kill*

you like the rat you are. I will tear out your tongue and make sure you can never reporduce.

Nick was looking over her arm. "One of your fans, I assume?"

"Most of them are bad spellers," she said.

"Let's hope most of them are bad at finding people. He sounds like the guy who ra…"

Nick cut himself off, but Pia completed his sentence. "…Who raped my mother. In other words, it sounds like my father."

"Oh no, not this again. Me and my big mouth." He sighed a long, disgusted sigh. "Are you taking any precautions to protect yourself from these crazies?"

Pia squirmed beneath her seat belt. Someone behind her was coughing up his lungs, or so it seemed. "I took continuing ed. martial arts while you were teaching your night classes. Don't you remember? With the scary lady cop who could smash bricks? I ended up with too many bruises. Besides, it seemed like a colossal waste of time. What are the odds an attacker would come at me with a knife the way he's supposed to so I could deploy my maneuvers? The way things are going in this country, he'll have a gun—with a scope. No contest. I decided I could use the time better doing something like yoga."

"That'll be a big help. You can impress him with your balance and flexibility. If you're going to write books that piss people off, you need to get serious about learning to defend yourself—emotionally and physically."

She lowered her tray table, realized she hadn't returned the letters to her purse, and snapped the tray table back to vertical. "Didn't you tell me once defending me was your job?"

"I'm not with you all the time." He shifted uncomfortably. His knees were pressed against the back of the next seat. "And I didn't take a martial arts class. I'd have to hit him with a book." He lifted the letter from her lap and re-read it. "You should take this stuff to the police."

"I've gotten several threats—from different senders, it looks like. Some actually sign their names, but most don't. People want to get a punch in from a safe distance. What are the police going to do? Nothing, unless I'm actually attacked."

"Oh, that's pleasant." Nick snorted and the lady in the next seat gave him a dirty look. He changed the subject. "Got any of those cashews in your handbag?"

"We ate them in Costa Rica."

"Oh."

Pia took the letter back, slipped it in its envelope, and folded it into her purse. "The people who want to control what other people think spin the facts and create time bombs like this guy."

"That's politics." Nick attempted to scrunch down in the seat to sleep, found it utterly impossible without removing his legs, and squeezed his eyes shut, instead.

"Why? That's what I want to know. Why do politics have to be so crazy?" she persisted.

He didn't bother opening his eyes. "Because people are crazy. You knew that."

When she opened her mouth to say more, he waved her away. How did he know she was going to speak when he had his eyes closed? Had the two of them been together that long already?

She opened the tattered magazine from the pouch in front of her, wondering how many species of bacteria it sustained. She wrinkled her

149

forehead at the magazine photos. Women in bikinis. Just the thing to cheer a disgruntled child of rape with an unexpected sunburn and death threats instead of fan mail.

When they landed, Nick and Pia were herded through Customs. This way, that line, up these stairs, follow this color. Widgets in a widget village. Pia imagined a giant child moving figures around. Nick would be the figure wearing a perpetual scowl. He was no fun when he was in this mood. She remembered photos of early airliners filled with people sitting in spacious seats before tables dressed with white tablecloths. They were dining using china and silver and wine goblets, enjoying their flight. Yes, ma'am. No, sir. More steak? The change had happened so slowly that the passengers who expected to be treated as guests instead of commodities were all dead now. The rest flew in their own jets.

Nick hailed a cab, and one swerved into an open space in the line of taxis waiting for fares before the next cab could pull forward. The swarthy driver of the car behind made a rude gesture and shouted something in an unfamiliar language. Meanwhile, a heavy man the color of old cottage cheese pulled himself out of the driver's seat of the offending vehicle and waddled to the rear of his car to open the trunk for Nick and Pia.

Pia watched him grunt as he clumsily stuffed their suitcases into the trunk. How did he stay so fat getting in and out of his cab, she wondered idly. Wasn't it odd that active people like nurses and cab drivers could be obese? She climbed into the back seat of the cab beside Nick, trying to enter the way she had seen celebrities in short skirts do it. A skirt had been happily cool and comfortable in Costa Rica. Now it felt drafty. The driver slammed the door shut behind her. The interior of the cab smelled stale and old.

"Where to?" the driver asked after he had puffed and wheezed his way behind the wheel.

Nick gave him the address of their hotel. They would rent a car tomorrow to visit Marguerite and pick up their car before they went home. No more planes unless flight was unavoidable—going to Hawaii, maybe, when a packed airplane trumped a ship teeming with seasick passengers.

The cab pulled from the curb, nearly colliding with the taxi ahead so that the other driver had to quickly jump to the side, suitcase in hand, to avoid being crushed against the open trunk. The alarmed driver shook his fist and swore.

"Big pain—going through all that security, ain't it?" asked the fat driver in the front seat of their cab, perhaps to distract his passengers from what had just happened. "You're lucky if you can get through with fingernail clippers."

"Just part of modern travel," said Nick, who was working hard not to say anything about the near miss. He made a face for Pia's benefit, one he calculated the driver wouldn't be able to see. He mouthed, "What the hell?"

She didn't respond. She was feeling dizzy from the changes in pressure, humidity, and altitude she had suffered in the past several hours. She concentrated on looking out her window to combat a feeling of nausea.

Nick pulled out the book he had started reading on the plane, a large volume describing the ecosystems of Central America. He could read anywhere.

No one spoke for a while, preferring to let the twang of singing on the cab's radio fill the void.

Pia could feel her headache growing worse with the motion. She needed some dinner, a glass of wine, and a long night's sleep. She wished Nick hadn't booked a hotel so far from the airport. He said he couldn't sleep with the sound of aircraft overhead. He'd seen too many movies featuring airliners careening off the ends of runways into nearby buildings, creating spectacular special effects fireballs.

The cab rattled on, taking a turn onto a smaller highway.

They passed directional signs. Pia realized with a start that there was no way they were going to the hotel Nick had booked. She knew the city well enough to be sure. "Isn't this a really long route to take?" she asked the driver. "Are you milking our fare?"

"I know what I'm doing," he replied. "You'll get where you're going faster than you think."

She poked Nick. "Something's wrong," she mouthed.

"What?" He was engrossed in his book. "What do you want?"

She could see the driver watching them in the mirror. "I just wondered what you were reading. How can you read in the car without getting sick?"

Nick didn't catch on to her attempt at secrecy. Apparently, he didn't watch enough spy films. He yawned and stretched. "I've always done it." His attention returned to his book.

She dug one of the death threat letters from her purse and scribbled on the back of the envelope: *Wrong way. He knows.*

"You dropped your bookmark," she said aloud. "Here it is."

Nick started to protest, but stopped when he had read the words. He looked from her to the driver. "Thanks," he mumbled instead. "I didn't notice it fell out."

She slid the envelope back into her purse. Nick didn't look at her, but she could feel him stiffen. "Excuse me," he said to the driver as he leaned forward. "Could you stop at the next gas station? I need to relieve myself. The airport bathroom was too crowded."

"You can wait," growled the driver. He seemed to realize that he had sounded too curt, so he amended. "We'll be there soon."

Pia could feel her pulse gaining speed. She and Nick were being driven somewhere against their will, somewhere they hadn't chosen. The possible reasons that leaped to mind felt unreal. In a James Bond film, they might be taken to meet a Mister Big, but no one would want to discuss world dominance or diamond smuggling with Nick or her. Neither of them knew any vital state secrets or formulas for rocket fuel. If no one wanted to *talk* with them, the possibilities dwindled. They weren't rich or famous enough to be worth ransoming. She took a deep breath and exhaled it as slowly as she could. She needed to clear her mind. The death threats weren't all idle. She and Nick were most likely being taken somewhere remote to be killed–being murdered, a family legacy.

Pia picked up Nick's book and motioned to Nick to keep talking.

He leaned forward again, doing his best to block the driver's view in the mirror. "Listen, I don't mean to be difficult, but I'm not kidding about the bladder problem. I had this infection in Costa Rica, see, and I don't have a lot of control…"

As Nick was speaking, he was gesturing more than he did normally. Behind the bulk of his body, Pia was writing in big letters on the blank pages at the end of his book:

Kidnapped. Call police.

She held the book in the window. The driver in the cab of the semi-truck beside them honked his horn.

"What are you doing back there?" the cab driver demanded to know.

"I was gesturing for him to honk," said Pia, trying to make the book inconspicuous. "I do it when I'm bored riding. Sorry. I didn't mean to bother you."

The cab swerved to the side of the highway and stopped. There were no buildings nearby, only a sorely neglected, littered field. The cab driver climbed out and Nick and Pia quickly followed suit. Should they run? Could they signal distress to the passing traffic?

"I didn't want to pee beside the road…" Nick began before he noticed the driver was holding a gun on them from inside his jacket to conceal it from the drivers zipping by.

"Give me that book," demanded the driver. He was no longer pretending to be polite. "Or your bodies will be part of the trash by the road."

Pia handed it to him. He found her message. "I'm glad you understand the situation, Ms. Garcia," he growled as he pitched the book into the field. "I was getting sick of being nice to you. Into the cab." It was an order. "Or I can shoot you where you stand."

Nick stepped between the driver and Pia. "And let you take us somewhere in the sticks? No, you'll have to shoot us here where there are certain to be witnesses. You'll be caught."

"And you'll be dead. These people don't give a hoot about what's going on beside the highway as long as we don't make them slow down."

"Now I really *do* have to go to the bathroom," said Pia, without looking at Nick. "I can't hold it when I'm scared." She stepped over the fence and started into the field.

"Stop there," ordered the driver.

Pia could feel him weighing the wisdom of shooting her. She pulled her skirt up to her waist, dropped her panties, and squatted, broadly mooning the traffic on the highway. "I'll just be a minute. You don't want to smell urine all afternoon." Traffic was slowing down. She could sense Nick assessing the situation.

She had devised a plan to make a run for it to give Nick a chance to act when she heard a siren that grew loud and then shut down. A police car pulled up at an angle behind the cab, its lights flashing. Two officers emerged. Pia hurriedly tugged her panties up as Nick leaped over the fence to her side.

The cab driver didn't meet the officers quietly. Nick yanked Pia to the ground as the cab driver fired at the squad car several times. The police ducked and fired, and in the end, the flabby white cab driver lay dead at the edge of the pavement only feet from a stiff crushed cat.

The officers advanced cautiously from the cover of their squad car. "Stay down," one ordered Nick and Pia. He had his weapon trained on them.

"We're the good guys!" exclaimed Nick, but the officer didn't lower his gun.

"This one's dead," announced the second officer, a stout Black man, after he had examined the cab driver and made a call on his radio. "We need to Mirandize these two and get them separated."

The first officer, who looked too young and pasty to be carrying a loaded weapon, nodded. He was shaking visibly. "You have the right to remain silent," he recited in a burst, as though that were the way he had memorized the words. "Anything you say can and will be used against you in a court of law–you have the right to an attorney–if you can't afford an attorney, one will be appointed for you–do you understand these rights–is there anything you'd like to say to us?"

The second officer nodded his approval. "Get your notebook ready," he advised his rookie partner as he took over pointing a gun at Pia and Nick.

"Yes, we have something to say," said Pia, feeling her heart dancing around in her throat. "We were kidnapped by this guy. He picked us up at the airport like a regular cab driver. And..."

Nick interrupted. "...Then he drove us out here, so Pia used my book to write a help message to the truck driver beside us. The cabbie threw my book out there in the field —and he threatened us with his gun..."

"...And I mooned the traffic," finished Pia. "I was trying to buy time."

"That's why the call came in as indecent exposure," the young officer told his trainer, who gestured for him to be quiet.

"I need that book back," added Nick, looking around for it. "It's difficult to find a copy."

The older officer, whom Pia assumed was some kind of trainer, ignored Nick. "Get all that down in your notes, then go ahead and cuff the guy and put him in the car. I'll cuff the girl and we'll keep her out here until backup arrives."

The young officer started writing in a little notebook he had pulled from a chest pocket of his shirt. Pia could see him mouthing the words as he wrote.

The older officer looked at Pia, who was clinging to Nick. Her expression must have reflected the shock she was feeling, because his tone softened a little. "We have to keep you apart until the investigators can talk with each of you singly. It's procedure. The cuffs are to ensure that you make it to the station and don't split on us when we're not looking. We need your statements."

The young officer was fumbling behind Nick now, trying to get the cuffs on properly. The older officer pretended not to notice.

A helicopter with a large news station logo whooshed overhead.

"That didn't take long," said the young officer looking up, and again, the older officer scowled at him.

Traffic on the highway had slowed to a near standstill as passersby strained to see what was going on.

"Get the guy into the car. We need to block off the road." In a single deft movement, the trainer clicked the cuffs onto Pia's wrists, but she could tell he left them fairly loose.

"I'm scared," she told him quietly as the rookie led Nick to their squad car and settled him in the rear seat.

"No point in being scared now," the older officer said, smiling. "Nobody's shooting."

She could hear the approach of other sirens as more police cars rushed to the scene, their lights flashing. Officers seemed to rush everywhere, stringing tape and setting out cones. The chaos felt like a mad party. The trainer motioned for one of the newly arrived officers to come to him. "This woman needs to go to the station for her interview," he told the other officer. "We have a guy in our car."

"The lieutenant's on her way," the unfamiliar officer said, "so why don't you give the guy to Harris to take in?"

The trainer nodded. He turned to Pia. "You'll go to the station now," he said.

"Thanks for saving us," she told the trainer as the unfamiliar officer led her away. She thought he smiled.

Pia sat without talking in the rear of the police car. She didn't feel like a guest. The car had a strange, rummage sale smell—like a sweaty locker room or old shoes. The radio was playing smooth jazz and the officer was tapping out the rhythm on his steering wheel. When they stopped at a red light, the older couple in the car beside them stared at her, probably wondering what Pia had done wrong. Did she look like a felon? She glanced down at her blouse and skirt. She wanted to pick off the sticks and weeds that stuck to her, but her hands were trapped behind her. The handcuffs clinked as she moved. She wondered what had happened to her purse. She felt unreal, as though she were acting in a play.

When they arrived at the police building, the officer walked with her through the double doors. He said something to a woman at a desk, who gestured down the hallway.

"Room two," Pia heard her say.

The officer took her to room two where he directed her to sit at the table inside. "Here you go," he told Pia as he unlocked and then removed her handcuffs. "I'll get you a statement form and a pen. Write down everything you remember about what happened in the order it happened—as much detail as you can remember. Eventually, somebody will be here to interview you. No rush. This process isn't quick."

Pia stared at the mirror along one wall. She had seen one-way mirrors in police shows on television. It made her feel exposed. Someone was probably watching her—for what? Did they suspect her of something? She wanted to cry.

The officer returned with the form, a pen, and a can of soda. "I hope you like Pepsi," he said. "The guy who's supposed to fill the machine hasn't come yet, so this is all that's left. I figured you could use something to drink. The coffee is practically syrup by now. It's been on since the last shift. Do you want a candy bar or anything?"

Pia took a long drink that made her want to belch. "Anything chocolate would be fabulous," she said. The prickly sensation of the Pepsi in her throat was helping her feel more normal. "What happened to Nick—the guy I was with?"

"He's here someplace or will be shortly," the officer told her. "In the meantime, I'll go find something chocolate for you. You've got a long evening coming."

<hr />

The paperwork and the interviews took hours. Day had ended and night was considering the distant approach of dawn. Pia was dozing on one of the black vinyl chairs in the hallway by the time Nick emerged from his turn with the investigator, who walked beside him. Pia stirred when she heard their voices.

"I'm sorry we need to keep your book for a while," the investigator was saying to Nick. "It's evidence. I'll tell the D.A. that you want it back, but I'm not promising anything."

"Did you give them those death threat letters?" Nick asked Pia when he saw her sitting there, cradling her purse.

She nodded. "Everything. And I told them I'd send them any others I find back in the apartment."

"We'll get in touch with you when we learn something." The investigator scratched his head—not in confusion but because he was itchy. "We know the cab was stolen. That's about it. Who can guess what sets a guy like that off?" He smiled at Pia. He had a round head, a broad toothy smile, and matted gray hair that made him look like a stringed puppet. His suit was rumpled. He didn't seem anything like the detectives in black leather on TV. "Mooning traffic was quick thinking, Miss. That may have saved you. People complain much faster than they jump in to help. Most don't want to get involved."

She tried to look pleased. "Thanks."

The detective continued. "I called a cab for you, and set you up in a different hotel than the one you booked. This guy seems to have had detailed information about you. We might as well be less predictable until we know if he was part of some larger group or a solo act."

"A larger group?" repeated Pia. "I'm worth a whole conspiracy?"

The detective shrugged. "You never know."

"I'm not sure I want to take another cab," protested Nick half-heartedly. It was his attempt at humor. Nick was feeling punchy, too.

The investigator gave a crooked half-smile. "I'm not surprised. Don't worry. This cab's legit. Here's my card. Call me if you think of any other information that might help us out, but don't say anything to reporters. You never know which bit is going to end up being important. In the meantime, get some rest. For a couple just back from Costa Rica, you two look bad."

Pia's mouth curled into a smile, but her emotions weren't involved. She was beginning to feel really terrible.

"I hope this hotel has 24 hour room service," said Nick as they relaxed into the summoned cab. "I haven't had anything to eat but candy bars. I feel sick. I need something big and heavy with lots of beer."

Pia didn't answer. She sat staring out her side window, watching the city shops whirr by, a blur of colors. Sale. Sale. Sale. Everything was for sale. Everything. And maybe everyone. She was tired...

They didn't talk much.

"When you think how close we came to dying, it's sobering," Nick said at last. "All our years of studying and working and planning, gone like that—two stiffs on slabs in the morgue."

Pia's insides were trembling—a delayed reaction she hadn't anticipated. She hugged her arms around her. She wondered if Nick could sense her personal earthquake. "If the patrol car hadn't been passing," she began, not knowing if she wanted to finish her sentence. She was shaking so hard, she wasn't sure she could.

"Yeah. That guy was crazy. He might have done it right there. What kind of an end is that?"

She heard herself voicing the words that were in her mind. "Murdered in a field."

Nick's mood had darkened. "How does it feel to be someone strangers want to kill? he asked without thinking.

"It's great," she replied, her sarcasm clipped and acidic. "I don't know when I've enjoyed myself more."

"Maybe you should think about focusing on book topics that don't tick people off so much," he suggested in automatic reaction, realizing as he did that he was walking into trouble.

"And maybe you should get a job flipping burgers and frying potatoes."

"I didn't mean to put you or your work down, Pia. It's just that I love you, and these threats are serious. I don't want to come home from work and find you murdered or missing. I'd say I can't be with you all the time, but what good did it do when I was? I felt helpless and pointless. I didn't like it. I feel like less of a man than I was a week ago."

"I'm sorry you've had a hard time."

He wanted to snap back at her continued sarcasm, but he stopped himself. He knew they were very near a pit of vipers, and he had better hold still.

17

"**Y**ou could've been murdered!" exclaimed Marguerite in alarm the next day as Nick and Pia sat on her sofa. They had told her about their scare. Footage was running on TV—in fact, it was the local lead story. Marguerite's face went pale and her breathing was quick and shallow as she watched the pictures taken from the helicopter. The camera zoomed in on the covered body lying beside the road. "Butchered like an animal," muttered Marguerite.

Pia thought she could imagine what her mother was seeing in her mind. After so many years together, she recognized the faraway look on her mother's face.

"Butchered," Marguerite repeated. She stood up, but she didn't seem to have anywhere to go. Slowly, she realized where she was and sat back down in the upholstered chair that Dorothy had owned so long ago. "Sometimes you wonder if surviving and remembering aren't more difficult than dying."

"Surviving is always a challenge," Pia agreed.

"I've been telling Pia we need to find a place to live where we can relax and regroup," said Nick, changing the subject. "We could get married and she'd have a different name. Then we could go somewhere far enough from here that the neighbors wouldn't have seen all the hype about the book—just until the media attention dies down. After all, Pia's book isn't an international bestseller or anything, just a flash in the pan from a small publisher. Hopefully, people will forget it soon. I can work almost anywhere if I don't expect to be paid much. Pia told me she'd think about it."

"Yes, yes, that's the thing to do! Leave the New York area." Marguerite turned toward Pia. "Your book is great, but it isn't worth dying over. You'd have to be in Congress or head of a movement or something to actually change those problems you outlined. The only people who read books like yours and take them seriously are the people who already agree with you—or the crazies."

"You're probably right there." Pia sighed. "I probably made the language of my book too academic and that's the reason so many people misinterpret what I was trying to say."

Nick snorted. "People like Don Watson don't misunderstand. They deliberately twist what you say so they can spout more of their nonsense. It's about who has control."

Marguerite nodded sadly. "His followers like to feel right and safe in the middle of the pack. Back when we had riots, they called it mob mentality. After a while, followers don't seem to have brains left. There's nothing they won't do."

Pia rose and walked to the window. "I want to think most people are better than Don Watson."

"They are," Marguerite assured her. "But most people are too busy, too stressed, and too fearful to pay real attention—like you said in your book. They operate on impressions. They want somebody else to be perfect and fix things."

Pia sighed and turned to look at her mother. "I wanted to make Matias proud, even if I'm not his child. I wanted to make Silva into the fool."

Marguerite nodded her understanding. "But Matias is dead, Sweetheart. It's good to try to make the world better, but if you die in the process, who's going to pick up the standard and run with it? You need to build a movement, like I said, not work alone. You have more impact as a group. People can easily ignore a single person—or blame you. If you want to make a bigger difference than just talk, you have to pick your battles. You tried to look at too much at once. Choose just one of your institutions and decide on the specific changes you want to see. Then you have a chance of succeeding—one triumph at a time."

"And stay away from religion!" Nick chimed in. "People think they're on a mission from God and they get crazy. Religion is too emotional and primal. It's too hard to sort the true believers from the pack. That's God's job."

Pia gave him a dirty look. "And you wonder why I don't want to get married. I wasn't writing about religion per se; you should know that. I was writing about leaders who lie."

Marguerite rose and went to slip her arm around her daughter's shoulder. "I don't mean to take sides, Sweetheart, but Nick's right. You don't belong in a religious fight. It's been going on for thousands of years. You aren't going to solve it, and maybe the confusion of it is part of what people are supposed to wrestle in this life. Maybe people are judged partially on who they believe. Education or politics—either one you choose needs more than enough reforms to keep you busy the rest of your days."

Pia kissed her mother's cheek. "Okay, okay, okay. I'll break my contract with Barbara Bright—or maybe bend it. There's a case for extenuating circumstances. She can't say much since I've already delivered most of the requirements. I'll tell her I won't do interviews unless they're with hosts who are both sane and honest."

"I guess you won't be doing any talk shows then," chuckled Nick.

Pia turned. "Don't get too excited. I just need to lick my wounds for a while. I'm not surrendering."

"You know, I have a great town for you," said Marguerite, rising. "It might have been a Mafia summer hideout in the thirties. I ran into it when I was traveling."

Nick threw up his hands as he made a face. "Terrific."

Pia ignored him. "I'll call Barbara."

———————

When Pia was seated in Barbara Bright's overly decorated office later in the week, she announced her intentions immediately. For a moment, she thought the middle-aged woman was going to take back the cup of gourmet coffee she had just delivered.

"Do you know how lucky you are to *have* an agent—much less one who works for you as hard as I do?" Barbara hissed through her carefully painted lips. "Do you have any idea?"

"I'm not doing the book circuit anymore—at least for the present," Pia said without answering the question. "I'm going to disappear for a while. I'm going to stop being a book whore."

"A publicity whore–be specific," corrected the hard, champagne-haired woman in the orthopedic shoes. "Each appearance means money in your pocket that you can nobly donate or whatever. This is the worst possible time to take a break. Your adventure being kidnapped with your boyfriend is money in the bank. I loved the part in the TV footage where the truck driver said you had a cute butt. Bingo! End of academic stigma! The only thing that would be better would be footage of your cute butt. You're a crusader or an outcast, depending on the point of view—but sexy. There was a peek of cleavage and a lot of leg in the shot of you getting in the cop car with your hands cuffed behind your back. Shades of S and M! I couldn't invent something that would have a better impact on your sales. I'm putting a clip on You-Tube as soon as I straighten out the credits. This is the time when you need to put yourself out there *more*."

Pia shifted in her chair. "Each appearance means I lose another piece of my self-respect."

"You're being melodramatic."

"You're protecting your percentage."

"Guilty as charged." Barbara flicked her hair with her unbelievable plastic nails. "What's wrong with making a few dollars?"

Pia took a breath. "It almost got me and the man I love killed. I'm having nightmares. I start sweating when I have to take a cab. That's what's wrong. The misleading publicity for my book has made me into a target for any maladjusted person in the country. Is that right or fair? No, of course not. Should I be able to say anything I can back up with information as being true and factual? I think so. But lots of people don't. Okay, done. I don't want to be a martyr, Barbara. My father was a martyr, and what did it get him?"

"Really? He was a martyr? This could be good!"

"No, not really. My dad was a sleaze-ball weasel scum-of-the-earth."

Barbara sat back and eyed her through her heavy eyelashes. "And what about your future as an investigative writer?"

"What about it?" Pia knew it was a lame answer—further proof that the talk shows had sucked out her brains. "I'll let you know where I am, but do your best not to call me."

Barbara leaned back in her fancy, adjustable desk chair with the imitation leather arms. "You're ungrateful, do you know that?"

"It has occurred to me before." Pia picked up her briefcase and her purse and walked out. Outside, the air seemed to be cleaner and fresher than before. But she had a feeling her troubles weren't over.

———◆———

The southwestern town of Camisa, named for the shirt-like shape of its mesa, wasn't much, which was the beauty of it, according to Marguerite. It could be reached only by car or bus—a two-hour drive from the airport. No one there cared much about the world because almost no one had a concept for it. People who moved away always moved back and knew better than to talk about their disloyalty in leaving in the first place. The world outside didn't know Camisa existed. Every so often, letters sent to Camisa were returned to sender "Address Unknown." Sometimes that was due to the postmistress–who everyone said was both mad and vindictive–sending back mail if she didn't like the recipient, and sometimes it was due to the zip code that didn't seem to be entered in all the postal system databases. Camisa wasn't even on the weather maps the city TV weather forecasters pointed to during the evening news. People in Camisa worried more about their tiny high school sports teams and old cars and how to work the social security system than they did about nearly anything else— with the possible exception of professional football. Camisa seemed like a perfect place to hide and recuperate.

Nick found part-time work in a university up north. Although his pay was pitiful, with his parents' help he rented a tiny apartment where he could stay near campus during the week until he could join Pia in Camisa on weekends. He and Pia found an old blue Victorian that needed new wiring and plumbing and insulation. It was cheap, so Pia rented it. Nick wasn't entirely pleased. It wasn't a great deal. He voted it the house most likely to burn up its occupants in the night. The antique boiler still worked, but not well. Drafts blew through the house like wispy ghosts looking for someone to haunt, necessitating heating bills that surpassed the rent. The walls smelled of old wallpaper. The kitchen had a hole in the ceiling that led directly and without discernable purpose to the second floor so that an intercom between levels wasn't necessary. But the stair landing boasted a lovely stained glass window, and the master bedroom bulged with a huge window seat that seemed ready to climb out through the frame some morning when the glass was open to sit in the giant cottonwood beyond.

Finding a way for her to supplement their income was a more difficult problem than Pia had anticipated. She had to use her birth certificate to get a driver's license, since she had accidentally thrown her driver's license away with the garbage before they moved. The town clerks were skeptical, so she needed to look for a job within walking distance while her identity was verified. She could write, but the newspaper was one that wouldn't hire anyone who wasn't born and bred locally. They could tell without asking whether she fit the requirement, because every native son in Camisa seemed to be related to every other one. She finally accepted a job as a clerk in a tiny shop that sold office supplies. Yes, she could make copies. She had almost finished a PhD, for goodness sake. That made her suspect. Why would anyone do such a thing?

She was standing behind the counter when Carl Minnelli entered. He was an imposing man–large, heavy, sweaty, but also a force. His chest pushed hard against his plaid shirt. He felt like arguments and conflict. Negativity ran down his face with his sweat.

"Can I help you?"

He glared at her. "You're the one who wrote that book. I heard about what you said from somebody who knows."

Her spirits sagged. So this was the reason people didn't run away. There is no *away*. What a waste of time and effort. Nick would be livid. He left his research for nothing. "Are you sure we're talking about the same book?"

"Yeah. The Communist one about pastors being dictators."

"Did you read it?"

"Hell no. Do I look like some kind of troublemaker?"

She decided not to answer his question. "Actually, the book is about many sorts of dictators. May I help you make copies? Do you need supplies? Why are you here?"

"I just wanted to see what you look like."

"Are you disappointed?"

"You look like I figured." He gave her another glance and turned to go. "You don't know as much as you think, Girl," he said almost beneath his breath to avoid the customer coming in. "You don't."

The cheery lady who had just entered looked curious. She resembled a plump blueberry in her dark blue sweat suit. Her dark brown hair was pulled back in a bun that was slowly unweaving itself.

"Apparently, I don't know enough," explained Pia.

The lady chuckled. "Who does? Somebody die and leave him in charge of judging?"

"I guess so."

The lady handed her a school poster. "For the elementary mothers," she said. "They have to know when picture day is or they raise a big stink. I had to fight to put the information in both Spanish and English. Some of the parents think we have to force immigrant parents to read English, even if they won't know to dress their kids for picture day—as if the Spanish-speaking mothers won't complain. I had no idea how much trouble being president would be. We need about a hundred copies. I have a paper to prove we're tax-exempt. I put it on the top there. I'm Theresa Peterson, by the way, president of the parents' group. I haven't seen you before, have I?"

"No, I'm new."

"Welcome to Camisa."

"Thanks." Pia took the master to the copier. "Do you know that man?"

"That's Carl Minnelli. He's about the most self-righteous son-of-a-gun around. He hates women and he isn't real fond of anyone else, either."

"At least it's not just me."

Theresa smiled. "You may hear more nasty talk. People are all hyped up about what you wrote in your book–or their version of what you wrote. There's a popular pastor in town who uses you as a villain to keep his sermons lively. I don't know where he heard about the book. He must have been thrilled when he realized you had moved in here. He doesn't usually have his crusades come to him. From what I hear, he keys off phrases you used. Did you see those cardboard cutouts of the mayor around town?"

Pia collected the pile of printed sheets. "I saw a man in the post office try to shake hands with one."

Theresa laughed. She handed a few bills to Pia—exactly the correct amount. She had obviously used the copy service before. "I almost did that myself the other day because of my bifocals. Felt like such a fool. The way I see it, certain folks here spend a lot of time dealing with cutouts. That's what I'm saying."

Pia went to the door to see Theresa out. Carl Minnelli was standing across the street, leaning on the exterior of the bar, staring toward her shop.

"Don't mind him," Theresa told her. "He doesn't do any harm. He's just ugly. I'm sure he was ugly when he was born. See you soon." She chuckled at her own humor and went on her way.

Pia heard a voice behind her. "What a folksy place."

She turned to see Nick.

"I came in the back door. Some guy in the parking lot said it would save a lot of walking. Doesn't seem safe to me. You should keep the back door locked. And if that mutant across the street bothers you, call the cops immediately. There *are* cops here, aren't there?"

"My reputation precedes me," Pia told him as she went to do as he had suggested. "The guy you call the mutant was just in here grumbling about my book. Oh, Nick, I'm really truly sorry I dragged you out here."

Nick made a sound in his throat. "You should be impressed he'd grumble about a book. I thought everyone here was illiterate."

She took a cloth to wipe the fingerprints off the glass countertop. "Oh, I don't think he read anything. He just heard from someone who heard from someone who read something on page forty-four."

"I brought you a can of mace from the big city. I want you to keep it with you."

She rolled her eyes. "If you say so."

"I do." He came to kiss her. "I hate the week without you. You have no idea how difficult it is to have a serious discussion with people these days—unless they have no idea what they're talking about. Then they have plenty to say. Everyone else wants to be politically correct."

"Well, we don't have to worry about that with me, do we?"

He feigned a laugh. "I trust your mother's taste in most things, Pia, but are you certain you want to stay in this town? I've never been anywhere that was more defensive."

"How long have you been here?"

"Besides the eternity we spent finding a place to live, a few hours. I didn't want to annoy you while you were working. I spent a lot of time in the diner fishing for information. You can learn a lot in a diner. Anyone from anywhere else is automatically suspect. I'm told we come here and try to make the locals look bad. The fact that I teach in a university makes me too ignorant to have opinions about anything important. They think I'm a stoner."

"A stoner science professor?"

"I was thinking of trying to fix those rotted boards in the deck, so I went to the lumber yard. What a lot of junk. Did you know the city council passed a law that you have to pay a percentage at city hall if you buy construction materials outside town? The idea is to protect the mayor's son-in-law. He owns the yard and hasn't carried a straight board in the past twenty years, according to my anonymous sources. He makes more money selling warped ones."

"You did learn a lot. Have you considered a job with the CIA?"

"I'll stay here with you if that's what you want, Pia. And if deliberately staying here isn't love, nothing is."

A neatly dressed male customer came in, and Pia gave Nick a perfunctory kiss. "Go on home and I'll make you dinner as soon as I get off." She dropped her voice to a whisper. "And don't say a word about restaurant food around here. The guy looking at the printer supplies owns most of the restaurants."

Nick had gone out when she got home, so she hurried to put a pot of water for pasta on a burner. A knock on the door prevented her from doing more.

A bearded man in a denim jacket and red cap that read "Great Foods" was on the porch. "Is the man of the house home?"

"The man will be here in a minute, if you can wait. Or you can talk to me."

He handed her a paper. "Citation," he said smugly, "for code violations."

"What codes? What's wrong?"

"Your trees need trimming, your sidewalk is uneven, and your yard has weeds over four inches tall. You have lots of work to do, Lady."

"We're renting. We just moved in."

"You're here now." He strode down the walk to his black pickup that was waiting at the curb.

"Thanks," she mumbled sarcastically. "Nice to meet you, too."

She was still standing in the doorway when Nick drove up.

"I found some wine!" he declared, triumphantly holding up a bottle like a recent kill. "I can't say it's the best, but it was this or cheap beer. I found lots of liquor stores but they don't carry much wine. Are you waiting to greet me?" He came up the walk to kiss her lightly on the mouth.

"Citations," she replied, not caring that he had no idea what she was talking about. "I'm collecting citations—for problems no one mentioned when we rented. Big problems."

Later, as they sat sipping bad wine and feeling the taste of spaghetti in their mouths, he took the list of citations from the top of the tower of packing boxes where Pia had left it. "I would think these should be owner problems," he decided as he read. "Are we—or you–being persecuted or what?"

"That's just it. I don't know."

"In a small town, just being an intelligent woman can make you controversial–unless you're one of the founding dowager empresses. I hear there's one here who can pretty much change the weather. Her family laid the first brick or something."

Pia tore the last bit of garlic bread apart. "Yes, I've met her. She was sweety-nice to me in the beginning. Then she found out I'd written a book—not a romance. And then she must have read something—probably just the highlighted nasty parts."

"Who highlighted parts if no one reads?"

"I imagine they have a committee dedicated to making sure no one thinks. They flip through books and look for certain nasty words. If they find them, they ditch the book."

Nick shook his head. "Like the time Yahoo blocked the breast cancer websites because they used the word 'breast.'"

Pia gulped the last of the wine in her glass. "How's your job coming?"

He shrugged. "Not bad for slave labor. Adjuncts aren't exactly revered. For a while, I thought they weren't going to give me access to a computer. My office is a former closet. I'm not compensated for the time I spend with individual students. Different world."

She leaned forward, emptying the last of the wine into her glass. "Coming here was a huge mistake. Would it help if I apologized again?"

"It's going to be an experience." He took the last bit of garlic bread and dipped it in his wine. "We'll adapt and be glad we're here only temporarily. Tomorrow I'll call the landlords and tell them they have problems to fix."

"Nobody's open on Saturday mornings, Nick—not even the downtown stores."

"Oh. Then I'll call on Monday from the university. And on Friday, when I get back, I'll go to City Hall and have a word or two with them about who's responsible for sidewalks. It'll be fine."

Pia slumped down in her chair. "They'll listen better to you because you're male. My impression is you don't want to be any kind of minority in this town—and that includes females. I think I might be suffocating."

"Come on, I'll help you clean up and then we'll get some rest." He pulled her hand to his lips and kissed it. "We'll stay until our lease is up and then we'll go elsewhere—unless something happens to make us move sooner."

"What would happen, exactly? Do you know something I don't know? We haven't found the conspiracy group, have we?"

"No. No conspiracy. We'll wait and see what's next."

18

Pia was attempting to mow the lawn with a dull-bladed old push mower she had found in the flimsy metal shed in her side yard when the neighbor walked over across the yards. She was young, maybe in her late twenties—short and thick but not really fat. Her long black hair hung onto a knit top that was meant to showcase her bulbous breasts. Instead, it emphasized the roll of flesh above her jeans she used to support the baby sleeping in her arms. She wore thick glasses she had to push up on her nose frequently. Behind them, her eyes were ringed with heavy black eye liner.

"Are you Lympia Garcia?" she asked. She was neither friendly nor challenging.

"They call me Pia."

The woman smiled. "Hi. I'm Elena Velasquez—from next door. I heard about you from my cousin. She works at City Hall. She knows about all the new people."

"Nice to meet you." Pia wondered what she should say next.

"You're not Mexican, are you?" asked Elena, seeking confirmation of a conclusion she had reached on her own.

"My father was from Argentina."

"I didn't think you was from Mexico. *Garcia* is hard to guess." The young woman paused, perhaps not knowing what to think of Argentina—maybe not knowing where it was. "People here ain't friendly to people from Mexico. There's too many of them."

Pia wasn't sure where to take the conversation. Her neighbor appeared to be Hispanic.

"My people came from Spain," the young woman explained proudly. "Conquistadors and stuff. We've been in this area ever since."

Pia smiled. "My impression is there are many people living here whose families have been here a long time."

"You're right," said Elena. "Except they don't all get along. They stay with their own—Mexicans with Mexicans, Italians with Italians, Chinese with Chinese, and whites with whites."

Pia directed the mower back toward the shed. It didn't even push easily over concrete, and it was totally overmatched by the resiliency of the weeds. She was going to have to find someone to sharpen the blades. She slammed the metal shed door shut and pulled the sweatband off her head. "There are Chinese people here?"

"You probably saw the restaurant just outside town. Don't eat there. People get food poisoning. My cousin works with the health department, and he says they failed an inspection. He found mouse droppings all over the kitchen—even a dead rat. It was all squished and gooey behind the stove."

"Good information." Pia felt a sudden wave of nausea. "Excuse me a minute, will you? I need to go to the restroom. I'll be right back."

She hurried into the house, barely making it to the bathroom before she vomited. Her eyes turned red and puffy. When she returned, Elena was waiting, sitting on the front steps.

"So, you're pregnant?"

Pia sat on a lower step. "You were talking about mouse droppings and a squished rat."

Elena laughed. "Girl, you ain't that delicate. You're throwing up, right? You look like hell right now."

Pia nodded.

"And tired. You look tired. You got shadows under your eyes. You missed a period, didn't you?"

"It was probably because of the move." Pia realized with a start that she was explaining herself to this girl she had never met before. Why was she having an intimate conversation with a stranger? Her head was starting to hurt.

"No, Girl. You're pregnant. This is something I know about." Elena laughed an unselfconscious laugh that made her sleeping baby bounce. "We don't have a GYN at our hospital. We're lucky to have a hospital. They don't do babies or broken bones. You got to go up north. You got insurance?"

"I'm on Nick's policy."

"That your boyfriend?"

"Yes."

"I seen him. He's kinda cute in his way." Elena leaned close. "Will he stick around when he finds out about the baby?"

"I think so."

"That's good, because the daddy of my first—man!–he took off so fast. I was still in high school and Jorge, he was living at home. His dad didn't like me so he give Jorge his truck and Jorge, he got a job up north. But then his new girlfriend had a baby, so he didn't get off like he thought. Now I got Manny. I don't love him like I loved Jorge, but at least he's here. We got a house—right next-door here, and that's more than Jorge will ever have. He drinks his pay. He does drugs, too. So if you need something, you call me. Manny and me, we help out. It's how we was raised."

Pia watched a squirrel scamper up a nearby tree. She couldn't imagine how she could tell, but she was certain her neighbor was right about her being pregnant. A nervous quiver skittered up through her abdomen to constrict her breathing. A baby. Now what? "I don't know much about this sort of thing."

"This is your *first?*" Elena was incredulous.

"Yes. Kind of an accident. Too much vacation."

Elena laughed. "I got three. It's good you didn't wait too late–you know, when you're old. Then you gotta take all kinds of tests all the time. My aunt did that. That baby has old parents." She peered at Pia through her thick lenses. "Well, maybe you *are* gonna have to take those tests. But they ain't bad. Something about diabetes. Hey, you know, we can babysit for each other!"

Pia gripped her stomach, thinking she might be sick again. "Not for a while."

"You don't look so good. I got a card with my GYN on it. I'll get it for you. You're gonna need somebody to give you all those vitamins and shit."

Pia sat down on the step. Santiago Silva was going to be a grandfather.

That Friday, as Nick rested in the living room sipping wine he had brought from the city, Pia chose the chair across from him.

"Nick, you know how you had a feeling something was going to happen?"

He nodded.

"It already happened. Nick, we're going to have a baby. It's kind of an accident—from the vacation, I think. I did the test. I'm going to a doctor next week, but I don't think there's any question."

He sat for a moment, staring at her. She wasn't sure if he was going to laugh or cry.

"I'll be damned," he said almost beneath his breath. "I'll be damned." His hazel eyes turned from brown to green. Slowly, he got to his feet. He came to stand in front of her. He dropped to one knee. She was about to stop him when he reached into the pocket of his suit coat and pulled out a ring box.

"You're kidding," she said. "You have to be kidding."

"No, no, I'm not." He opened the box. "Now don't laugh. This is me being romantic here. Lympia Marie Garcia, will you marry me? Please? I love you."

"How did you find out?"

He shrugged. "I didn't. I ordered this weeks ago. The lady says we can have it sized, but I matched it to one of your other rings—the one you thought you lost."

"You didn't know about the baby?"

"How could I? Didn't you just tell me? Would you agree to marry me if you thought I was doing this because you're pregnant?"

"No."

"I didn't know; I swear. Thank God I ordered the ring when I didn't know. That's the magic of this, and I don't believe in magic. I really want to marry you, Pia. I think I've mentioned it before–a few times."

He reached out to take her hand. His fingers were shaking as he tried to slip the ring on her finger. When she moved to help, she realized she was trembling, too. How odd, when they had known this would happen for so long. But the world seemed to be tipping, sliding sideways into a fresh reality. The blue-green of the stone gleamed within its gold setting. On her finger, it seemed to glow.

He smiled up at her. "Aquamarine is the birthstone for March. It's supposed to cool the temper and enable the wearer to be more level-headed."

"Is that a joke?"

"No. It's what the lady told me. She was all about symbolism. To me, the color suggests cool seawater—like in Costa Rica. The other birthstone for March is jasper, called the martyr's stone—dark green speckled with red that's supposed to signify the blood of Christ dripping down from the cross. I figured you didn't need a martyr's stone. Your family has had enough martyrdom. Besides, it was kind of depressing and ugly. I remembered you said diamonds are tainted by the abuse of the men who mine them in Africa. But if you *want* a diamond, we can exchange this. The lady said so. I want you to be happy."

She smiled at him. "I feel more level-headed already."

He grinned back at her. "Does that mean you'll accept?"

She pulled him to his feet. "Yes. I accept." They kissed, taking their time to enjoy the sensations. "I love the aquamarine. I never would've thought of it."

He kissed her again, playing this time like a boy discovering sex. Pia was giggling. He seized her face in his hands and whispered in her ear, nibbling seductively before he spoke. "How about if I call and get us dinner reservations in the city, and we can spend the weekend in a hotel there?"

"Nick, it's already dinner time, and I'm starving."

"How about tomorrow then? There's no restaurant here fancy enough for this celebration. You can drive the car home, and then come to pick me up next weekend. I want to spend every possible minute with you."

She nodded, laughing. "Sure."

He was muttering happily to himself as they walked to the dining room. "A husband and a daddy, almost at once. Holy shit."

When they had eaten their fill, Nick leaned back in his chair, enjoying a second glass of wine. "How do you want to do this thing— the wedding?"

Pia was folding and refolding her napkin to make it stand at attention as she imagined a formal reception. "I think we should plan to have it near Mom even though that will be more difficult than having it here would be. We don't have any real friends or family here. We're kind of an oddity. No bride should feel like an oddity. Besides, Mom has to attend, and she doesn't like to travel these days. I have an old friend from college who lives in New York. She would probably be happy to be my maid of honor, and you have What's-His-Name, the beer drinker from grad school–or you could ask your brother."

"So you want the whole long white dress, flowers, and tuxedo thing—with bridesmaids and a reception?" He tried to look like he was excited, but she knew him too well.

She smiled. "The biggest, fanciest weddings I've ever attended didn't seem to help the couple stay married, and they're so extravagantly expensive—mostly show. To me they feel like The Prom, Part Two."

Was she testing him? He kept his expression carefully noncommittal. "My parents will pay. They know your mom can't afford to finance a wedding."

Pia pushed her plate forward, away from her. "Then we shouldn't have a big wedding. This wedding needs to match us, who we are right now."

"My parents would rather have a show for their friends. My mother's been planning what she'll wear to my wedding for years. Actually, I think she might have the theme and colors and all the trimmings detailed in a scrapbook somewhere. She's been hoping she can persuade whoever I marry to go along with her plans. She loves to make plans, and she loves to dress up."

Pia shrugged. "Oh well. Maybe she and your father can renew their vows in a lavish ceremony—or they can bully your sister into behaving—when she finally finds a groom."

Nick laughed. "She'd do it. Okay, if we're not going to run with the white dress thing, what are we going to do?"

"First, we need a date—before the baby comes. I'll go shopping in New York with Mom and buy a dress I like. You choose some slacks and a shirt. We hire a minister who doesn't mind unconventional weddings, and we pick a spot—maybe in the park where I used to walk with Mom, Allen, and Dorothy. I have a lot of happy memories there."

She looked at Nick, into him. "I'm not a traditional person, Nick. Nothing about my life has been traditional. I don't have any family but Mom—any family I'd be willing to recognize, that is. I don't want to sit in an empty church that echoes like a tomb with a lot of strangers wondering why I don't have very many people on my side. I don't want to invite anyone who doesn't know for certain that you aren't marrying me to give the baby a name. I don't want to listen to an organ that usually ushers people out of this world. I think that's creepy—not an auspicious beginning. I've had enough death in my life already. I don't want to wear a white dress that looks like a museum piece or have bridesmaids who match. I'd like our wedding to feel like an authentic celebration. If we could do it, I'd prefer to be married on a tropical beach, but to make our deadline, we can't wait for you to finish your academic year. Anyway, I'm not sure Mom would fly. Maybe we can reserve a reception room in that Italian restaurant you like. Your dad can pay for lots of food and wine and lively music. What do you think?"

He came around the table to kiss her on the top of her head. "I think I love you more than I thought was possible. Any wedding that pleases you, pleases me. But, to be perfectly honest, I'm glad you don't want to go the courthouse route—something quick and clandestine. A wedding shouldn't feel like a legal proceeding. I'm more sentimental than that. I want to make sure everyone knows how proud I am to be marrying you—how proud I am of you."

"We won't have time for a real honeymoon." She twisted in her seat so she could look into his face.

He leaned over to kiss her. "Not yet. Only not yet. The delay will be temporary. I intend to celebrate our honeymoon as often as possible for the next fifty years or so."

"Only fifty years?"

"With options after that."

She smiled. "I can try to reserve the gazebo in the park for the ceremony. Then we'll be ready for anything but a freak blizzard."

"With our luck?" Nick laughed and started gathering the dirty dishes from the table. "You'd better pick out some cute white boots."

19

*M*atias was waiting for her, standing by the gnarled tree that shaded the stream. He drew a handkerchief from his pocket—it was the lacy one he had given her—and wiped the blood from his face. "You see?" he said, his voice its old soul-reverberating baritone, "It's all right now."

People somewhere were screaming. Marguerite covered her ears. It was her. She was screaming. She turned quickly as she realized Silva was standing beside her, the cattle prod in his hands.

Matias stretched out a bloodied hand. "Here, my love. We'll go to America. Come away with me."

Silva grabbed her arm. "No, Señora, you can never leave me," he growled. "Never, never, never. The baby is mine!"

———————

Buzzer. Buzzer. Buzzer. Marguerite stirred and opened her eyes. She was lying on the sofa in her living room. She rose and walked to the intercom. Her heart was pounding. "Yes?" she answered, half-afraid she would hear Silva's voice.

"Mom? It's Pia. I'm here."

Marguerite pushed the button to release the door lock and went to open her apartment door.

A scarred man with a shaved head opened the door across the hall. He was wearing gray sweats. "Are you okay, Maggie? Is everything okay? I thought I heard you crying out again."

"Yes, yes. I'm fine, Ralph. I was just dreaming. My daughter's here."

"Okay. Okay then." Ralph closed his door.

Pia arrived in the hallway as his door clicked shut. "Who was that?" she asked as she kissed her mother hello.

Her mother ushered her into the apartment, closing and locking the door behind her. "His name is Ralph. I can take you to meet him. He has what they call PTSD—flashbacks–from Viet Nam. He says I have it, too. So when he hears me cry out, he comes running. We're quite a pair, the two of us. He thinks he's in Viet Nam, and I think I'm in Argentina."

Pia embraced her a second time, as though to crush the nightmares. "I'm so sorry, Mom."

"You'd think they'd go away," Marguerite muttered as she sat down on the sofa. "You'd think the nightmares would finally go away."

Pia sat in a chair to face her. She folded her arms awkwardly over the small mound of her belly.

Marguerite seemed to rally. She forced a bright smile. "Ah, here you are, looking radiant and beautiful!"

"I look like I swallowed an elephant, like the serpent in *The Little Prince* drawing."

"You look wonderful. I can't tell you how delighted I am that you decided to visit me. What did you do with your suitcase?"

"It's on the landing. I can bring it up later. Nick wanted to come, too, but he couldn't be away from work long enough." She stood up and stretched. "I could use a glass of water. Do you want anything?"

"No, I'm fine, but I should be waiting on you."

"Not necessary. I need to walk around as much as I can." Pia went into the tiny kitchen and poured a glass of water from the faucet. The kitchen wasn't as clean as she remembered it. Her mother must be in pain again.

She returned to the living room, to sit beside Marguerite this time.

"And how does Nick feel about the baby?" asked Marguerite. "I imagine he's thrilled."

Pia nodded. "He's already planning schools and all that. His parents are happy, too, or they say they are. I suppose they're waiting to see what the baby looks like. If it looks European, they'll celebrate."

Her mother smiled. "I think you're underestimating them. It's pretty hard to be a cold-hearted grandparent."

"Maybe." Pia drank from her glass, placed it on the coffee table, and drew a long breath, exhaling it slowly. "Mom, I have a difficult question to ask, and I want you to answer truthfully."

Marguerite made a sound that said she was mildly insulted. "I'll try."

"Are you going to be able to love this baby if it looks like Silva?"

Her mother reached out to caress Pia's cheek. "Ridiculous child! Of course I will. I'm the grandma. I'll love it as I love you and Nick." She stroked Pia's hair. "Silva is a bad memory. He means nothing any more. Your baby will look like my grandchild."

Pia sighed. "I hope so. I don't want it to remind you of...bad memories."

"Oh my darling, don't give it another thought. This baby will be like you were when you were born. You were fresh and new and clean—straight from Heaven. I was terribly worried that I wouldn't love you, but once I saw you, I knew I'd been worried for nothing. This may sound mad, but I think you were meant to be Matias's child—our child together, and by the grace of Heaven, I think you are. Silva was just a means. Your soul is the soul of our love child."

Pia leaned close to hug her, tears welling in her eyes. "I believe I'm your love child, too." They remained in a soft embrace outside time as the universe moved around them. At last, Pia pulled away. To prevent herself from crying, she took another drink from her glass.

"Nick says he wants his baby to have his name—as well as mine—from the beginning. So we're planning to have the ceremony before the baby arrives. Nick's parents would love to stage a grand event, but Nick and I want to find someone who'll marry us here, in the park, with you to give me away. We'll wear regular clothes, because we want our marriage to be a part of our real lives—nothing that's just show. We want to be under the open sky—one union, under God—no extra trappings, just love. What do you think? Will you give me away?"

Marguerite hugged her, letting her tears flow freely. "Of course, Sweetheart. Matias will be there, I know, but I'll give you away. Just a moment."

She went into the bedroom. In a few minutes she returned, carrying a small jewelry box. She placed it on the table as carefully as she would if the wood were fragile crystal and lifted the lid. Peeling aside a layer of red velvet, she lifted out a necklace—a Christian cross on a gold chain. "If you like—don't do it if you don't want to—but if you like it, you can wear this as I did in my wedding to Matias. It belonged to his grandmother. Maria gave it to me to keep before I left. It's one of the few things I saved."

'It's perfect," muttered Pia softly. "Mom, it's perfect."

———✥———

"Mom loves our ideas for the wedding, but not nearly as much as she loves the idea of being a grandma," Pia told Nick when she had

190

returned to their house in Camisa. "She says she thinks I was meant to be the child of Matias and her. She believes I was granted that soul."

Pia paused, waiting for Nick to be as touched as she was.

He nodded. "That's nice."

She supposed she had offended his scientific brain.

"Yes." Pia sighed and continued. "So, the wedding is all set for the first weekend the minister is available—before the weather turns cold."

"Great work!" He pulled her into his arms and kissed her soundly. "I've wanted this since we first met, since we first made love. Thank goodness for the baby or you might never have relented. You know, I think I knew you were pregnant before you did. Dads have this sense about such things."

She punched him in the arm. She couldn't say for sure if he was joking.

The ceremony happened without fanfare in a city park gazebo. Children ran by, never realizing a wedding was happening. A ball bounced to the minister's feet. Someone hit the back of Marguerite's folding chair with a flying disk. But the wedding worked. Pia wore a long skirt with her deep blue silk blouse decorated with Maria's cross necklace and wrapped herself in a shawl against the fall chill. Nick wore slacks and a sweater. His parents stood out in their crisp wool suits—the only people properly dressed in the party. Pia's girlfriend from graduate school brought a bouquet of scarlet roses for Pia to carry. Nick's red-haired friend Mike roared with laughter without much provocation—as he often did when he'd had a couple of beers. His laughter served as their music until George, another of Nick's friends, arrived with a guitar—late as he always was—and entertained everyone who cared to listen.

In the Italian restaurant, the party grew more festive. George had called a couple of his buddies to fill out the sound of the guitar with percussion and a flute. The owner of the restaurant joined in, singing a couple Italian arias as he could fit them in. Everyone applauded and laughed. As people sang impromptu solos and danced, Cynthia Graves pulled Pia aside.

"Just for a moment," she told Pia. "I know I haven't been very welcoming to you," she confessed quietly. "I didn't want to become attached to you in case Nick wasn't serious. Harold had high hopes for Nick's career. We were afraid he'd be distracted from his goals by the young women who chased him—often for his money, I'm sure. Scientists aren't usually sexy. But you're the prettiest girl he ever dated—and the smartest. I read your book. Harold wasn't keen on it, but I thought it was very brave of you to be so open with your opinions. Now that you're expecting, I hope you'll consider moving back here where your mother and I can back you up and Nick can return to more ambitious work. He's really quite talented, you know."

"Yes, I know."

Cynthia gave a nervous little laugh. She appeared to be perfectly groomed in her cream-colored ensemble. Her age had been smoothed and dyed. Her hair and make-up were modern but not trendy. Her carefully painted lips looked almost too flawless to speak. She could have been a work of art. "In my day, wives gave in to their husband's ambitions. I was studying to be a nutritionist, but Harold needed extra help in his office. I'm proud of all he's accomplished; don't get me wrong. I was glad to be of help. I guess I'm saying I understand why you want to write. I just hope you know Harold and I won't interfere if you decide to live closer."

Pia smiled. Perhaps because she was pregnant, but for the first time, she could see the pain of motherhood in her mother-in-law's eyes. She could see the hopes and worries and love. She wondered if Nick could comprehend just how much emotion sat with its hands neatly folded in its lap behind his mother's tasteful contact lenses.

"I love Nick very much," Pia told Cynthia softly. "More than you know—probably more than I show. I love our child. I can't guess what the future holds for any of us, but we'll always have a place in our home and in our hearts for you and Harold."

Cynthia nodded her head several times, quickly, perhaps shaking little tears back inside, away from exposure. "I haven't quite adjusted to the idea of being *Grandma* yet."

Pia gave her a tidy kiss on the cheek. "You have plenty of time. The baby won't talk for months. You can be called whatever you like."

A few guests snapped photos they'd share later, but there were none of someone with wedding cake in her face or an odd Uncle Floyd stuffing his mouth with olives. The atmosphere was intimate and uninhibited. As the dancing continued, Harold took off his suit coat and tugged Cynthia into a close slow dance that made her blush. He told the restaurant owner how his first job had been as a waiter under the owner's father—now deceased, a confidence that made the owner break into another aria.

Peter, Nick's younger brother, stood tall and square like his father. An aspiring football player who had been persuaded to pursue real estate development, he never seemed quite comfortable in a suit. His ready smile worked well for him but not quite well enough to make up for the fact that he didn't actually understand or like real estate, but he never lacked for a lovely young lady on his arm. His dates seemed to be interchangeable—all with ample bust lines and long, platinum blonde hair—so that the family never called his dates by name for fear of using the wrong one. He gave an awkward but sincere speech about how much he admired his older brother:

"I take this occasion to honor my older brother Nicolas and his new wife. He has always been a role model for me, although we don't have anything in common that I can think of. I'm supposed to tell a funny story about him and the only one I could think of happened when we were little. He ate a worm in order to get into his friend's secret club. When I tried to copy him, I threw up, and he took me home. He's been a wonderful brother and a good professor and I'm glad he finally found a decent girl who was willing to marry him. Pia is hot. I toast my brother Nick and his wife Olympia!"

Nick's sister Kathleen helped Marguerite catalog the gifts–for the couple and the baby—a wedding reception and baby shower combined. Kathleen was spectacularly uninteresting, having spent her life trying to please her mother, who wouldn't be pleased. Sadly, Kathleen had inherited her father's face. She sat as far away from Marguerite as she could manage and still be able to hear her, as though she might contract independent thought if she sat too close. Kathleen smiled without reason so often that Marguerite was relieved when the list was finally finished and she could take her leave.

The guests ate tiramisu instead of wedding cake and the restaurant owner sent anyone who asked for them home with leftovers. No one walked away hungry. Pia thought it was a very satisfying day.

"How was that, Mrs. Graves?" asked Nick later as he pulled his wife close in the huge, soft bed of the hotel. "Was that a satisfactory wedding?"

"I liked it. How about you?"

"I didn't have to wear a tux. How could I complain?"

"Did anyone ask about my father?"

He leaned close. "If someone did, I don't remember." And he kissed her.

After an extremely abbreviated honeymoon, Nick had to be back at school, and by Monday morning, Pia was standing in the office supply store in Camisa, sticking labels on new merchandise, feeling lonely and forgotten. She recognized that she was more emotional than usual these days, but crying seemed like a good idea. The citizens of the town were nicer to her now that she looked maternal. Single women were always suspect. A pregnant married woman didn't disturb the natural order of things. Something about all those realities made her feel tremendously sad.

A man she knew came into the shop—Herb Whitney, the town fire chief. Herb had graying hair that stuck out from beneath the baseball cap he wore. His craggy face reflected long hours in the sun over many years. He wore a navy "Fire Chief" sweatshirt that he had pulled low over his khaki canvas pants. He always smelled vaguely of smoke— sometimes from cigarettes, sometimes from burning wood, often from both at once. He blinked his gray eyes repeatedly, as though trying to clear them of something.

Pia was glad when he came in, because he usually took the time to stand and chat a little.

He had brought her a small gift, a silver serving fork in a box obviously gift wrapped in a store.

"I hear you got married," he said with a smile. "Congratulations."

"Thank you. And thank you for the pretty fork. We didn't have one. That was very thoughtful."

"Gloria picked it out." He looked a bit uncomfortable, as though he thought the gift was silly but his wife had talked him into it.

Pia decided to change the subject. "That was quite a cold snap this morning," she began, opening the way for conversation.

"That time of year," he said. He handed her the equipment lists he needed to have copied and glanced around the room, checking to see if they were alone. "I won't be stopping by any more after this week. I've been fired."

"Fired!" Pia fed the master into the copier and pushed the buttons. The machine hummed into action. "I heard from one of the county chiefs that you're the best, most qualified chief this city has ever had. He said city response times have been great, and he's glad because his mother lives here. Besides, you're nice." She smiled.

Herb looked down. He wasn't comfortable with compliments.

"What's the problem, if you don't mind my asking?"

"I sent a truck to a fire outside the city—that big warehouse just barely beyond the city limits—you know, up there on Union. I knew the county volunteers would take a while to get there and I hoped a quick response might keep the damage minimal. A flare-up could've taken out the west side of town in this drought."

She pulled the copied sheets out of the distribution tray. "Well, that certainly sounds like a firing offense. What else?"

"Nothing else. I moved here from outside. I changed the ways a few things were being done—procedures were really screwed up–and I sent a truck beyond the city limits. I shouldn't be talking about all this to you, and I'd appreciate it if you'd keep our conversation to yourself. I guess I'm telling you because you're an outsider, too, so you might have an idea what I've been up against. I feel better letting off steam. My wife is tired of hearing about it."

"Can't you appeal to—who? The City Council?"

"No. They know." He was wise enough not to provide more details. "I didn't want to disappear without telling you why I was gone, that's all. You've been a bright spot in this town. I wanted to tell you so."

She made a face. "Your being fired is just wrong. Somebody should do something."

He smirked. "You could run for office. There's a space on the City Council that's up, and you live in town. They usually have the same people year after year, but Pete Martinez died. You wouldn't be their first pick—especially with the hoopla about your book just dying down, but they're running out of choices. The old-timers try to run everything. There might be enough newcomers in town just now with the drilling and all to get you elected. It's too late for you to help me—I'm gone. I have another job lined up already, and my wife is delighted to move. She can't wait to be closer to shopping and better schools. I hate to leave on a sour note, but I can't say I'm too broken up." He picked up his papers and tapped them into a neat stack. "Don't get me wrong. There are lots of good people here, but they keep quiet. You can't lead if no one is following. But a smart, clean person like you could make a difference here. You aren't the type to shrink from a fight."

"City council! But I'm pregnant."

Theresa Peterson stepped into the shop just as Pia finished her sentence. Her yellow sweat suit made her look like a child's version of a nice, round sun. "Well, congratulations, Dear, but that's not new news. I brought you a gift from the parents group. It's a set of one-sies in different colors." She brought an extravagantly wrapped baby gift to the counter and placed it there with a copy of Pia's book. "You can't have too many one-sies."

Herb Whitney turned to her. "We were talking about Miss Garcia here…"

Pia interrupted. "Ms. Garcia Graves," she corrected. She looked at Theresa Peterson. "The wedding was this past weekend."

Theresa pretended to frown. "You should've had the wedding here, and we could've had a party. We should probably have one, anyway."

Herb Whitney interrupted. "We were talking about Ms. Garcia Graves running for the Council seat vacated by Pete Martinez. Talk her into it. She'd be good." He looked to Pia. "Just having you run might wake up a few folk."

Pia followed him to the door. "May I hug you goodbye?" she asked, following the customs of the town.

"Sure." He gave her a big hug and grinned at her belly. "You've gotta be a good role model now! Show that baby what you're made of." He was whistling as he left.

Pia turned back to her friend. "I can't believe people who live here don't want the best services possible, but it looks like they'd rather keep bad service in the family. Herb is leaving."

"That is a shame," agreed Theresa.

"So what do you think?" Pia asked her. "Do you think I should run?"

"Well," Theresa hesitated to answer. "Thirty copies, please. Here's the master. I can't imagine that you could be elected—you being number one, a woman; number two, pregnant; and number three, a newcomer. But you never know around here. I read your book like you said. I put it on the counter there. You certainly aren't afraid to tackle controversy. That makes you unique in this town. And you have your name on a book. That makes you almost famous. You're educated and well spoken. All of us in the parent association would back you. We'd like to have a friend on the council. Why not run? What do you have to lose?"

The machine started spitting out the copies.

Theresa continued, stepping closer conspiratorially. "We need to know we have someone who isn't corrupt." She dropped her voice as though someone outside the store might be able to hear. "Last year, a couple of high school girls got raped by three of the football players. The police said they didn't have enough evidence and the boys were never charged, but those girls were raped, sure enough. The boys graduated and the girls got sent away. Nobody on the parent association wanted to say anything, but something's not right. The police chief keeps saying we don't have drugs in this town, when we all know we do. No one wants to raise children in a town that isn't safe. So yes. I think you *should* run. It can't hurt. Here's my number. If you decide to run, give me a call. You'll have a campaign. I guarantee it."

When she had her copies in hand and was ready to leave, Theresa paused in the doorway. "And congratulations on getting married. I think your Nick looks like a nice man. I'm glad he's stepping up."

Pia bade her goodbye and stood watching through the window as Theresa walked away. So they thought she needed a man to claim her baby, someone to take care of her. They had no idea what kind of a woman they were dealing with. She thought of Matias standing up for his values and of all the times her mother had told her how sorry she was that she hadn't taken a stand. Marguerite had said good people pay the price for the outcome, whether they get involved or not, so they might as well jump in and do what they can. Pia began scribbling a list of documents she would need to fill out her application. She had decided she owed it to the baby to show him or her that Silva genes wouldn't rot the barrel.

20

"**W**hat the hell are you thinking!" Nick exploded when Pia told him what she was considering. "City council! In this town? We came here to lay low, and you decide to run for office? You don't even belong here." She had made the decision without him, and he definitely did not agree. He stood in the dining room, watching her set the table. His stance broadcast his anger.

"You're going to get into small town politics on purpose?" He began pacing back and forth in front of the window. "Having a job, a new marriage, and an impending baby isn't enough for you? Do you have any clue what goes into a campaign? I thought you'd had your fill of being in conflict." He paused to glare at her. "You've seen the other people on the council. Let me ask you this, are you *nuts*?"

He could tell as soon as he'd said it that he had pushed her off the fence—the opposite of his intent. Being away from her so much had dulled his skills. He was tired and cranky and she was moody. He was playing a very poor game.

"No," she replied coolly. "I am not…nuts."

He forced himself to take a long, deep breath and let it out. "I didn't mean that. I just can't figure out, why you? Why does it have to be you to run? Do you even qualify? Have you lived here long enough? God, Pia, can't they find somebody else—somebody who's from here and isn't pregnant?"

"No. You don't get it. Nick, I need to make a difference–like Matias. Don't you understand that? I need to do what he couldn't."

"A difference!" He swallowed whatever he was about to say next and began pacing the room again. "I think we've been here before. Who's going to try to kill you this time? Who's going to put you down and make you feel like shit? You know, ideals are great, but they have to relate to the real world. Sometimes you have to do what makes sense. What are you going to do with the baby?"

"What's that supposed to mean? Am I going to roast it or what?"

He planted his hands on the table so hard that he made the glassware quiver. "Don't be flip. You know what I mean. You say you want to be a crusader like Matias. It didn't make him a better father. He couldn't even *be* your father. He had to give up his rights to some sicko. He had to watch while his wife was brutally attacked. Do you think he felt like he'd made a difference then? And *had* he made a difference? Had he?" Nick grabbed a napkin and crushed it in his fist. "Dammit, Pia, he gave up his life and his family and what did anyone get back for his sacrifice? We all just keep paying and paying."

Pia crossed her arms over her chest and stared at the floor. "What's this really about, Nick? We aren't talking about me throwing myself in front of a military junta, so what is this about?"

Nick drew a ragged breath. His face was red. Pia had never seen him so upset. "It's about us being an old-fashioned mom and pop like the ones I had when I was a kid. I thought that was what we promised when we got married. You're putting the baby and me in the back seat. You want us to follow you around while you play councilwoman for a town you don't like so you can feel like you're doing something important. If you ask me, this whole damned town isn't important. The baby and I haven't had a chance to become your family yet, and we're already being treated like footnotes in your life story. This decision isn't just about you, you know. It's about us."

She didn't move. "Is this an ego problem?"

He made a funny sound in his throat. She thought for a moment he might throw something.

She kept her voice low and even. "You knew I wasn't going to be the kind of mother who sits at home all the time, finding her greatest pride in a clean toilet bowl and shiny kitchen floors."

He took a deep breath and let it out slowly. "Let me tell you what I thought. I thought you were going to be the kind of mother who would give our child a chance to be born healthy, to have a solid start, before you started working. I thought I was coming home today to help you start packing, because you told my mother we were going to move back east to have the baby. Do you have any idea how excited she and your mother both are? My sister is taking babysitting classes! I thought we were going to share the joy as an extended family. I thought you'd be selfless for a while."

"So you think I'm self-centered."

"Right now? Yes, yes, I do. When do the baby and I get a turn, Pia?"

She stared at him, meeting his eyes this time. "What if I asked you to give up *your* work?"

He came around the table to stand directly in front of her. His gaze was fierce. "Look at me, Pia. Take a good, long look at the man you married. Look at my grade book and my pay stubs and my shirt without all its buttons. Look at the piles of nonsense the administrators force me to generate day after day. Look at the fact that I haven't done any meaningful research since you threw away your PhD. And now you're going to obligate us to stay in a backwater hole for years instead of months without any real discussion? Give up my work? You didn't notice, but I already have."

She walked into the doorway to the kitchen and stopped. She didn't turn as she spoke. "I have an obligation to go to this meeting tonight. Theresa Peterson set it up to determine if I have enough backers to run. I'll see what happens, and then I'll make my decision."

"You do that," he muttered. "You make *your* decision. I'll be in the bar. It's my turn to get vomiting drunk."

———

Pia felt sicker than ever as she walked into the conference room behind the Savings and Loan where the meeting was to be held. The air was already fetid from the people crowded into the small space. Gray metal folding chairs were set up in short rows in front of a homemade podium. Theresa Peterson was there in the front row, looking cheerful as always in a green pantsuit. She was sitting sideways in her chair, chatting with three other middle-aged ladies who were seated behind her. There were a couple men of varying ages seated elsewhere. And at the front of the room sat the woman Nick called the Dowager Empress. She had her own little table set to the side of the podium. Her name was Helen Suarez, and she was sitting with Carl Minnelli. Her graying black hair was upswept into a French twist that anchored the maroon frames of her glasses behind her ears. She wore an orange jacket that overlapped her black skirt and a white blouse with lace on the collar. Her face was pinched and severe. She made Pia think of Halloween.

"Come in, Dear," Helen said, smiling benevolently. "You can stand at the podium so we can all see you. And we'll ask the questions. We want to be sure we're funding the person with the best possible chance of both winning the election and serving our town well."

Pia walked across the linoleum floor to the podium, feeling like she was back in the rear of a police car with her hands cuffed.

"Very well, then," chirped Helen, "I believe Theresa wanted to begin. Theresa?"

"First, congratulations on becoming Mrs. Nick Graves." Theresa pivoted to address the women behind her. "He's a science professor up north, you know." She turned back to Pia. "Second, I want to ask about your education. Would you share the details of your education with us, please?" She smiled at Pia, clearly convinced she had won the day for her new friend already.

Pia detailed her degrees, ending with the fact that she had earned what some called an "ABD," or "all but dissertation"–meaning she had completed her comprehensive exams for a PhD but hadn't finished the dissertation process. "I can submit my Vita, if you wish," she said, hoping that the academic term for a resume would impress someone.

"And why didn't you finish your degree?" asked Helen sweetly.

"The committee didn't like some of the premises on which my work was based."

"Did you have an opportunity to go back and redo that part?"

"I had seven years to complete the degree."

"Had?" Helen smiled.

"So far I've opted not to go ahead."

"You quit?"

Pia tried to sound unconcerned. "Yes. I quit." She almost said she had quit to write her book, but then she decided the book she had written might not be a big selling point with this audience.

Helen glanced down at her notes. "Mark, you had a question?"

"Yeah." A tall thin man with a fringe of white hair touching his big white ears cleared his throat. His splotchy flushed face looked like the first stages of a heart attack. "Helen says we can't ask about your pregnancy without violating your privacy, but let me put it this way: You've been open about having some *medical issues*." He glanced at Helen who smiled and nodded.

He continued. "With your issues in mind, how do you plan to manage your personal life and still fulfill your duties?"

Pia tried to appear pleasantly imperturbable, although her stomach was churning. "The same way the men with families do."

One of the men chuckled, "You're going to let your wife handle the kids?"

The group laughed.

Pia smiled politely as though she were mildly amused. "It takes two people to create a family. In my house, it takes two people to raise one—or it will once the family arrives."

The joking man sat back in his chair. "That's why she got married. She's gonna let her husband do the babysitting." Someone muttered something else and several people snickered.

Helen consulted her list. "Carl? You're next."

"Is it true you push young women into abortion and out of the church like it says in your book? Aren't you an atheist?"

Pia allowed herself a small sigh. "My book does not say that, nor do I. My book is about the ethics of authority figures—hence the title. You'd have to read it to understand it. And you're not permitted to ask questions about my religious beliefs—even here."

"Jen?" called Helen, consulting her list. "What did you want to ask?"

Jen was very young, her thick brown hair pulled back into a ponytail. She was wearing jeans and a knit top with "Honey Pot" written on the front in sequins. "First, do you have any experience serving on a council or any other government body, and second, what good works have you done as a resident of Camisa—I mean, like have you volunteered at the animal shelter or anything?"

Pia's mouth kept smiling. "No, I have no direct experience with government, although I did run work teams and management training workshops when I was a graduate teaching assistant. I know I can bring fresh ideas and enthusiasm to addressing the problems in the town. I haven't yet participated in the local nonprofits. I'm hoping this position will help me decide where to dedicate my energies."

"No involvement and no experience," Jen summarized, knowingly, looking at Helen.

"Finally," said Helen, looking smug, "I have a couple questions that are of a confidential nature," she turned her head to address the occupants of the room, "so everyone here must remember what we say is strictly off the record and legal only because this isn't a job interview." She returned her gaze to Pia. "We will certainly not share this information with the general public, but as your funders, we must know who we're empowering. After all, as Jen pointed out, you haven't been active in our town, so we have no basis from which to judge."

Pia could feel a trap being set. "Yes?"

Helen's voice slid forward. "It has come to my attention, Mrs. Graves, that your birth certificate lists your father as 'unknown.' That is, of course, none of our business, but I am left to wonder what line of work did your mother pursue?" Her tone suggested lewd possibilities. "She's listed as a writer, but what did she write?"

Pia was angry. "How did you gain access to my birth certificate?"

"You aren't answering my question."

"It *isn't* any of your business, but my mother used to write travel books. She was an international author."

Helen never stopped smiling. "And so it was in her 'travels' that she gained a child of questionable parentage? We have to be sure you're an American citizen, you see."

Pia was feeling dizzy. She glared back at the dowager empress. "I could show you my passport, but I won't. I was born in New York, and I'm the daughter of an American citizen. It was in her travels that my mother was brutally raped by a member of the military junta in Argentina, while her husband was being tortured to death. Is that gory enough for you, Mrs. Suarez?"

Helen's eyes lit up, but she pretended to maintain her decorum. "A rapist! You're the child of a rapist."

Someone made an odd sound like air being sucked in.

Helen was not deterred. She gushed with artificial empathy. "Being thus conceived must be a difficult burden for you to bear, Mrs. Garcia. You can't predict which traits you might have or which might be expressed in your child."

"I can predict that he or she won't have to be mean and small-minded," said Pia picking up her purse. "You've already given the gossips of Camisa plenty to talk about, Mrs. Suarez. Count yourself successful in that way. But in the end, you all lose. I would've been a huge asset to this town, but I withdraw my application for candidacy. My husband was right. I'm wasting my time here. You can go fuck yourself, Helen. If you think this little meeting was legal or ethical, you obviously don't get out much."

Someone gasped.

Pia marched out of the room, whispers swelling behind her. She was struggling to pull her coat on when she realized someone was holding it for her. Nick helped direct her arm into the sleeve. She looked up at him, her eyes moist.

"You did it again," he said gently, and she nodded.

"I'm proud of you." He slid his arm around her. "You weren't a victim."

"Let's start packing up the house," said Pia as they headed for the door. "I'll spend the rest of the pregnancy with my mother. They don't *want* someone to make a difference here. I have better things to do."

He smiled. "I'm with you."

21

Marguerite had her spare room prepared for guests before Nick and Pia arrived. She moved slowly now. She looked emaciated and bald and far older than her years. She watched the news coverage on television each evening, and her nightmares had increased. "People are fodder," she told her imposing friend Ralph from across the hall as he finished making the extra bed. "Regular people are just fodder for whatever end the powers have in mind."

Ralph agreed as he stepped back to admire his work. In his worn fatigues, he might have been a prototype for the aged warrior. The bed in the spare room was a model of military precision.

When Marguerite opened the front door to Pia and Nick, they stood for a moment, staring at her.

"Mom, what happened to your hair!" exclaimed Pia.

"Ralph shaved it for me. It was thinning, anyway, and I got sick of trying to fix it."

Nick tried to smile. "You look like a Marine. Very powerful."

"I should be as strong as Marines," muttered Marguerite, ushering them into the spare room. "Ralph emptied the drawers in the dresser." She gave a wave toward the man who was still standing there. "He'll find you whatever you need. Just make yourselves at home. I'll fetch some tea."

Ralph did his best to smile. "There are more hangers in the back of the closet, if you need them." He looked tough and slightly scary in his patched fatigues with his missing fingers, scarred face, and pronounced limp, but his voice was deep and gentle. His jaw quivered the tiniest bit as he faced Pia. "I gotta tell you while she's in the kitchen. Your mother has cancer pretty bad. Nobody's optimistic. I don't guess she'd say it, and I'd appreciate it if you wouldn't mention that I told you."

Pia tried to hold in the whimper she felt. "Oh dear god. As if she hasn't had enough."

"Yes, ma'am." He swallowed hard. "That bastard who tore her up left her this legacy. But she's got grit. She ain't going down easy. You come from tough stock. I've been keeping an eye out for her, her being alone and all. She hasn't wanted for anything."

Pia kissed him lightly on the cheek. He seemed embarrassed, but he didn't pull away.

"Thank you, ma'am," he said quietly. "I appreciate it."

Nick touched Pia's hand. "It's a good thing you're here, Pia. She needs you."

Pia nodded, but she was thinking that she had come to be mothered, not to do mothering. She was going to have to rally forces she wasn't sure she had.

Once they had settled into the spare room, Nick and Pia couldn't help but notice Ralph was a regular visitor in Marguerite's apartment. In fact, he had his own key he was careful not to use while they were around. "Don't mean to be a nuisance," he'd say when he arrived at the front door with groceries or light bulbs or extra towels. He was comfortable in Marguerite's kitchen, but Marguerite had to insist he join the family for meals—some of which he cooked himself. He didn't talk much, but he always seemed to be handy when anything needed to be moved.

When the time came for Nick to return to his job teaching, Ralph lingered until all the goodbyes were finished. He pulled Nick aside on the landing of the stairway. "Here's my phone number. I'm home most of the time. You stay in touch," he instructed. "I'll take the watch here."

With Nick gone, Ralph stepped up as the official jar opener and grocery bag carrier. Pia suspected that lifting was painful for him—he never showed her why he limped—but he insisted. His affection showed in his touch. He seemed to grow taller around her mother, a damaged old tree that would never surrender its post as shade and rest. She could see that her mother had grown accustomed to leaning on him.

———

Pia's pregnancy progressed more normally in the relative peace of the little apartment. Ralph drove her to her doctor's appointments in his proud old Chevy, and Marguerite kept an eye on her supplements. Nick's mother called intermittently, self-consciously asking how things were going. At last she ventured to Marguerite's apartment. Harold dropped her off. She had never been there before. She draped her designer coat over the back of a chair, taking care to suspend the bottom edge off the floor. She was wearing sleek black slacks with a wine-colored silk blouse and bolero jacket—her idea of Argentine chic. Her high-heeled boots clicked across the floor.

"I hope you don't mind my coming by," Cynthia told Pia and Marguerite as she sat on the edge of the sofa by Pia's mother. "I brought a few things." She presented a special cream for Pia's skin and an elegant handmade baby quilt in a chic department store shopping bag. She stared at Marguerite's bald head briefly, then hastily looked away.

"Of course we don't mind," Marguerite assured her. "We've been hoping you'd come."

Pia tried to remember what her own voice sounded like when she was being herself, because she felt strange with Nick's mother in the living room. The atmosphere hung heavy with words that weren't being said. "Thank you so much for the gifts."

"They're nothing, really." Pia could see Cynthia's eyes traveling around the room. "It seems very... comfortable here." She had chosen her words carefully.

"Yes, it is," agreed Pia. She was wondering what the adjectives Cynthia had discarded might have been.

"I'm blessed to be able to have my daughter near during this time," Marguerite told Cynthia. "I was worried she'd stay out west and you and I would miss the whole thing."

"Yes!" Cynthia nodded. "I felt the same way." She turned toward Pia. "Have you had any more trouble from people objecting to your book?"

"No, nothing. I've completely disappeared." Pia realized how unfortunate her word choice was as soon as *disappeared* was out of her mouth. She glanced at her mother, but Marguerite didn't react. "I mean, the attention of the public doesn't stay in one place long. When I write again, I'll be more judicious about my marketing."

Cynthia nodded, aware that Marguerite had fallen silent. "That might be a good idea, although—as I told you—you write very well and I'm sure people *should* think about the issues you raised."

"Yes."

An awkward silence followed.

"You two need some time to chat with one another," Marguerite said at last. "And I need to rest." She rose slowly and faced Nick's mother. "I'm so glad you're in Pia's life. My pregnancy with Pia wasn't quite normal—I wasn't well at the time–so she can use your advice. Besides, a pregnant woman can't have too much tender loving care to see her through." She smiled. "I don't mean to be rude leaving you alone, but the two of you need a chance to build a relationship."

Pia was sorry to lose Marguerite's presence. The air seemed to turn chemically cold as it would with too much air conditioning. She smiled a lips-only expression at Nick's mother. "So, how is Harold doing?"

Cynthia was struggling to look agreeable, as well. "Oh, he's fine— high cholesterol, of course, and high blood pressure, but essentially fine. He still works out at the club. He has a nutritionist these days to direct his diet. So do I." She changed positions on the sofa, leaning toward Pia. "I don't want to pry, but is your mother alright?" she asked in a hushed tone. "She looks so...tired."

"Not really, to be honest," Pia replied after checking to see that her mother had closed her bedroom door. "She won't say anything, but she has cancer."

"Oh, I'm so sorry. I worried when I saw her without hair. They have cute turbans for that now." Cynthia avoided looking directly at Pia. "I can ask my doctor for the name of a good oncologist, if you like. You know, they can do a lot for cancer these days. It's not a death sentence like it used to be."

"I hope not."

The older woman heaved a huge sigh. "Listen, I don't mean to be indelicate, but I know Nick hasn't been making that much money and neither have you. Of course, you will in the future, but for the moment, a baby and cancer are a lot to handle. Do let Harold and me contribute. Harold makes enough for all of us."

Pia nodded. "I appreciate the thought. You're already paying for Nick's apartment by the university and the storage unit for our furniture from the house. That's plenty. We're okay for the time being, but we'll let you know. We aren't about to let the baby want for anything."

"Of course I didn't mean to suggest that you would." Cynthia heaved a second sigh. "I'm not terribly good at mothering. Nick probably told you as much."

"He told me he loves you."

Cynthia smiled. "How sweet of you to say so, but no, I wasn't very good. I don't think of the right things to do or say. I just don't think of them. Your mother was kind enough to say I know about pregnancy, but my health was managed by a whole team for most of my pregnancies—except for Nick, when Harold was just getting started. I don't know what to offer that you'll find helpful. So please speak up when there's something I can do. I would really appreciate it. I want to be a good grandmother."

"I promise."

Cynthia straightened her posture, drawing whatever dignity she sensed she had lost close to her like a protective cloak. "The baby won't have to call me *Abuelita*, will he?"

"No, why would he—or she?"

"I just wondered, since you're from Argentina and they speak Spanish. Our housekeeper said the baby might call me that, but she's from Mexico, so maybe it's different in South America. I saw an Abuelita package in the grocery. I understand it's supposed to be cute, a nickname from a brand of chocolate, but it doesn't seem dignified to me. I hope you don't mind. I think *Grandmother* would be more appropriate."

Pia tried not to smirk. She remembered her mother using the brand of Mexican hot chocolate tablets Cynthia had seen. *Abuelita* meant *little grandmother,* the Nestle chocolate with a grandmother image.

"I don't see why the baby would call you anything in Spanish," she told her mother-in-law diplomatically. "My father was the only family member from Argentina." Pia noticed the deepening worry lines in Cynthia's forehead. "My father and I aren't in touch. I've never been there—at least since I was born. My Spanish is strictly high school."

Nick's mother pursed her carefully painted lips. "I'm sorry. I must have misunderstood Nick. He gets so defensive when I ask questions. Half the time I don't know what he's talking about."

Pia felt a strong movement inside her. The baby wanted to be recognized, and Pia couldn't blame him...or her. She thought of how much she had hated the unexpected revelation of her secret parentage. Identity shouldn't be a surprise—a shock. Suddenly, she couldn't bear the strain a moment longer. She looked at the woman before her, someone who made good taste into an assignment, who pretended to live in rarified air. If Nick's mother had any hope of becoming worthy of being a grandmother, she couldn't waste a second of preparation time. Cynthia needed to begin adjusting to reality as soon as possible. Judging from what she had said so far, she had a long, difficult road ahead of her. "Cynthia, there's something you should know because I don't think it's something to hide—especially not from family. I believe in truth, even when it's painful."

Nick's mother looked concerned. "Yes?"

Pia took a deep breath and exhaled it to gain a sense of momentum, an action that seemed to discomfit Cynthia even more. "Matias and

Marguerite Garcia were seized by military thugs while the military junta was running Argentina. They were considered dissidents. My mother was horribly brutalized and raped and then her husband was tortured until he died. I am the child of that rape."

"A child of rape? The baby's grandfather was a rapist? Oh my god," exclaimed Cynthia in a whisper. "Oh my god." She looked like she might faint.

Pia stiffened. "I can't imagine the courage my mother has needed to raise me with love. She probably owes her cancer to the electrified cattle prod the rapist used. She could legally have aborted me, but she didn't. I haven't always appreciated what she endured, but I'm starting to get an idea. I'm telling you because I don't want you to run into any surprises later and think I deceived you. We are who we are. I have no doubt Nick and I can raise an extraordinary child you'll be proud to call your family."

Cynthia stared at the floor. "Does Nick know?"

"Does he know?" Pia shifted her position. "Yes. He's known as long as I have."

"Oh." Cynthia checked her watch and stood up. "Harold will be coming for me, so I have to go now." She walked toward the door. "Nick can make his own choices," she said slowly. "And we'll adapt." She looked at Pia. "I'm sorry, Dear, but this is difficult for me. I had such high expectations for my Nicolas, you see—very high expectations." She slipped on her coat and opened the door. "Do take good care of yourself and your mother." And she let herself out.

A few moments later, Marguerite emerged from the bedroom. "How did it go?" she asked Pia.

"Fine," Pia answered after the briefest hesitation. She smiled for her mother. "It's all fine."

A couple days passed before Nick called and asked Pia if she could take his call in private. His voice was tight and fast. She carried the phone into her bedroom.

"What is it?" she asked, afraid of what he might say.

"I just talked with my parents—about your mother's rape. I wish you would've told me you were going to share that information with my mother. I could've helped."

Pia felt herself shrug. "The time seemed right."

"I guess in a way it was your story to tell. But, damn! Mom's throwing a fit about having a rapist in the family. I can't believe people who are well educated can sound so ignorant."

Pia leaned back onto the bed. Sitting had become difficult, trying to bend around her immense middle. "I'm not shocked, but if Cynthia is, so be it. We just won't say anything to my mother. She feels guilty enough already, and she didn't do anything wrong."

"I told Mom that she and Dad don't get to choose their family, any more than we did. Their only choice is whether or not they want to stay in touch."

"What did they say?"

Nick made a disgruntled sound deep in his throat. "Mom says they're thinking about it. I've read the *nouveau riche* tend to be haughty, and I guess that applies to my family. Mom believes Dad's bank account makes her into royalty or something. I don't know what she'll eventually decide about us."

The baby kicked hard, making a statement of sorts from within. "How about you, Nick?" asked Pia. "Will you be okay if your parents choose to disown you because of me?" She tried to imagine his expression through the silence on the phone.

"You're my family, Pia, you and the baby. You're more than enough for me."

Her relief made her laugh. "Good answer. Will you be home soon? The baby's getting anxious."

"I'm already packed."

———

Nick arrived a few days later–after the end of the college semester, which ground to a halt just in time for the slightly premature birth of his daughter. The little girl was born in early December—Sagittarius, theoretically the sign of people extroverted and free. Pia was researching every sort of sign—star signs, Mayan signs, Tarot, Numerology, even the Chinese signs. She was desperate to find a clue about the person she was about to raise. Nick indulged her, although he couldn't stop himself from explaining that he thought Pia was being fanciful, seduced by her erratic hormones into a lot of superstition. They were using Nick's laptop to review the predictions they could find online when Harold and Cynthia came into the hospital room. A mist of expensive scents floated in with them on their camelhair coats and cashmere scarves.

"Good looking baby, Pia! Congratulations!" Nick's father announced as he deposited an enormous flower arrangement on the windowsill. He came to kiss Pia's forehead. "We saw her in the nursery on the way in. About that rape thing–you know, my grandfather was a shrewd businessman, but he lost everything because he was a drunk. I've got his knack with a buck, but I don't touch hard liquor. With family, you take the good and rise above the bad, that's what I say. Right, Cyn?"

Cynthia kissed Nick on the cheek. "I suppose so. What will you name her?"

"We were considering *Amy*," Nick replied, glancing at Pia. "It's a name that hasn't belonged to anyone we know."

"We wanted her to be a fresh start," added Pia.

"Not a bad idea, and it's a good, strong name—*Amy Graves*–good for business." Nick's father drew an envelope from his suit jacket. He handed it to Nick. "Just a little something for the new family."

A dark-skinned nurse entered, carrying the baby in a bundle. "She wanted to meet the grandparents," the nurse explained to no one in particular. She glanced around the room, assessing the situation, then, without waiting for either a request or permission, she handed the baby to Cynthia who was standing the farthest away from Pia's bed. "I'll be back in a little while," she announced as she walked out the door.

"There you go, Momma," declared Harold cheerfully. "Your first grandchild."

Cynthia's warring emotions played across her face. The baby snuggled against her. "Please. Please, you take her, Harold." She passed the bundle to him.

He tucked his finger into the baby's tiny fist. "She's a fine baby, Nick. She has a purpose, this one. She's going to do us all proud."

Cynthia tugged her coat closed. "Come on, Harold. We'll miss our plane."

Harold passed the baby to Nick. "Momma's gone and booked the family on a holiday cruise. We're supposed to meet the kids in the Bahamas then eventually connect with my cousins in New Zealand. But I told her we had plenty of time before our flight to stop in and say hello." He kissed Pia's forehead a second time, perhaps to make up for Cynthia's obvious discomfort, and shook Nick's hand vigorously. "You take good care of our granddaughter!" he exclaimed. "I'm going to spend this trip thinking of ways to spoil her rotten—Grandpa's privilege. Keep a list of anything you need." And he followed Cynthia out the door.

Nick looked to Pia. "I guess we don't have to worry that the grandmothers will compete with one another for her attention."

Pia smiled ruefully. "Apparently not."

———❈———

Amy was oblivious to the controversy she had begun. She seemed to embrace her role as the vanguard of a different line. Her eyes weren't open at first, but eventually she gazed at the world with big blue eyes that laughed even before her mouth learned how. She had her mother's way of staring into people.

Marguerite delighted in her granddaughter—especially since the baby's blue eyes were entirely unlike Silva's—more like her own. Marguerite would sit and sing in soft tones no one else could hear for hours on end. She didn't feel safe carrying the baby. The weight seemed to be too much. But she loved to sit with Amy on her lap, laughing at being alive.

At first, Ralph was afraid to hold Amy, but when Pia insisted, he sat gingerly on the sofa, cradling the squirming bundle, rocking her gently to and fro until she fell asleep. "I was married once, before the war," he said without any preliminaries one day.

Everyone stopped what they were doing, startled to hear him speak of himself.

Ralph didn't look up. "She took our baby—my ex. Said I didn't have a claim on it since I wasn't there for the birth. I was overseas. Damn if I don't miss being a granddad."

Marguerite, who was sitting beside him on the sofa, reached out to touch his hand.

"Amy's lucky to have you as a grandpa," said Pia from the kitchen doorway. "You're welcome to cuddle her any time."

"Yes, you are," agreed Nick, slipping his arm around Pia's waist.

———

Christmas came and went, as did New Year's Day. Harold called from Tahiti and had caterers deliver champagne and hors d'oeuvres to the apartment. No one mentioned the fact that Cynthia didn't talk on the phone. Her choices didn't seem to matter any longer. They all sat together—the four adults and the baby—not really watching the Rose Parade or football, but using them as background noise for piecing a jigsaw puzzle into a whole. No one spoke about the invisible force that held them there together, although they all sensed it. The air around them felt like a warm sigh—a moment of calm. A clock in the kitchen ticked away the respite.

As soon as the doctor permitted, Pia took the baby in her stroller for long walks in the park—sometimes with Nick or Ralph and sometimes by herself. When the snow was too deep, she carried Amy in a sling, wrapped in all the blankets she could manage. They both liked the snow. The heavy whiteness slowed the incessant traffic of living and gave the trees more visual weight, new elegance, as black and white design. It was on just such a day of snow and intermittent sunshine that the unthinkable struck.

22

P ia walked alone farther than she ever had before, feeling the heat of Amy in her sling. She was thinking that Nick would be leaving the apartment to teach spring semester soon—his last semester so far away. She had left him at home typing new course schedules into his laptop as he thought about the clothes and other items he needed to pack. She hated the thought of lying alone in their bed, having nothing to hold but a cold white pillow as she listened for movement in the crib. Nick had grown expert in detecting precisely when her postpartum depression was simmering. He would wrap his arms around her and talk in low tones about the beautiful life they were going to create as a family. He would make her herbal tea and rub her back. For someone who thought in numbers, he had keen instincts for balance.

She thought about her mother—with Ralph today at yet another chemo appointment. Marguerite had already warned her that the day might come when she would quit the appointments and let Nature take its course. Pia didn't blame her for yearning for an end to the pain, but she couldn't imagine a world without her mother in it. Poor Amy would grow up knowing no grandmother but Cynthia. How terribly sad.

Pia was so focused on her thoughts as she walked that she didn't notice the neighborhood changing around her. She didn't notice the group of young people strolling just behind her. She heard rather than saw the car that swerved toward them from a side street. She felt the bullet before her brain heard a barrage of explosions.

———————————

She didn't remember much about what happened except for falling down and down and down. Slow motion. Or maybe not. Thinking, "Don't fall on the baby!" Not thinking. The snow. The sidewalk. And pain. Had she hit her head? Was she on the baby?

Someone screaming. Shouts. Hands touching her, lifting her. Sirens. More sirens. And lights. More hands. More lifting. She kept asking who was taking care of Amy, but her mouth wasn't making sounds. No one told her Amy had taken the brunt of the shot. Amy didn't survive.

When Pia eventually awoke in the hospital after her emergency surgery, she made them tell her. A part of her already knew. She was bandaged where her child should have been. She didn't cry. She didn't breathe. Someone called for oxygen. It didn't help. She gasped and clutched her heart. There wasn't enough air in the universe to sustain her. At last she grew still—not dead and not alive–a woman with no threads to tie her to living.

Nick was sitting beside her. He looked haunted, like someone in a death camp who has seen too much. Ralph stood above him, his hand on Nick's shoulder. They couldn't speak. Words were hard wooden things—not made for exploding hearts. Nick held Pia's hand. She gripped him—as tightly as she could. If she let go she might drift off into nothing. She might become nothing.

"She saved your life," Nick said at last in an empty, dry voice. "Amy deflected the bullet just enough for it to miss your heart."

"It's all wrong," Pia mumbled, not knowing if she said it aloud. "It's all wrong." She looked up at Ralph. His eyes were a sepulcher, a dark grave that drained his living.

"How's mom?" Pia asked him.

"Better now she knows you're safe," Ralph replied. But his voice said that was still not good at all. "She'll be glad when you're home."

A nurse came to the door. "A police officer is here to collect your statement, and there are reporters who want an interview. The doctor says you can talk a little if you wish. What do you want me to tell them?"

Pia's first thought was "Go to hell," but she said, "No. Tell them no."

The nurse withdrew.

"You weren't the target." Nick sucked in a long breath. "It wasn't about you at all. Just stray bullets from a drive-by."

"Stray." Pia spat out the word, then repeated it, hearing the sound inside her head. "Stray dog. Stray hair. Stray bullet."

"I'm gonna go now," Ralph told her. "Your mother will be needing me. I'll tell those buzzard bastards outside to leave you alone."

Pia wanted to say, "Thank you. I love you," but she didn't. She merely said, "Okay."

"God," said Nick when Ralph had gone. It wasn't a prayer and it wasn't swearing. He was beseeching. "I'm so sorry, Pia. God, I'm sorry."

"You!" She exhaled a short, disgusted burst. "It's my fault. I'm the one who took her out. It should've been me killed."

He lifted her hand to kiss it. Tears welled in his eyes. He looked for all the world like a small boy, a boy in terrific pain. "Would it be evil of me to say I'm glad it wasn't you? Forgive me, Pia, but I'm really glad it wasn't you."

She looked at him, into him. The immensity of his love forced its way into her broken heart. She started to weep, realizing she hadn't wept before. The tears fell easily—pain in liquid form, streaming, dripping, spotting her hospital gown. Nick was crying, too. He sat beside her, holding her, gently, as though her bullet hole was a crack that might spread.

A nurse came to the door, looking to see what was going on. "You need to calm down," she said to Pia. "Your monitor is all over the place. The surgery was very close to your heart. Do you want a sedative?"

Pia pulled away from Nick. "Not unless you can give me enough to kill me." Nick made a noise, so she added, "I'm being sarcastic. I'm okay."

The nurse eyed the two of them. "The psychologist will be here soon."

"Tell him to stay home and hug his kids," Pia told her. "He can't do anything to help. No one can. Nick and I will survive. That's the hell of it. We'll survive."

The nurse frowned a little. "I'll ask the doctor for a sedative. She'll have to okay it since you had a blow to your head."

Pia cut her off. "And it will numb the pain. I don't want to numb the pain. I want to feel it. I want to wash myself in it, wallow in it. I want to drink so much of it that it loses its potency as poison."

Nick stroked her hair. "Bring a sedative if you can," he told the nurse. "When she's asleep, I'll go get a stiff drink."

———◆———

Pia's days in the hospital stretched into weeks. Nick quit his job and came to sit with her every day. She lay staring out the window at the building next door for hour after hour.

"Pia, you won't talk to the chaplain and the psychologist says you won't talk with him, either," Nick said at last, a note of despair in his voice.

"No, I won't."

"Why?"

"He wants to make me feel better."

"And that's wrong?"

"It's wrong for me."

"What about me?"

"If you want to feel better, then *you* talk to the psychologist."

Nick sighed. "The doctor says you don't want to heal."

Pia rolled her head to look at him. "I should be dead, Nick. *I* should be dead."

He looked toward the door where he could see Marguerite approaching in her wheelchair. "Your mother is here."

Pia straightened slightly. "She shouldn't be. There's nothing she can do."

Nick shook his head. "You tell her. I'm going to get a cup of coffee."

He walked out, nodding to Ralph as Ralph pushed Marguerite's wheelchair to Pia's bedside. Ralph gave Pia a little half-smile and followed Nick down the hall.

Marguerite's face hung like forgotten flesh. She wasn't scowling, exactly, but she didn't bother with pleasantries. "I heard you say you should be dead."

"Yes."

"I thought I should've been dead when Matias was murdered."

Pia rolled her eyes. "I know, Mom. You told me."

Marguerite took a moment to reply. Her irritation crouched beneath her voice. "I don't mean to bore you, Lympia Marie, but I have a question. "Why do you think I didn't die with Matias?"

"You weren't involved in the politics. You were American. You were prettier. I don't know, Mom. Why?"

Marguerite's lips pursed momentarily, before she spoke. "I thought perhaps it was because of you. I thought perhaps I lived to bring you to this world."

Pia rolled her eyes again. "Sure, Mom."

Marguerite leaned forward. "I could be wrong, of course. Ralph tells me most of us never know why we're here, why we survive when someone else doesn't. Maybe we find out on the Other Side. But I still think my reason is you. And today, Pia, today it looks like you refuse to be worth the trouble. I don't know why Amy died for you, but she did—by design or by accident. Either way, it seems to me if you have any love or respect for either one of us, you owe us a serious effort at living."

Pia sat up, her voice bitter. "Like Amy's death meant anything. Like I'm supposed to pay you both back. You think it's my duty to do something outstanding—be a hero—be a saint?"

Her mother's tone fell low and hard. "I think you need to stop being a self-centered coward, get yourself mended, and get out there and be a partner for your husband. Did you even notice that he's lost weight? He lost his daughter, and now he's worried he's going to lose his wife. You owe him, Pia." She reached out to grip Pia's arm in her cold fingers. "Maybe you're going to have an ordinary life and never know why you lived when Amy didn't. Maybe the world needs your ordinary life. Maybe it's not about you at all, but about another baby in the future—maybe a grandchild you'll never meet, maybe somebody you'll influence at your work or on the subway. Who knows? But one thing is for sure—you aren't going to have a chance in hell of finding out what you can make of your life as long as you're in this bed."

Marguerite released her grip and started for the door, wheeling herself slowly. "I'm not coming back here to visit you, Pia. Either get better and come home or say goodbye now. I don't have time to dawdle. I've set Amy's memorial service for next week, and I'd sure like you to be there."

Ralph came inside far enough for him to be able to direct Marguerite's wheelchair. He had been standing just outside. He closed the door behind himself as he wheeled her away.

Pia stared after them, feeling her emotions melting down her cheeks.

Nick came in a few minutes later, cradling the end of his cup of coffee. He stopped abruptly when he saw tears running down Pia's face.

"What's wrong? Where's your mother? Where's Ralph?"

"They left. Mom yelled at me. She looks terrible." Pia reached over to pull out a tissue for her runny nose. "Nick, do you think I'm a selfish coward? Tell me the truth."

He sat down, slowly placing his cup on her tray table. "What do I think? I think you feel like I do."

She looked at him, seeing his agony unrestrained for once. "Yes, I guess I do." She reached for his hand and he gave it to her. They sat in silence holding hands until the nurse came in with dinner.

———◆———

Pia dedicated herself to her doctor's orders after that and improved quickly.

"You can stop sitting here driving yourself mad staring at the walls," she told Nick as she prepared for therapy. "Get out and get busy. I'll behave."

He smiled. "You, behave?" He kissed her forehead. "I have an appointment with Dr. Leibowitz at the university. He thinks he might be able to get me some work as an assistant on the project we started before…before you and I went to Costa Rica. We need the money, and you're right. I need to be busy. I need to be very, very busy."

She watched him as he poured himself a glass of water from the pitcher on her tray table. He didn't usually expose his pain to her. Even now, he tried to smile. "When I think of Costa Rica…damn, can you believe the life we've had together so far?"

She shrugged. "Maybe my mother's wrong. Maybe I'm a curse instead of a blessing. Think about it. I wouldn't blame you if you wanted to bail out."

A nurse entered. Nick downed his water in a single long drink, and watched the nurse help Pia slip on a bathrobe and situate her in a wheelchair.

Nick's voice had a torn edge, as though it was stretched too tightly over ragged emotions. "I had a roommate who kept telling me we never know what's good or bad until our stories are completely told. I can't wait to find out what was good about all this." He pulled on his jacket. "Take care of yourself. You're stuck with me. I signed on for the long haul, and I meant it." He brushed the top of her head with a kiss.

She gave him a last look before the nurse wheeled her from the room. "Thank God," she said quietly.

Pia was released before the memorial service and given permission to attend since it was a small affair Marguerite had insisted on setting up at her local church. The baby had been cremated and only a few friends were invited. Marguerite paid to have a stone with Amy's name and dates engraved on it inserted into the church garden. The cremains were set in an urn beneath the stone.

"I won't have Amy disappear," she declared when Pia protested.

"Mom, it won't change anything."

"I won't discuss it. I'd do the same for you." Marguerite attended the dedication in spite of the fact that Ralph had to carry her to and from her wheelchair.

Ralph had already taken Marguerite home by the time Harold and Cynthia arrived at the churchyard. Peter and Kathleen followed after them like naughty children. Their tans were conspicuous.

Harold came to Pia first. "I'm sorry we're late. We came as quickly as we could. You have our deepest, deepest sympathy. How could a thing like this happen? What's going on in this city? Where were the police? We should sue somebody. My god, that beautiful baby! And how are you? Nick said it was really close for you—close to your heart. You look pale."

Pia stared at Harold as though she had never seen him before. His face was red. "Yes, the wound is close to my heart."

He gave her a cautious hug.

Pia couldn't respond. She felt herself turning to rock. She turned her head.

Harold embraced Nick next. "We should've been here for you, Son. We should've been here. I'm so sorry. We met some friends in New Zealand and went with them into the mountains. Your mother had trouble finding us a flight out. There was a typhoon in the South Pacific. Everything was down."

Nick nodded. "That must have been rough." His father caught his sarcasm, but it flew past his siblings.

"The surf was awesome," interjected Peter.

"It rained all the time," added Kathleen.

Cynthia moved to Pia. "I don't know what to say to make you feel better," she began, her voice quavering. "I can't even imagine..."

"You don't have to," interrupted Pia bitterly. "Your problem is solved for the moment. You can go back to your nice tidy life as though none of this ever happened. No abuelita. But you haven't gotten rid of me—the contaminated one."

Nick slipped an arm around Pia. He paused to look at his mother. "And you never will, if I have anything to say about it," he said flatly. "As far as I can see, she's too good for this family, Mom. She never would've treated you the way you've treated us."

He helped Pia to the car.

Harold turned to his wife. "You asked for that," he said without emotion. "Maybe we all did. I'm ashamed of us. I'm ashamed of myself. We missed our only chance to know our first granddaughter, and we did it on purpose."

———————

Pia was sure her mother was embarrassed by her daughter's failure to cope. She imagined Marguerite avoiding her. She knocked quietly on the doorframe of her mother's bedroom the next morning.

"Mom?"

"Yes, come in." Marguerite looked worse for the strain of the memorial service. "Please leave the lights low. It's a kindness to both of us."

Pia sat in the chair near her mother's bed. "I came to apologize."

Marguerite waved a dismissive hand. "No need. You and Nick are hurting. You should be. It'll soften somewhat if you keep moving on. Movement is life or the other way around. People who stagnate wither. But I'm glad you're here. We need to talk."

Pia wished she could make an excuse and leave. She thought she knew what was coming next. "What is it, Mom?"

"I stopped my therapies. I don't know if Ralph told you."

"No, he didn't, but I guessed you would."

She reached for Pia's hand. Her fingers were cold and boney. "Sweetheart, I hate to do this to you—especially now. But my time is coming fast."

"Yes, I know."

"I'm not sure how to say this. I'm grateful if you love me enough to feel sad for my passing, but you can't let it defeat you. I'm ready to go. I've had plenty of living. I'm tired. I hope you can find a part of you to be relieved for me. Please try."

Pia knew the words her mother was waiting to hear, but they stuck in her throat—dry and puffy like pods of seeds before a winter wind.

"Pia, promise me."

"You think I can command myself not to be sad?"

"I think you can command yourself not to quit."

Pia drew a long breath of air and exhaled it as a painful sigh. "I promise."

Marguerite squeezed her hand. "Good. Ralph says he wants to see me through to the end here in my apartment where I'm

235

comfortable, but I told him to call hospice if he needs to. The end may not be at all pretty. And once I'm in enough pain, I may not know or care where I am."

"I'm with Ralph. We'll take care of you."

"You're both incorrigible. And Nick?"

"He's at the university today, but he'll come home whenever we call."

Marguerite released her hand. "Ralph wants to set up a cot in here. He has basic medic training. It's up to you to say something if you feel like he doesn't belong. He wants to take the burden of caring for me off you, so you can finish healing."

Pia smiled. "He belongs. In fact, I want you to know Nick and I will take care of Ralph as much as he'll let us after you...after you've gone."

"Good." Marguerite lay back against her pillows and closed her eyes. "Thank you. And don't be too hard on Cynthia. She may grow up yet."

Pia did her best to look cheerful, but she was pretending and everyone knew it.

The hollow parasitic beast of loss didn't shrink; it was growing daily. It held Pia's emotions in a tight grip that deadened her ability to cope.

"Let's go for a walk," Ralph told her one day.

"Walks haven't worked out well for me."

"I wasn't asking so much as directing," he said. "You and I will go for a walk now while your mother is resting. Your doctor says walking's good for you."

She stared at him. He had never ordered her around before. His expression was inscrutable.

"Now would be good," he said flatly.

She slipped on her coat and went out the door he held for her.

She had never realized how people reacted to him, to his scars, his limp. They stared, then looked away. Were they afraid he'd speak? Were they just afraid? Even at his age, he still looked intimidating. She took his arm in defiance of the stares. She had to hurry to match her pace to his.

He didn't say anything for a while. He took her to the park where he motioned for her to join him on a bench.

When he finally spoke, he began with a rush of air as though he had been rehearsing a speech in his mind. "Losing somebody you love like we all loved Amy is the shits. But you can't let it defeat you. Self-pity is no kind of way to honor somebody. You're gonna have to climb out of this pit. Your mother needs you."

Pia sighed. She was already ashamed of herself. "I know," she said. "I'm trying."

"In the war, we lost lots of brothers. You go on. You show them you're gonna live your life the best you can, since you're the one still alive. That's how you make their deaths count."

Pia nodded, wondering how many more of these lectures she would have to endure.

"This wasn't so easy for your mother, losing her only grandchild. It wasn't so easy at all. She didn't have the strength for this. It's taking her down."

"I know."

He adjusted his position. "But that's only part of what I come to tell you." He took a few moments to stare at the pigeons bobbing up and down the pathway looking for bits of food. "I got some news for you. You just say if you don't want to hear it. Maybe I'm butting in where I've got no right." He looked at her, but she didn't know how to respond.

"What news?" she asked, worrying about where he was going.

"I hope it's news that'll settle your mind some. When your mother told me her story—about the torture and all—and how she was afraid someday that bastard would find out about you and look you up to hassle you, I got to thinking. I called in favors from people I know who are good at finding things. Some of us in the war were good at that. I asked them to find that scum Santiago Silva."

Pia could hear her heart pounding and leaping in her chest. "And?"

"There are plenty of Silvas in Argentina, so it took a long time to be sure we had the right one. He's alive. Living in Buenos Aires. He did a little time for what he did, but he's been out for years. He's living with a son who ain't at all good in the head. Nobody's saying nothing, but some think his kid has syphilis that never got treated. Others think his father caused irreversible brain injury. He's still that kind of violent scum."

Pia stared at her fingernails. "If I were a better person, I might say I was sorry."

"No reason. Things have a way of happening to people who do bad things."

"If you say so."

"Anyway, I just wanted to tell you what I found. I'll make sure Silva doesn't make more trouble. I'll sure do that. You can rest easy. Don't say nothing to your mother. Even Silva's name upsets her. I don't want her thinking about him anymore, but maybe you should know—know I'm watching that bastard."

"Thank you." They sat for a few more moments. "You're a good man, Ralph."

He shrugged. "You take the missions you're given, you know?"

He stood up and Pia followed his lead, pretending not to notice that he had to use a few seconds to stretch himself vertical and make certain his leg was in place.

"Your mother deserves better than what she got," he muttered, half to himself.

"Yes," agreed Pia. "Yes, she does." She couldn't help wondering if he thought her mother deserved a better child.

23

Marguerite lay in the bed that had become her world. The quiet of the apartment next to the tumble of sounds in the street made the space around her feel like a tomb. She could hear the clock in the kitchen marking time as it clicked past. She didn't have many clicks left. She could feel it. She thought of poor little Amy who had never even touched her feet to the earth before she was sent away from it. Would she be waiting on the Other Side? Was there another side?

A wave of pain rippled over her nerves and finally settled into a routine. She sucked in a breath and thought of Matias. She dreamed of him sometimes, vivid dreams when he would come to embrace her and they would be young and healthy as before. Some said such dreams were real. She thought she smirked. How would she, of all people, know what was real and what was not?

Sometimes the dreams were the same old nightmares. She could tell she was still alive because of the nightmares. They waited behind every old smell or sound. They waited to have their way with her in the night. At least when she was gone from living, they should have to be gone, as well. Surely.

Now and then, she saw again the streets of London where she had started her travel book career—the pub and barkeep that seemed to live outside time, relics of another age. She sometimes imagined she had found her father there, the father who had walked away. Perhaps if there were another side, he would stop for her this time. He would turn and greet her as he had when she was little, spreading his arms into wide wings to enfold her.

She heard a sound at the door. Pia and Ralph were back. She thought of Ralph. The Universe presented gifts when you least expected them. He came to touch her naked head with his big, scarred hands. When he touched her like that, it was a kiss, an embrace. It was the purest form of love, asking nothing, expecting nothing. Matias would like him. He would thank him and accept him as a brother.

"So, how are you doing? Can I get you something?"

Ralph didn't look like an angel, if angels were as people said. Was it wicked to love two men?

"I'm fine," she told him. "Maybe some fresh water would be nice, if you don't mind."

"I don't mind."

He left the room and was replaced by Pia. "We bought you some of your favorite tea."

Her mother took a moment to respond. She had to answer the pain first. "Thank you. There, on the chair, my purse. Take the money."

"No, Mom. We don't need money. We took care of it."

"There!" Marguerite ordered. "I pay my own way."

Pia lifted the same old purse from the chair. It was worn and repaired and stained. "You need a new purse, Mom. I've been saying that for years."

"Never," breathed Marguerite, struggling to open the bag. "These stains. I never told you. They're his blood. And mine." She pulled out her coin purse where she kept carefully folded bills. The strain was too much. She motioned for Pia to take the purse. "You get the money. I'm tired. I'm very tired." She closed her eyes.

Pia held the purse away from her, staring at the stains.

Ralph came with a glass of water and a pill.

"Is it time for another pill already?" asked Pia.

"Who cares." He pulled a chair close to sit by Marguerite, helping her to place and then swallow the pill.

"Won't you use them up too fast?" asked Pia. "They count them out to fit the schedule."

He shrugged. "I got some I can share," he said. And Pia understood why his forehead seemed to have extra lines lately.

After a while, Marguerite relaxed a little, dozing perhaps.

They heard a commotion at the front door. Someone opened it with a key.

"Nick's here," said Ralph.

Both Pia and Ralph went to greet him. He held Pia for a long moment, kissing her and fondling her hair, before he moved to shake Ralph's hand.

"How's Maggie?"

Pia answered. "The pain gets worse all the time."

"Maybe we should take her to a hospital."

"No!" The emphasis in Ralph's voice made Nick pause as he hung his coat in the closet.

Ralph seemed to sense he had been too forceful, so his tone was calmer when he continued. "She doesn't want to be with strangers when her time comes. The three of us can tend her well enough. Hospitals are for sick people. They aren't much good for the dying. Too many rules. We've got a hospice nurse coming to tell us how to get on. That's plenty."

Nick started to say something about finding a hospice facility to take Maggie in, but he realized he knew what the response would be.

"In the old days, people used to tend their own family members. I'm glad we can do that for her."

"We never leave one of our own behind," muttered Ralph as he returned to the bedroom to sit on the chair by the bed.

Nick carried his suitcase to the spare room with Pia close behind him. "Doesn't that hurt him to sit on that hard chair like that?" he asked softly so Ralph wouldn't hear.

Pia nodded. "More than you know. He gives her his pain pills."

"Wow." It was a flat exclamation, a short skid to a stop. "I'm glad he's here."

Pia began sorting the lunch items from the papers in his briefcase.

"And how are you?" Nick asked her, although he could see the deep shadows beneath her eyes.

"I'm okay."

"This is a lot for you to handle all at once." He drew an uneven breath that betrayed the grief he was trying to hide. "Actually, it's a lot for us both."

He wasn't really talking to her, so she didn't answer. She didn't like to think about the sorrow he didn't mention. She didn't want to imagine what losing his daughter had meant to him. She thought she couldn't endure another ounce of strain. Her gift to him would be for her to maintain her sanity.

The days dragged with the clicks of the clock that seemed to grow louder and more obnoxious with each minute. The clicks absorbed the air in the room, replacing it with dark tension, as though the four of them were trapped in a pit, waiting for an invisible beast to devour them. In a way, they were right.

Cynthia and Harold came. They brought flowers, creams, and a big bottle of single malt Scotch.

"We want to do what we can to help," explained Cynthia, looking plain and weary.

Pia accepted the flowers and took them to the kitchen for water.

Cynthia followed her. "I need to apologize, Pia. I've been unkind, and I never meant to do that. I just wanted to run away for a bit—to give myself room to adjust. I didn't mean to be hurtful."

Pia nodded. "I'd be a hypocrite to judge you. I've said some terrible things to my mother myself. Life rips us open once in a while, and we get to see what we're made of. It isn't always a pretty sight."

Cynthia dropped her voice until it was barely above a whisper. "You wouldn't think a person could survive being raped by a cattle prod."

"She won't," Pia said, without looking to see how Cynthia was reacting.

"Oh," muttered Cynthia, and then again, "oh."

The final days of Marguerite's life dragged out like years in a deep dungeon—dark, inhuman, and filled with torture. The hospice nurse kept her deeply sedated, but at the end, drugs couldn't overcome the pain. She cried out at erratic intervals until the neighbors both upstairs and down complained, and Nick had to play the television at high volume to cover the sound.

When she passed, the three were with her, watching. She had been quiet for a few minutes—barely breathing. And then the road ended. One minute she was there, a sigh, and she was gone. A body lay in her place. Instantly the world inside the apartment flew off-balance, one soul removed. Nick turned the TV off. Ralph went back to his apartment. And Pia sat still, staring.

The strangers came—the strangers who wrapped up the body, placed it on a gurney, and took it away. Marguerite would be cremated like Amy, but there was a waiting list. It would be a few days. Then Pia, Nick, and Ralph would do the scene from the church garden all over again, this time with Ralph paying the bill at his own insistence. Pia didn't notice who else attended the service. She retreated to an interior world cushioned by sobs. Nick sent his parents home. They had nothing to say that would help.

———✦———

At first, life seemed to return to its regular pace. But soon Pia would burst into tears at odd times—eating, showering, sorting the mail. Commercials on television would set her off. One day they couldn't find her. Nick and Ralph were frantic. They discovered her sitting in the fetal position in the back of a dark closet, weeping onto her knees. Nick wanted her to see a counselor, but she refused. No more counselors. No more well-wishers. No more. No more.

Ralph tried to convince her to exercise, even if she did no more than walk around the park with him. She couldn't get her legs to cooperate. She sat on the sofa, looking at the TV that was often not on.

She stopped sleeping through the night. Nick would wake, feel the chilled space beside him, and go to find her sitting in a chair by the bed where Marguerite had died. She started talking to herself, holding conversations no one could hear with people no one could see.

"What can we do to make this better?" Nick asked her, but she just shook her head.

"Pia, you have to come through this," he told her grimly. "You have to. Please. I can't stand the idea of hauling you off to a psychiatrist and pumping you full of drugs. I need you."

She forced herself to see him. "Yes, I know. I know. I know. Be patient. I'll find a way. I won't give up. I promised Mom. I'll find a way."

24

Ralph was startled when he heard a pounding on his apartment door, answered it, and found Pia standing there—her eyes wide, her dirty hair dangling in greasy strings beside her face.

"I have to go!" she declared. "I have to go see the man who started all this."

He seated her at his little nicked dining table and gave her a beer. His gray sweatshirt bloomed with sweat spots. His set of weights lay on the floor. He worked out harder when he was upset.

"Are you talking about Argentina?"

"Yes! I have to go. Please, Ralph, give me the information. I have to go. I have to see Santiago Silva."

Ralph sat back in his chair, studying her. "What are you going to do when you meet him?"

"I don't know yet. I don't know what I might do. But I have to see him. He's a monster in my mind. He haunts me. I have to see what he is, really. Please, Ralph. If I confront the man, maybe I can begin to push my life back into reality. I need reality."

He considered for a few minutes. The scar on his face seemed to twitch.

"Okay. Okay, I'll take you. I'll need a new passport, and God knows, I'm gonna set off the alarms going through security. But I'll take you. I'd like to see the son-of-a-bitch myself."

Nick came running in from the other apartment.

"Oh, thank God!" he breathed when he saw Pia. "Here you are. I was in the bathroom when you disappeared. You scared me. You could've said something about where you were going."

"We're going to Argentina, Nick," Pia told him. "Ralph and I."

"Argentina? Whatever for? Maggie said you didn't have any relatives there."

"Yes, yes, I do." She turned her piercing dark eyes on her husband.

He had never seen her look so cold, so fierce.

"I'm going to meet my father."

Nick looked to Ralph, but Ralph was staring at the table.

"No! I forbid it. This is crazy. This is sick. Ralph, tell her this is madness. Silva doesn't know about you, Pia. He couldn't. Leave sleeping snakes alone. Why make trouble where none exists?"

"Because–can't you see? He's the beginning of the evil. He's the beginning!" Pia stood up, defiant. "Ralph found him. He's there, Nick. He's living there in Buenos Aires. And I have to see him. I have to. You can't forbid me. I'm not your child."

"You're my wife, I love you, and you aren't yourself right now. Ralph, tell her!"

Ralph finished drinking his beer and wiped a hand across his lips. "Sitting here ain't doing any of us much good. Maybe she's onto something. When you've got a problem and your figuring starts going in circles, you go back to the beginning to find a fresh approach."

"Go back to Start. Do not pass Go. Do not collect two hundred dollars," mumbled Pia.

Nick threw up his hands. "Then I'm coming with you. God knows how we're financing a trip like this, but I'm not letting the two of you go without me. Somebody has to be objective. I'll call Dr. Leibowitz and my dad. Dad feels guilty enough that he'll bankroll us even if I don't have a good reason why we're going. Paying him back will be the problem."

Pia sighed a long, relieved sigh. "I think I'll go take a shower," she said. "I have work to do."

———◈———

Over the long hours of the flight, the three remained silent, trying to sleep, trying to find distraction in the magazines. Ralph entered Customs first.

"Reason for your visit?" the Argentine agent asked curtly.

"Just looking around Buenos Aires–tourists. Never been here."

The agent poked here and there among the clothes in Ralph's suitcase. An old man with an old man's things. "Enjoy your visit."

The three picked up their rental car and ate at outdoor stands, being careful to drink only bottled beer. They exchanged a little money and shopped in the market, buying trinkets tourists might buy. The people of Argentina rushed around them, hardly seeing them, never really looking. At last, their car sat outside the low unkempt house that matched the address Ralph had recorded.

"Wait until I get in," he instructed. "I'll go first to make sure we have the right man."

After Ralph had closed the car door, Nick exhaled loudly.

"Pia, what are we doing here? What difference can any of this make? It won't bring back Maggie or Amy. It won't change anything."

She didn't answer. The conversation was a re-tread. She hugged the stained purse that hung from her shoulder and stared out the window. Nick understood that the discussion was ended.

She saw someone answer Ralph's knock—a swarthy man with graying hair—thick, curly graying hair—hair not entirely unlike hers.

Pia leaned forward to get a better view. He didn't look like a monster. He looked like any other man—aging, bending, losing what he had been. He was insignificant beside his evil. As he talked with Ralph, he was growing animated, gesturing. His face twisted into a scowl. Ralph shouldered his way into the house.

"Let's go." Pia jumped out of the car first. She ran so that Nick had to hurry to catch up. They stepped into the house through the open front door.

They might have been stepping into the depths of a swamp. The air was a fog of stench. Pia covered her nose. In a moment, their eyes had adjusted to the darkness. Ralph stood beside the curly-haired man, his arm around Silva's throat.

"Lympia Garcia Graves," Ralph announced, "This is Santiago Silva."

"You have some connection with the detentions?" asked Silva. Pia could see he was puzzling over who these threatening people speaking English could be. He glanced backward toward Ralph, his fear in his eyes.

"Some," answered Ralph, looking down on him.

Nick was wandering around, trying to determine the source of the wretched smell.

"You! Stop! Go out of my house!" ordered Silva. "All of you, go! You have no right!"

Nick ignored him.

"We have more right than you know," growled Ralph as Nick opened first one door and then another. "What are you hiding?"

"Oh my god!" Nick exclaimed when the last door was opened. "Oh my god."

Pia went to look. Ralph stayed beside Silva, keeping him prisoner with his enormous arms.

"Oh dear god." Pia backed away, her hand to her mouth, as she saw into the room.

"There's a man in here chained to the bed," Nick reported to Ralph. "At least I think he's a man. He looks like somebody from a concentration camp. He doesn't seem to have a clue what's going on. What you smell is his shit and rat shit and food from who-knows-when spread around the floor."

"Mama!" wailed the son.

"You have no authority here," huffed Silva. "My son Lucas is very sick. I tend to him as I must. Go away and leave us alone."

Ralph tightened his grip. "One of the women you raped in the ESMA was a young wife named Marguerite Garcia."

"We punished only the dissidents, the terrorists," muttered Silva. "I cannot recall their names."

"You tortured her husband to death—a good man named Matias Garcia."

"As I said…"

"You cut out his tongue so he couldn't even say goodbye to the woman he loved."

Silva glared at each one in turn, looking for the connection. "We saved this country, and one day when the civilian government collapses, people will cry for us to save them again."

Ralph had hardened. His gaze had gone cold. Pia could see the Special Forces warrior he had been. She could imagine camouflage on his cheeks. He jerked Silva's head back. She saw a flash and realized Ralph had a knife—a nondescript kitchen style knife he must have purchased with the trinkets in the market. A knife that would dull quickly. It had only one good slash in it. Enough.

Ralph raised the knife to Silva's throat.

"I'm gonna kill you, Santiago Silva. I'm gonna slit your miserable throat before you can swallow your spit." He held the knife to Silva's neck with a skilled hand. "But I wanted you to see this, the beautiful daughter you'll never know—the child of your rape. I wanted you to realize the happiness, the family, you'll never share. And I hope like hell you're about to experience the pain you gave your victims."

"No, don't!" Pia begged Ralph. "Don't kill him! Can't you see he's not worth it? I came here wanting to kill him myself, but he's not worth it."

"Don't do it, Ralph!" cried Nick. 'You're better than that."

"He ain't worth saving," replied Ralph. "I killed so many in the war—some were good people, I'm sure, so I'm already bound for Hell. This one's no good at all. I'm just delivering the execution that should've happened a long time ago."

"No, *Señor*." There, just inside the front doorway behind them, stood a uniformed Buenos Aires police officer, his hand on his gun. He was at least middle-aged, of a medium build, athletic, with a neat mustache trimmed above his lips. He kept his tone even, speaking in careful English. His steady gaze pinned Ralph in place—two warriors meeting. "This execution is not for you to do." He stepped into the room, assessing the situation. "I saw your car outside. Silva has no visitors."

"Please, Ralph," pleaded Pia, ignoring the police officer. "You're my father now—the only family I have. Mom wouldn't want this. She loved you. We love you. Please don't do this thing—certainly not for me, and not for Mom, either. I can't live with it. You'll die here in prison. I can't stand it! I need you."

Ralph didn't move. "He killed Maggie. He mutilated her."

Silva's eyes betrayed his fear. He could feel the blade. He looked to the officer.

The officer stepped forward, slowly drawing his gun and pointing it at Ralph. "You, by the bedroom, release the son Lucas from his chains. The key is here on this hook by the door. Use a cloth–your shirt, perhaps, or a handkerchief–to wipe away your fingerprints once the lock is open. Throw the key on the floor. Take care. Our technicians are thorough."

Nick didn't ask questions. He hesitated only briefly, glancing from the gun to Ralph, before he went to do as he was told.

Ralph was eyeing the officer's weapon. "I can kill Silva faster than you can shoot; you know that."

"*Si*, this I know, but you will give me the knife, *Señor*."

Pia's hand was on her heart. "Please, Ralph!"

He was staring at the officer. "You'll take me in on charges, anyway. I might as well do something useful. Killing this scum bag would make the world cleaner."

The officer stopped only feet from Ralph. His voice was still calm. His stare didn't waver. "There will be no charges if you give me the knife, *Seño*r. I swear."

"Please, Ralph." Tears were running down Pia's face. "You'd be killing me."

Ralph seemed to soften, although he didn't change his focus. "Pia, he knows about you now. He'll make trouble."

"I don't care. Let him try. You're more important to me."

Slowly, Ralph turned the knife away and handed it to the policeman. He released his grip, and Silva twisted away.

The policeman holstered his gun and pulled on a pair of gloves from his pocket. He wiped the length of the knife between his gloved fingers. "Step aside, *por favor*, *Señor*," he said politely to Ralph. Ralph obeyed, looking to Pia.

Silva sneered. "This is a civilized country, Swine. We live by law. You can't touch me! I have friend…"

But before Silva could finish his taunting, the officer plunged the knife deep into his chest.

Silva fell, shock on his face. He mumbled something no one could understand. His life gurgled out, puddling on the floor.

"Step away," the policeman ordered the Americans. "You don't want blood on your clothes."

Ralph began to laugh. "Well, I'll be damned."

"This man is guilty for attempting to murder the soul of my country."

Lucas had wandered out of his room, looking without actually seeing, alternately moaning and laughing. He was little more than a yellow skeleton held together by dried skin and rags of clothing streaked with filth and dried white sweat. His wide, dark eyes seemed huge and sunken in his pale face. His age was impossible to gauge, although he was clearly no longer a child. His dark, curly hair fell to his shoulders, matted and ragged. He dropped to the floor and wiped his feces across his father's face. Nick stood behind him, his face ashen.

"Here," said the officer. "Something you found." He handed the knife to Lucas who turned it over and over in his hand. Lucas stabbed the body as the officer had done, laughed, and stabbed again.

"I heard a fight," the officer continued. "And I came inside only to discover that this poor lost soul had killed his father. The son and I, we will create the scene. You have come to the wrong house, *Turistas*. You must leave now and find a plane back to your home. Take your car away quickly, before the neighbors return from their work. I must call in this tragedy."

"Why did you do it?" asked Pia. "Why now after all these years?"

The officer looked at her, noting her dark hair and the deep tones of her skin. "People said the disappearances were crimes of opportunity. Long have I prayed that I would have a chance to honor the memory of our murdered citizens, to give them justice so they can find peace. A brief prison sentence was too little for this one. He was mad with cruelty. You have helped me ensure that this attack was fatal, a problem I had not solved previously. When Lucas is convicted, he will receive far better treatment than he has ever known from his father. This is his justice, as well. No one will ask many questions. No one will weep. The only regret most will have is Santiago Silva suffered too little."

"*Gracias, Señor*," Ralph told him, gesturing for Nick to leave. "You've avenged a fine woman, her mother—among the many others."

The officer nodded acknowledgement. "I am not a violent man. This was my duty."

Nick reached out to take Pia's hand, but she was staring, staring, staring at the nearly mummified man Lucas.

"Lucas is my family," she told Nick. "That poor wretch is my half-brother."

Lucas seemed to sense his name, and he looked up. His gaze met Pia's and, perhaps without realizing, he gave her a half-smile.

She could hear Nick's voice beside her. "Your brother has saved you, Pia. Twice, no three times, innocents have protected you. This is how the evil ends."

Pia returned her brother's smile. "*Gracias, mi hermano*," she said, but Lucas didn't seem to hear. He had sent his attention elsewhere. She followed Nick out the front door.

Nick slipped behind the steering wheel as the three hurried to go. Pia sat beside him. He pulled the car onto the street and headed for the traffic in the distance. "I don't know what to think. Should we tell somebody? Can we trust that guy not to be setting us up? I don't want us to spend the rest of our lives in South American cells."

"We're taking a chance," admitted Ralph settling back in the rear seat. "But I believe him. I think it's time for us to go to the airport. We'll buy something special on the way, something that might be worth a trip to Argentina to a bunch of crazy American tourists, and we'll go home. We have a few hours before our flight."

They rode in silence for a while, until their car became an anonymous other in a stream of cars on a main street.

"I'm glad you didn't kill him, Ralph," Nick said at last, "for all kinds of reasons."

"Me, too," added Pia. "Thank you." She reached out to caress Nick's cheek. "Thank you, too, Nick. Thanks for being here. I love you so much."

Nick nodded. "If I didn't love you more, I wouldn't be here. Life with you is never dull—surreal, maybe, but never dull. Damn, that was disgusting. Silva isn't going to notice any difference between the world he's been living in and Hell."

Pia leaned back against her headrest. "I feel like I've lived a thousand lifetimes." She sighed heavily. They passed a shop with huge eyeglasses portrayed on the sign, and she stared at the sign until it was behind them. "Death isn't an out. It's a lens—a way to see."

"You got that right," said Ralph in a low voice. "You got that exactly right."

Acknowledgements

*M*y heartfelt thanks...

To David Harris for acting as my technical advisor and partner,

To Tom Bird for not letting me quit,

To Jilly Gwin for pulling me out of my writing rut and prodding me to complete my story,

To Esra Beyatli for her thoughtful contributions and optimism,

To Meghan Harris Russell and Chelo Diaz-Ludden for help with marketing,

To Rama Jon Cogan for his guidance and promotion,

To Jeffrey Pill for years of encouragement and mentoring,

To Kay Evans and Jean Crisler for keeping my body and soul connected,

To Laura Goodrich for being my fan since middle school,

To my extended family for their patience and support,

And to the Trinidad Writers' Guild for listening.

About the Author

S usan Adair Harris brings a widely diverse background in screenwriting, academic writing, play writing, and editing a professional online photography magazine to her first novel. She has recorded audio books for the Library of Congress Talking Books program; taught theatre, communication, and language arts courses in secondary and post-secondary institutions (including college courses in a correctional facility); and coordinated a regional adult education resource center. She both designed and delivered regional and state adult education professional development training. She has served as an officer on the boards of a tourist steam train, a state association for adult educators, and a rural fire department auxiliary. She broke and trained her own horse (or vice versa); helped raise a family plus numerous dogs, cats, horses and a donkey; hiked the Rocky Mountains; and sold original oil paintings and charcoal drawings. Susan currently resides in Southern Colorado with her husband and a very vocal cat. You can follow her on Facebook, Pinterest, or Twitter or at susanadairharris.com where her books will be featured. Her blog is available at personaljourneyswithgramma.com.

Sample Discussion Questions for
Death Lost Dominion

1. How did you react to the beginning of the book after you learned the specifics were based on actual historical accounts?
2. What part does culture play in the relationships represented in the story, and how authentic do you think the depictions of culture were?
3. Which relationships in the novel seemed to you to demonstrate the purest unconditional love? Which represented superficial love?
4. How do Marguerite, Pia, and Nick change by the end of the book?
5. What do you think the blood-stained handbag symbolized? Did you discover other symbols?
6. Which plot points, bits of dialogue, or passages struck a chord with you as either important or improbable? Was the book surprising or predictable?
7. How are the following themes expressed in the book and how realistic are they?
   a. Forming and maintaining personal identity.
   b. Prejudice against
      -- victims of rape, AIDS, or PTSD
      -- people who exhibit differences (i.e. disabilities, economic class)

-- mothers who choose abortion, adoption, or single parenting.

    c. Self-sacrifice and its motivation.

    d. Living fully after surviving.

    e. Death as a lens for understanding life.

    f. Another theme you identified.

8. What do you think would've happened IF...

    a. ...Marguerite hadn't kept the baby?

    b. ...Marguerite had told Pia as a child about her real father?

    c. ...The baby had not been with Pia on her winter walk?

    d. ...Ralph had carried out his plan for Santiago Silva?

    e. ...Pia had brought her half brother home?

    f. ...The book continued into a sequel?

    g. ...Another change of your choice had happened?

9. How would you describe the morality (living according to standards of right and wrong) of these characters:

    a. Marguerite

    b. Santiago Silva

    c. Pia

    d. Nick's mother Cynthia

    e. Ralph the Marine

    f. The Argentinian police officer

    g. Another character of your choice

10. Did you find the ending satisfying—why or why not?

11. In a movie version, who would you cast in the main roles and why?

Recent Reviews

This One Delivers Smiles and Tears – "The title of this beautifully crafted story suggests it is about death. To this reader, it is clearly a story about the struggles of three lives tainted by violence but sustained by unconditional love. The author masterfully brings her main characters situations and gives us a view of how they find the inner strength to overcome. The question of why we are here on this often cruel world does not go unanswered. Finally, this powerful author teaches us lessons about survival and how to live with the decisions one must make to carry on despite the curves life can throw us purposefully or accidentally. You will see some of yourself in Pia and remember her for a long time. Susan's story gives us an exciting and fulfilling reading experience.

~Ben Boyd, Jr., Author of AZ2016 NEO,
The Qixi Virus via Amazon.com

An Excellent Book – "I loved all the characters in this book and thoroughly enjoyed reading it, even when it was sad. The ending was totally unexpected! Would love to read more from this author."

~Bonnie C., via Amazon.com

Book Changes You – "This 'hard to put down' book is rich with life and compassion. It tackles difficult subjects bringing tears and chuckles throughout. It's a book you keep thinking about – it doesn't leave you for quite some time. Great dialogue. A very worthy read!"

~Kay, via Amazon.com

Survival – "…I recommend the book for readers who desire a sincere view from a gifted author as she writes about how we relate to our fellow humans. There is hope in the book and I still think about the characters, particularly Marguerite and how she raised her daughter. It is a "page turner;" hope to read future novels from this new novelist."

~Stellate, via Amazon.com

Hard to Put it Down – "This is a wonderfully written book about a very difficult story. I found it hard to put down. I found myself really caring about the characters and getting caught up in the tragedies of their lives. Some interesting twists will cause you to think and have great conversation with anyone else who reads the book. It would be a good book club read! I recommend this book but don't expect a light-hearted summer read! Susan is a good writer…we need to read more by her!"

~Jim, via Amazon.com

Did Not Want the Book to End – "Enjoyed very much. Did not want the book to end, but could not put it down. Characters and story line captivate and haven't had the same reaction of not wanting a book to end since *Thorn Birds*. Don't miss it. Good Job Susan!!"

~Terri, via Amazon.com

www.ingramcontent.com/pod-product-compliance
Lightning Source LLC
Chambersburg PA
CBHW070849250626
47159CB00003B/997